Four Weddings AND A Duke

USA TODAY BESTSELLING AUTHOR
MICHELLE McLEAN

Entangled Publishing, LLC
644 Shrewsbury Commons Ave., STE 181
Shrewsbury, PA 17361
Visit our website at www.entangledpublishing.com.

Amara is an imprint of Entangled Publishing, LLC.

Edited by Lydia Sharp and Liz Pelletier
Cover design by Bree Archer
Stock art by Fotolit2/Depositphotos, xbujhm/
Depositphotos, unnaugan/Depositphotos,
FairytaleDesign/Depositphotos
Interior design by Toni Kerr

Print ISBN 978-1-64937-329-8
ebook ISBN 978-1-64937-330-4

Manufactured in the United States of America

First Edition June 2023

AMARA

ALSO BY MICHELLE McLEAN

*To all the plants I've inadvertently killed over
the years–I couldn't keep you alive,
but I can give you a hero who knows
how to treat you right.*

CHAPTER ONE

If given the choice between rolling about in a field of manure or attending the wedding of his cousin and her prince, Alexander Reddington would happily choose the manure. A childish sentiment, perhaps. And at over six feet and fourteen stone, Alex was most definitely *not* a child. In fact, some found him downright intimidating judging by the wide berth many gave him every time he entered a room.

Yet, here he was, little better than a mere schoolboy, tugging on his overly tight cravat as the line of elegantly dressed aristocracy slowly filtered into the cathedral.

"Stop that," his mother murmured. "You'll ruin all that hard work your poor valet did wrestling you into decent clothing this morning."

Alex grumbled under his breath, though he did stop trying to undress himself. "I fail to see why my presence is required here."

Her quiet sigh was the only outward sign of her annoyance, and one that showed how sorely he tested her nerves. Her genteel demeanor was rarely shaken. And that most often occurred when dealing with him. He had the grace to regret upsetting his mother, though he couldn't help his feelings on the matter.

"Lady Elizabeth is your cousin on my side, and Prince Leopold is your cousin on your father's side, and they wished for you to be at their wedding," she answered. "Even if they did not, you are now the Duke of Beaubrooke and are expected to be seen at these occasions."

The pit of dread that had taken up residence in his gut ever since that illustrious mantel had been dropped on his shoulders churned, and he swallowed back the bile that threatened to erupt. Yes, he was expected to be seen. He was expected to do a great many things now. Things he'd never wished for, prepared for, or had any inclination to perform. It mattered not.

"Distant cousins, Mother," he clarified. "Very distant. Leopold had never stepped a foot west of the Rhine until he arrived here for the ceremony. He wouldn't know who I was if he tripped right over me. Not to mention there are so many people here, they'll never know if I am actually in attendance or not. I have important work to do—"

"Oh, hush." She waved her hand as though she could erase all his arguments. "You have nothing to do that won't be accomplished just as well later."

He rolled his lips together and sucked in a deep breath through his nose. "I hate weddings," he muttered.

His mother patted his arm. "That is unfortunate, my son. Because yours is next."

Alex gritted his teeth. He didn't need the reminder. Despite being a score and ten, the woman still had a knack for getting under his skin. But then, he supposed that was true of most mothers.

He was happy for the bride and groom, of course, as it was, by all accounts, a love match. Certainly a reason for celebration. He simply failed to see why he needed to be a part of it. Or why he must linger once the vows were made when so many others were willing to stay and wallow in the revelry until dawn.

Getting through the ceremony and following ball would be difficult under any circumstances for a recluse such as himself. But on this particular occasion, it was even more challenging to harness his desire to leave when the manuscript he'd been waiting on for months had finally arrived that morning.

Timothy Lambert, the current Assistant Keeper of the Archives at Oxford, had sent word that a new manuscript he'd found possibly contained information they'd been looking for regarding ancient methods of plant grafting. Alex had spent the last several years studying different methods from around the world, using them to create his own hybrid species. And while he'd had some successes, his passion project continued to fall short.

And now, the help they needed might just be contained in the pages currently waiting for him in the small office he kept at Oxford. Putting in an appearance at this wedding, a tedious undertaking in comparison to his research, was the last thing in the world he wished to be doing right at that moment. Even if he'd known the couple well, social occasions were…not his area of expertise. But duty called.

A duty that should never have been his.

He rubbed his chest at the familiar ache the thought of his brother, Charles, always created. Charles had excelled at this kind of thing. Enjoyed it even. He was always the social butterfly, the one everyone loved. It should have been him attending these events, not Alex.

The thought also made him feel a bit more kindly toward his mother. She'd been through enough over the last year. The last thing she needed now was her only remaining son having an attack of the vapors because he'd had to leave his greenhouse.

"Very well," he said, pulling his mother's hand through the loop of his arm and patting it. "I shall attempt to enjoy myself." Or at least do a better job at pretending he enjoyed any of this.

She beamed up at him, and he gave her hand a squeeze, trying to shove thoughts of the manuscript from his mind. It would be there waiting for him no matter when he returned home.

It took them another twenty minutes to get inside the cathedral, and his mother immediately abandoned him to lend her support to Lady Elizabeth's mother, who was beside herself at such a grand affair.

He should take his seat closer to the altar, where the rest of the bride's extended family and friends were seated. But that would necessitate walking past hundreds of eyes eager for a glimpse of the relatively new and semi-reclusive Duke of Beaubrooke. A man heretofore rarely seen at such events tended to draw attention. A circumstance he avoided whenever possible.

And as his mother was no longer at his side but happily ensconced with their family, he could minimize his exposure somewhat and find an out-of-the-way corner in which to sit. Oh, he'd pay the consequences later. But it would be worth it.

Unfortunately, there were few alternatives, as any available seating was rapidly filling up.

He finally spotted an empty seat near one of the pillars, where his nearest seatmate would be a lady who was turned toward the pillar and seemed to be studying her lap.

The choir began singing the first few notes of the processional song as Elizabeth's and Leopold's considerable number of immediate family members began to slowly make their way up the aisle to their prime seating in the front. Where he should be.

Alex quit debating his choices and hurried toward the chair near the pillar, then dropped into it, eliciting a gasp from the woman beside him.

"Pardon me," he said, gazing into the startled, bespectacled eyes of his new seatmate.

. . .

Lavinia Wynnburn slammed shut the small book she'd smuggled into the cathedral in her reticule and yanked her spectacles off her face. Her mother had admonished her no less than a dozen times prior to their departure to leave both spectacles and books at home. Neither apparently had any place at a high-society wedding.

Lavinia agreed to a point. That point being that she couldn't see a thing without her spectacles unless it was right in front of her. The quizzing glass, which *was* fashionably acceptable enough for her mother to permit her to wear, only allowed her to see from one eye at a time. Hardly practical. She'd meant to hide both her spectacles and her book away before anyone noticed. But apparently the cathedral had filled with guests while she'd been lost in the story.

And of course, it couldn't have been a kind older woman who'd discovered her, but a rather stern-looking gentleman who was watching her with an air of surprise. As well he should. Her mother would be cross. She hadn't meant to get so engrossed in her book. Her family had arrived as early as possible, so she had snuck away to this quieter corner, intending to go back to her seat before the ceremony began. But…here she was.

With a man sitting right beside her.

A considerably handsome man, she noted, with a sharp jawline, well-defined chin. A full mouth set in somewhat stern lines, but he had what looked like…she lifted her quizzing glass…yes, the smallest dimple in his cheek. It would likely deepen quite becomingly when he smiled. If he smiled.

She followed the lines of his face past his fairly average-looking nose to his deep brown eyes, framed by impossibly long lashes and dark brown eyebrows that rose in a sardonic arch—

Oh, good heavens!

She dropped her quizzing glass, and her book slipped off her lap as she belatedly realized she'd been perusing the poor man as though he were goods for sale at the market.

He grunted when the book hit his foot, and

she gasped, clasping a hand over her mouth.

"I'm terribly sorry—"

"Allow me," he said, bending his large and fairly impressive frame to reach down and retrieve the book.

"My thanks," she mumbled. If only the floor would open up and swallow her whole.

After a moment, she risked glancing up at his now slightly blurry face looking at her like he was waiting for her to respond to some query. Oh goodness…he'd probably asked her something and she'd been too busy wishing she could disappear to listen.

"Pardon me?" she said, hoping he didn't find her the biggest nincompoop.

His brows raised again. "I offered my apologies for encroaching on your company."

"Oh. Not at all. I mean, I do not mind."

He nodded. "I'm afraid there's not much seating left."

"Yes, it is rather crowded."

"Quite."

His gaze left hers, and she took the opportunity to surreptitiously slip her book back into her reticule. To no avail, it seemed, since his eyes were immediately drawn to her movements.

"Interesting choice of pastime for a wedding," he said. "Are you not enthralled by this…matrimonial spectacle?"

"That's an interesting turn of phrase to describe a wedding ceremony," she said.

"I did not mean to offend—"

She held up a hand. "I didn't say I disagreed."

That sent his eyebrow up to his hairline again. "Is that so?"

She lifted her shoulder in a delicate shrug. "It seems a lot of fuss to go through just to begin one's life together. But then, most I know quite enjoy the fuss and go out of their way to manufacture it. Rather like the insistence on hosting a grand ball every time a Tuesday rolls around."

The gentleman barked out a laugh that he hastily covered with a snorting cough that had the surrounding crowd glancing their way with raised brows and disapproving fan snaps and her raising her quizzing glass to ensure he wasn't choking.

He recovered admirably, a finger rubbing over his lips to erase his smile as if it had never been there.

"There's nothing wrong with a bit of fuss now and then, is there?" he finally asked.

"Certainly not." She dropped the quizzing glass and let it swing from the chain about her neck. "I suppose I'd simply rather deal with the legalities of a marriage, and celebrations in general, in a less 'spectacular' fashion."

"Fascinating," he said, his expression unreadable. "You may be the first woman I've ever heard say such a thing."

Whether or not that was a good thing, he didn't seem inclined to share. Which was just as well. She had no desire to share that it wasn't necessarily the events themselves to which she objected. More so the crowds.

Well, to be more accurate, it was the crowds who objected to *her*. Such occasions invariably made her feel she was either under malicious scrutiny or unbearably alone. It was far more appealing to simply not go.

"If you prefer to avoid balls and other such spectacles, what do you spend your time doing exactly?" he asked, his tone curious.

"I find a great many diverting things with which to occupy my time."

"Such as that book?" His gaze flickered down to the reticule on her lap.

She closed her eyes briefly, her cheeks growing warm at the realization that she'd not only been caught reading in public—by a gentleman, no less—but she'd also been caught reading a rather romantic novel that her mother would surely not approve of…if she knew she was reading it, of course.

Lavinia cleared her throat. "It's just an amusing little story. Nothing noteworthy." She silently apologized to the anonymous author as the story was anything but *un*noteworthy.

"Ah," he said, leaning somewhat closer to

be heard over the sound of the music that was beginning to flood the cathedral. "Well, whatever it is, I don't blame you at all. I'd much rather be reading than sitting through this entire thing, as well."

Her eyes widened. "Truly?"

She should hold her tongue, but the thought of finding a kindred spirit in this sea of social butterflies was more temptation than she could resist.

"So do you dislike social occasions?" she asked. "Or perhaps it is just weddings in particular?"

He glanced back at her while she prattled on.

"I find them dreadful. I always end up on my own in some corner. Which isn't the worst thing, truly. However, if I am to keep my own company all night, I'd much rather do it in the comfort of my own home where I at least have my books with which to amuse myself."

His gaze lingered on her again, perusing her until her heart skittered through its beats and she had to draw in a shaky breath.

"Do you not enjoy conversing with other young ladies?" he asked, taking advantage of her pause for breath.

"Not particularly." The words left her mouth before she had a chance to think them over, and she tried to find a more diplomatic answer. "It depends on the lady."

His lips pinched together, whether in an effort to keep from smiling or frowning, she could not be sure.

Finally, he said, "That is true of a great many things, I'm finding."

Before she could unravel that complicated little ball of wool, she glanced up and caught the blurry movements of a lady trying to get her attention. She quickly raised her quizzing glass, and her anxiously waving sister Kitty came into focus.

Drat! The ceremony would begin any second. Her mother must be furious.

Lavinia jumped up, startling the poor gentleman and everyone else sitting near them.

"I'm sorry. I must go. I…"

She opened her mouth, but her mind emptied of all thought when her gaze met his. And he looked like he might say something, but the stares of those around them were becoming more than she could bear. She bowed her head in a quick farewell and spun on her heels, hurrying around the pillar to Kitty.

"Mother has had me looking everywhere for you!" Kitty said, grabbing her hand and hauling her quickly away to where her mother and her other sister, Harriet, were sitting a few sections up. Thankfully near the wall, so she didn't have to crawl over anyone to get to her seat.

"What were you doing speaking to the

duke?" Kitty hissed as they sat.

"What duke?" She'd only talked to one man, and no duke would have spoken with her like he had.

"*The* duke," Kitty clarified. "The one holding our fates in his hands."

Her mother's and Harriet's heads both jerked toward them.

"That was him?" Lavinia recalled their conversation, and her face went hot under her mother's glare. Then, just as quickly, she felt all the blood drain out of it. "I didn't know…"

But she was saved from further interrogation when everyone rose, indicating the imminent arrival of the bride.

"We'll speak of this later," her mother whispered.

Lavinia stifled a sigh. Sometimes putting off the inevitable was a worse punishment.

Not that punishment was needed. The sheer humiliation from having sat beside the Duke of Beaubrooke and rambling on about nonsense—no, worse than nonsense. About how she felt about marriages and celebrations and social occasions. To the man who was considering her as his bride.

She hadn't wanted to wed him in any case. Not really. Though she hadn't expected him to be as…visually appealing as he was. That wouldn't have helped with the necessity of performing the duties of his duchess, however, duties for which she was supremely unsuited. The Duchess of Beaubrooke would need to be visible, sociable, personable. Not words typically associated with Lavinia.

No matter. What's done was done. She couldn't go back and make him unhear the words she'd spouted. So, she turned her attention to the lovely Lady Elizabeth as she pledged her love and loyalty to Prince Leopold.

Perhaps the duke would forget he'd ever met her. And with any luck, her sister would forget what she'd seen.

She should have known better.

...

The moment their carriage doors shut after the interminably long ceremony, Kitty rounded on her.

"How did you come to be sitting beside the Duke of Beaubrooke?" she asked before the horses had even begun maneuvering down the crowded streets.

"I didn't sit beside him. He sat beside me," Lavinia said.

"What's the difference?" Kitty asked, her nose adorably scrunched.

"Intent."

"Yes, yes, but what did he say? I saw you conversing."

"Oh dear," her mother said, rubbing her temples with her fingers. "You have not even been introduced yet. What must he think?"

"It wasn't so terrible, Mother," Lavinia tried to assure her. "He apologized for encroaching upon me —"

"As he should," her mother said.

Lavinia ignored that. "And then we spoke of the wedding, briefly. There wasn't much else."

"Well, thank heavens for that," her mother said.

Her father gave her mother an absent-minded pat on the knee before he went back to gazing out the window. He tried not to get embroiled in the affairs of the women in his house. He'd likely never find any peace otherwise.

Harriet raised a brow and Lavinia bit her lip. Her sister had always been able to see right through her.

"Out with the rest," Harriet said.

Lavinia pursed her lips together briefly, and then blurted it out. "He may or may not have caught me wearing my spectacles. And reading."

Her mother threw her hands up. "Sweet Jove's beard, what will I do with this child," she muttered before leaning over and yanking the silver flask from her husband's pocket and taking a large swig.

Lavinia's mouth dropped open and her father stared dumbfounded at his wife. Her mother took a tremulous breath and handed the flask back.

"Is there anything else?" she asked.

Lavinia debated the wisdom in imparting any further details and decided steadfastly against it. If her mother knew she'd not only confessed to reading a romance novel but then clobbered the poor man's foot with that same book, the contents of her father's flask would be as good as gone.

She shook her head, carefully avoiding Harriet's eyes.

Her mother sighed. "Lord save us," she muttered, leaning her head back on the bench and closing her eyes.

Harriet said nothing, though the intensity of her gaze was enough to make Lavinia squirm. But her sister needn't worry. After spending time with the duke, filling his ears with how much she despised social occasions and celebratory affairs, Lavinia had certainly ruined any chance she may have had with him. And everyone would soon know it.

Their social circles were deceptively small, and word spread quickly. Everyone knew the duke needed a wife who could, and would, happily handle his social affairs and conduct herself as befitted a duchess.

More so than other society wives, as the

duke was a bit…eccentric.

And ever since their fathers had decided upon their unusual arrangement several years before, there had been much conjecture on which of the Wynnburn sisters would become the Duchess of Beaubrooke. Lavinia was well used to the speculation on which sister would be his bride and had frankly assumed it wouldn't be her.

She had just never realized that the first emotion to envelop her heart upon categorically ensuring she would never be the duchess was…disappointment. Curious.

Whether it was from the loss of the man—doubtful, as she'd just met him—or the potential she'd briefly had to become something other than what she'd assumed she always would be, she didn't know. And didn't want to examine it too closely.

Perhaps it was the dimple. A well-placed dimple had brought down more stalwart women than she.

She sat back against the cushions of the carriage and watched the blurry world outside the window. This was what she got for leaving her library and trying to converse with another human being. No good ever came of it.

CHAPTER TWO

Alex glanced around the ballroom, resisting the urge to yank at his cravat again. His cousin's "intimate" wedding celebration consisted of nearly one hundred people. Not nearly as sizeable as a typical ball perhaps. Certainly smaller than a ball celebrating the marriage of a prince and a lady of the court could have been. But not intimate by his estimation, either.

"Now, the Wynnburn sisters will all be in attendance tonight, so it's an excellent opportunity to observe them and make your choice," his mother said, and Alex grimaced.

"Must you phrase it that way? It sounds like I'm picking out a side of beef, not a wife."

His mother pursed her lips and smiled. "Oh, come now, darling. This is how such things are done. And it's far more civilized than just drawing one of their names out of a hat."

Was it? It didn't make much difference in the grand scheme of things, and the hat method was more efficient. But belaboring the point would be futile.

"I thought Charles had chosen the eldest daughter," he said.

His mother's lips pinched slightly, a reflex

at the painful memory of her cherished first-born son, but her voice was steady when she answered. "He favored her, certainly. She is quite accomplished and would make an excellent duchess. But he hadn't made his choice official or even gotten around to actually courting the girl yet. He'd only called on her once before…well…"

She cleared her throat, and Alex gave her hand a gentle squeeze.

"Thankfully, things hadn't yet progressed with them, or she wouldn't be in the running at all. And your father's agreement with the earl only stipulated that his heir would marry one of the earl's daughters. So you needn't choose as your brother might have. Whomever you choose will be *your* wife, after all."

"Indeed—"

A woman's laughter rang through the room, and they both turned to look. The woman's laugh was what he could only call confident. Loud, attention-grabbing, almost aggressive, but not in a way that was off-putting. It drew him in. Demanded he become a part of the merriment.

He hated merriment.

Perhaps that was too strong a word. He simply found it unproductive. Wasteful. Too fleeting to be worthwhile?

Suffice it to say, he avoided it when possible.

"Ah," his mother said, nodding toward the woman. "That would be Lady Harriet."

Alex's gaze sharpened, and he looked at the woman with new interest. Harriet stood slightly in front of the rest of the group, laughing and chatting with several young men while she flirtatiously fanned herself. Clad in a bejeweled and embroidered gown that reminded him of the yellow primroses in his greenhouse, she was as vibrant as the diamonds dripping from her throat and adorning her walnut brown hair, her laugh infectious and lively.

A younger version of her stood in a soft white dress at her side, her gloved hand pressed becomingly to her giggling lips. She wore a few less jewels, her gown slightly less embellished, but both women were lovely, seemed socially adept, fashionable, and in remarkably good spirits. They effortlessly held court over their group of admirers, men and women alike, and seemed to hold everyone captivated. All characteristics that would make for a fine duchess, as he'd need someone who could manage the social side of their lives. He certainly had no wish to do it himself.

His mother nodded in approval. "Lady Harriet is the eldest, there on the right in the yellow gown. Her youngest sister Lady Katherine, whom they call Kitty, I believe, is there beside her. Either would make a fine choice."

He frowned slightly, glancing around. "And where is the third sister?"

"Lady Lavinia. Hmm, I'm afraid I do not see her. That's odd."

She perused the crowd, and he followed suit, though he had no idea for whom he actually searched.

But then his eyes widened when he spied a large potted palm in a secluded corner...and the woman sitting beside it, nearly hidden by its enormous leaves.

The same chestnut-haired beauty from the wedding. His breath quickened ever so slightly. She sat in near solitude, her gown presentable but unadorned, ribbons rather than jewels in her hair, quizzing glass swinging from a thin, gold chain. She seemed far more interested in the potted plant beside her than anything or anyone else. He could unquestionably relate.

Though...was she...talking to the plant? His lips twitched. Again, he could relate. There was no better creature to spill one's thoughts to than a good plant. They did nothing but listen with a sympathetic ear and kept their thoughts to themselves.

She laughed, and he raised a brow. Hmm. In all the years he'd been speaking to his plants, they'd never spoken back. Certainly not amusingly enough to make him laugh.

"Well, no matter," his mother said with a sigh. "You'll make her acquaintance soon enough."

It took him a second to remember that his mother was referring to the elusive middle Wynnburn daughter. Right. He must make the acquaintance of the Wynnburns. And perhaps, once he'd fulfilled his duties for the evening, he could have a seat near his mystery woman again and find out why that palm was so amusing.

"Now," his mother said, taking his arm to gently steer him toward the waiting women, "I would advise you to spend time with each lady. A dance with each, perhaps?"

"A dance is hardly the best way to speak privately with a woman."

"Yes, but it will allow you to meet without placing too much pressure on either of you to converse overly much. You can always chat with them afterward, and we will certainly call on them tomorrow, in any case, so that you may get to know them better. But a dance is a good first step."

She nodded her encouragement, her hand on his back, not-so-subtly pushing him toward the group.

He sighed. "Very well, Mother."

She beamed, and he couldn't help but smile at her. Her smiles didn't come as readily as they used to. He missed seeing them. If dancing with the Wynnburn sisters would make his mother happy, then dance he would.

She reached up and kissed his cheek. "You're a good son," she said. "I know you don't want to do this. I'm sorry that this responsibility is falling on your shoulders. But with your father's death and your brother following him so soon after..." She paused and swallowed hard, and Alex's heart ached for her all over again.

"Are you all right, Mother?"

She waved it off and gave him a watery smile. "I'll do. In any case, what happened with your father and brother just proves how important it is for you to quickly marry and produce an heir of your own. If you were to..." She swallowed hard again. "If...well, you know, then the title and estate both go to your father's horrid cousin Bernard. And I refuse to give that man the satisfaction of becoming the next Duke of Beaubrooke. So I'm afraid it's up to you."

He forced a smile and gave his mother's hand a quick kiss. "Do not worry. The dreadful Bernard shall be kept at bay, and you'll be bouncing a grandchild on your knee in no time."

The happiness that shone from her face at his statement was worth whatever internal strife this situation caused him.

So. Now he just had to choose a woman with whom to propagate and spend his life with, from among three strangers. One of which he knew distressingly little about, except for the fact that she was the middle daughter. The other two, despite appearing the type of woman who made a good duchess, frankly, terrified him at the thought of being his wife. Lady Harriet and Lady Kitty, from what he could tell from a distance at least, seemed affable, effusive, and unreservedly friendly. The type of people he'd usually avoid like a spade to the foot. He much preferred the company of his plants and manuscripts to actual people.

He'd need to get along with the woman when they were alone...well enough, at least, that they produced at least one child. Two would be preferable. And his studious ways did not tend to inspire passion, or even placid interest, in the women he knew.

That was until he'd suddenly stepped into his brother's shoes. A ducal title was apparently enough to overcome even the most reluctant maiden's disinterest.

His mind strayed to the woman who sheltered beneath the amusing palm. A woman after his own heart, it seemed. One more comfortable with plants, books, and solitude than crowds and frivolity. However, he had at least two of the earl's daughters to dance with before he could seek out her company.

Alex took a deep breath and made his way to the Wynnburn women.

. . .

Lavinia squirmed in her chair near a tall potted plant, doing her best to hide her boredom behind a smile. It wouldn't fool anyone who looked closely. But then, no one ever looked closely. They saved those looks for her sisters.

Which let her get away with far more than she would have otherwise. Normally, she could have escaped by now, but with her mama determined for all three of her daughters to make a good impression with the duke, there would be no reprieve. For the moment, at least.

"What are you doing back in this corner? And stop slouching," her mother said.

Lavinia sucked in a startled breath and dropped the leaf she'd been rubbing, immediately getting to her feet. Her mother's gaze raked over her with a critical eye. Thankfully, she nodded, finding no fault. With her appearance, at least.

"Reticule?" she asked, and Lavinia held it out with a sigh while her mother quickly patted it between her hands.

"All books and spectacles have been left at home, as promised," Lavinia said.

"We must be on our best behavior

tonight," her mother said. "I have been assured that the duke will attend, and he will no doubt wish to dance with at least one of you."

Her gaze strayed to Harriet, and Lavinia nodded toward her. "He'll want to dance with Harriet, surely. And sitting quietly in the corner is hardly misbehaving."

Her mother scowled at her. "Must you always speak your mind instead of just listening and obeying?" She didn't wait for an answer, her attention turning back to the glittering throng dancing and conversing before them. A good decision on her part, as Lavinia's answer would not have been well received.

Harriet's tinkling laugh rang throughout the room, drawing a smile from every man within hearing distance. Her mother's pride as she gazed at her eldest shone clear and true. It was well placed. Harriet was indeed a daughter of whom to be proud.

"The duke is his own man," her mother finally said, apparently attempting to be diplomatic. "His father's arrangement with your father only stipulated his heir must choose one of our girls. Which one he chooses is entirely up to him. Therefore, *all* my girls will be ready should his eye turn upon them. No matter if the duke chooses you or not," her mother continued, "you must still find a husband. So we shall be at our most charming this evening. Yes?"

"Yes, Mother," Lavinia said, though a host of other retorts begged to be released. None of them would do her any good. And her mother, after a vague smile and pat on the cheek, had already turned her attention back to her sisters.

"Oh heavens! The duke is approaching," her mother said, clasping her hands together. She hurried off, fluttering a hand at Lavinia, which was likely meant to tell Lavinia to follow her. But as she hadn't heard the actual words, ignoring them seemed feasible.

"Is it safe to emerge?" a man's voice whispered from behind the potted plant.

Lavinia spun around, smiling when she caught sight of her dear friend.

"Nigel, stop doing that! You startle me every time."

Her friend, Lord Nigel Bainbridge, had been darting back and forth from the palm for the last several minutes, dodging one woman or another. The man had left a string of broken hearts from one end of the country to the other and seemed determined to use her palm to escape the consequences of his actions.

He peeked out from behind the plant and gave her a little bow. "You are looking very lovely this evening."

She grimaced. "You needn't try and flatter me, Nigel, though I appreciate the sentiment."

She knew very well the pale-mint-green dress did little for her complexion. But it had been her only choice, as the seamstress had been too busy tailoring Harriet's and Kitty's dresses to finish Lavinia's. The one she now wore was stylish enough, being one of Harriet's castoffs. But a dress for Harriet's tall, lithe form didn't translate quite as well to Lavinia's shorter, plumper frame. She was one sneeze or too-eager breath away from the seams disintegrating altogether.

"Perhaps I was merely aiming for a few compliments of my own," he said, posing with his chin in the air so she might admire his attire.

"You are impeccable as always," she said, nodding toward his sharp black suit, every line in place, the sapphire pin in his cravat accentuating the sparkling blue of his eyes. His blond hair curled in thick, fashionably tousled waves about his ears and face. He was, in a word, delightful. It was a feat that he'd managed to remain unmarried for so long.

"My thanks, my lady," he said with a charming smile that was wasted on her.

"What are you doing lurking back there?" she asked.

"I'm not lurking, dear girl. I was merely waiting for an opportune moment to make my presence known."

"Hmm," she murmured, not believing him

for a moment. "How did you get an invitation to this ball anyway?" she asked, changing the subject. "You aren't personal friends of either the bride or groom that I am aware."

"True. However, I am friends with Lady Elizabeth's favorite tutor who was invited and who was able to extend that invitation to me."

Lavinia shook her head. "Your connections are truly astounding."

"Thank you."

"It wasn't really a compliment."

"But I shall take it as one anyway. Why are you sitting back here keeping company with this poor plant instead of moving about the dance floor, enticing some poor sod into unholy matrimony?"

She rolled her eyes. "My sisters have that occupation well in hand. I am merely here to enjoy the spectacle."

"Ah yes, the infamous Wynnburn sisters. Harriet, the eldest, prettiest, and infinitely most acceptable, holding court as she is wont to do, surrounded by her friends, admirers, suitors, and, of course, your dear mamá. Who is naturally bursting with pride at having birthed such a paragon of womanly perfection. *Two* such paragons, since our darling Kitty is standing there beside your sister in her full maidenly splendor."

Lavinia snorted and swatted at him with

her fan. "You're ridiculous."

He gasped in mock outrage. "I am no such thing. I am merely extolling the virtues of the most—actually, *two* of the most—eligible ladies on the market. Not that they overshadow you for an instant."

"Um hmm," Lavinia mumbled with the eye roll that comment deserved.

Oh, she agreed with him on her sisters. Kitty's effervescent sweetness made her the giggling, smiling darling that one couldn't help loving. The perfect complement to Harriet's cunningly quick intelligence, elegance, and sophistication. They were the best of everything society had to offer.

Lavinia, on the other hand, was just…well, she was just *on the other hand*. There. Present. Alive but only remembered when she mistakenly breathed too loudly. Loved but… overlooked. Which stung occasionally, yes. Though it had its perks.

"I speak only the truth," Nigel said, with enough sincerity she almost believed him.

"My dear Nigel, there are more similarities between myself and this plant," she said, the leaf she touched leaving a velvety green smear on her gloved fingers, "than between my sisters and me. They are…what they are." She waved a hand in their direction. "And I am, for the most part, tended to enough to keep alive but otherwise left alone."

Nigel frowned, and Lavinia pressed on before he could protest.

"Don't mistake me. I'm not complaining. Truth be told, it is far preferable to those rare moments when my mother is reminded of me and aims that determined focus my way."

Nigel chuckled. "Your mother isn't that bad," he said, though he kept his voice low enough only Lavinia would hear him. Astute of him. Her mother was not one to be trifled with.

"Although," he said, tilting his head to regard her, "it *is* painfully apparent that your dear mamá will not rest until all three of her darling daughters are wedded and bedded."

"Nigel, really," she said with a small gasp, not that she was really shocked. Nigel was nothing if not irreverent about any and everything.

"Am I wrong, then?"

"You may have a point," she conceded. "However, I think my mother is quite content to leave me to my own devices until my sisters have made their brilliant matches. I will likely marry the first gentleman who asks me to dance at this dreadfully boring ball, thereby saving me from an evening of talking to a plant, and they…well…" She smiled and gestured at the flock of well-suited men gathering about her sisters.

Nigel slapped a hand to his chest. "I am

utterly wounded you find me as engaging as a plant."

Lavinia laughed. "First of all, I was referring to the actual plant," she said, gesturing to the thing with her thumb. "And secondly, whilst I shall always be happy to dance with you, as a suitor, you do not count. We've been friends for far too long for you to ever be anything more than an affectionate but often annoying brother-figure."

"Well," he said, straightening and smiling down at her. "I guess I'm not too saddened by your looming spinsterhood, as it leaves you free to enjoy my company longer." He gave her a roguish wink that had her lips twitching.

She reined it in and gave him a mock glare. "That's possibly the first argument you've used that actually makes me *want* to start courting."

"Your Grace," her mother said, her excited voice carrying over to Lavinia's corner.

Lavinia's stomach went topsy-turvy, and she stumbled to her feet, smoothing her dress out. Though she needn't have bothered, as her mother and sisters were far enough away from her that they'd forgotten her existence again. And the palm offered enough protection that the duke hadn't noticed her, either. So she assumed, at least. It was hard to tell without her spectacles, but upon inspection through her quizzing glass, he didn't appear to be looking in her direction.

"Ah yes, the darling Duke of Beaubrooke enters, and we must all fawn over him," Nigel muttered in her ear.

She shushed him. "Your dislike of him prejudices you."

"Yes, it does. And with good cause."

"According to you."

"Which is the only opinion you should require," he said.

"I am capable of forming my own opinion, thank you."

His low chuckle drew a smile from her. "You are very capable, to that I'll agree."

Lavinia turned her attention back to the dance floor, glancing at the duke through her quizzing glass now and again. What she would say to him when they were finally forced to speak, she couldn't imagine.

In fact, when he realized that the woman who had prattled on and on about how much she hated social gatherings and all the fanfare was in contention, theoretically, to be his duchess, he'd likely be horrified. The woman who would host all his social events and raise his children to be functioning members of their society? He'd know the instant he realized who she was that she would never do as his wife. Her cheeks flamed all over again at the thought.

Still, if he happened to speak to her, she

wanted to salvage whatever good impression she could so as not to ruin her sisters' chances. So…best behavior it must be.

The duke bowed his head toward Harriet and offered his hand. Lavinia ignored the disappointment swimming through her gut. It was hardly surprising that he'd chosen Harriet first. Well, at least now Lavinia could relax a bit.

She sat back with a relieved sigh and watched her sister dance with the duke while her mind wandered.

The wedding of the duke's cousin had been truly lovely, the celebrations that followed equally so, the affection between the couple palpable. Lavinia had never really given much thought to whom she would wed. But with her current situation with the duke, it had certainly been more on her mind. And after watching Lady Elizabeth wed a man she obviously deeply loved, Lavinia couldn't help but desire something similar for herself.

If she must marry, that is. But in lieu of a love match, she hoped for someone with whom she was companionable, at the very least.

Was that the duke?

She very much doubted it. Not when Harriet and Kitty were also choices.

Speaking of whom…Harriet and the duke were spinning in their direction, and she ducked a bit farther behind her potted palm, to Nigel's amusement. Time for a subject change.

"Enough about me," she said. "Tell me what's going on with you. Have you found that information you were looking for yet? Wasn't there supposed to be some clue in some long-lost manuscript about the mixing of particular plants?"

"Yes," he grumbled. "But your dear duke seems to have gotten his hands on it first, and I must wait my turn."

"Oh my. And you do so hate being patient."

"You have no idea."

"Poor Nigel."

His gaze flickered to the duke, who seemed to be quite a bit closer to them. Nigel's eyes narrowed slightly, but Lavinia patted his hand.

"Don't worry, Nigel. You are one of the most brilliant men I know. I'm sure you'll get your grant."

His gaze came back to her, and he smiled. "From your lips to God's ears."

She laughed. And abruptly choked it off as Nigel straightened with a garbled *oop* sound, and then disappeared. The duke had apparently come too near to their corner again.

In fact, Nigel had quite the good idea. There was surely a nice alcove somewhere that she could settle in with her book until her family was ready to leave.

Lavinia could be honest enough with herself that she'd admit she found the duke handsome and more than a little intriguing. Nigel had been complaining about him for years. And anyone with enough mettle to rile Nigel was a fascinating person indeed. While the duke seemed a bit dour during their brief interaction at the wedding, he hadn't been unkind. He was a studious man. That much she knew from Nigel. Which meant they had much in common. If she must marry—and her parents would be certain that she must— she could do far worse than a duke who loved his research.

Unfortunately, her chances were slim. While the duke might be a good solution for Lavinia, she was fairly certain she would not be the best solution for him.

CHAPTER THREE

"Sit still, Kitty," Harriet commanded, dragging the brush through their sister's hair as best she could while Kitty tried to squirm away.

"Oh, it's brushed enough." Kitty tried to bat at Harriet's hand, but Harriet thumped her on the head with the back of the brush and Kitty subsided, albeit with a pout reminiscent of her toddler years.

"I've almost finished," Harriet said.

"I know." Kitty sighed. "I just wish we were still at the ball," she said, swaying on the stool in front of her vanity mirror. "I could have danced until dawn."

Lavinia groaned and adjusted the damp cloth over her aching eyes. Trying to navigate the evening with only her quizzing glass invariably led to aching eyes, no matter how many candles and chandeliers were lit.

"I wish we could have left earlier," she said.

"Oh," Kitty groaned, tossing a comb at her. "You're always such a spoilsport."

Lavinia chuckled and tossed it back. "I am not."

"You are! You might actually enjoy yourself one of these evenings if you came out of your corner and spoke with people. Maybe even danced with a few nice young men."

"Hmm, perhaps. Though I thought the purpose of attending tonight's ball was to make a good impression on the duke in particular."

"Well, I did that easily enough," Kitty said. "And then I made a good impression on a few more," she said with a giggle.

"Kitty!" Harriet admonished.

"What?"

When Harriet merely glared at her, Kitty rolled her eyes.

"Oh, come now. Neither one of you can tell me that you are happy with this arrangement," Kitty said.

Harriet shrugged. "It's the way of the world. We must marry, and our parents want us to marry well. Is that so surprising?"

"Of course not," Kitty said. "But I would have preferred they simply matched one of us with him instead of this strange…competition."

Lavinia frowned. "I don't think it's a competition as such. I think Father wanted to give us some choice in the matter rather than randomly pairing one of us with him."

"Ah, but do we have the choice? It seems as though it is the duke who will decide."

"You know as well as I do that Father would never force us to wed someone we do not wish," Lavinia said. "No matter what the duke prefers."

"Well, good," Kitty said, settling back so Harriet could return to brushing her hair. "Because while he's handsome enough, he is much too somber for me."

"You don't wish to be a duchess?" Harriet asked.

"I'd rather be happy than a duchess," Kitty answered, and Harriet paused for a moment, looking at her thoughtfully before dragging the brush through her deep brown tresses.

"He'd be a good match for either of you, though," Kitty said.

Lavinia glanced up, startled. "What do you mean?"

"Didn't you enjoy speaking to him at the wedding?" Kitty asked.

"Well, yes. But we didn't really say much."

Kitty shrugged. "Perhaps not. But having met the man myself, I can tell you, you'd get along swimmingly."

"Perhaps…" Lavinia said, carefully keeping her face as blank as possible.

"He's just as preoccupied with his dreadful plants as you are with your books," Kitty said. "When we danced, he didn't speak of anything but his plant experiments. He spent more time staring at the potted palms in the corners than he did looking at me."

Kitty didn't often encounter people who would prefer to gaze upon a vibrant succulent rather than her own vivacious visage. But the duke was...unique. To say the least.

The indignation and incredulity in her sister's voice had Lavinia burying her face in her pillow. As did the sudden realization that he very possibly had been staring at *her* in the corner. Then again, with his penchant for plants, perhaps he was merely *that* interested in the palms.

Harriet groaned. "He did spend quite a bit of time near the hydrangeas now that I think of it."

Kitty giggled, and Lavinia shook her head. "Oh, you two. Surely he's not that bad."

They both looked at her with eyebrows raised, and her lips twitched.

"Perhaps he simply needs to be introduced to new diversions, something to entice him out of the greenhouse."

"Such as?" Kitty asked.

Lavinia pursed her lips. "I quite enjoy the works of Mrs. Clara Pope. I'm certain he'd find her paintings diverting if he isn't already familiar with her."

"Oh, certainly," Kitty said in a teasing tone. "Mrs. Pope. You mean the artist who is renowned for her botanical paintings?"

Lavinia opened her mouth to retort but snapped it shut again. Very well, that was a valid point. Still... "That's not all she paints. She's actually better known for her miniatures," she muttered.

"Yes, yes," Harriet said. "Just please keep in mind that he *is* the Duke of Beaubrooke now. He has a duty at these social events. He cannot sit in a corner, jabbering on about tiny paintings for an entire evening."

This time Lavinia rolled her eyes. "His only duty is to his family and the people on his estates," she said. "He does not have a duty to flit from one party to another, entertaining the whole of society."

"Of course he does," Harriet said, pinning Lavinia with an exasperated gaze. "How else do you suppose that wealthy gentlemen remain wealthy? They need to curry favor with the right gentlemen and make connections with the proper people. He has a responsibility to his peers and his heirs. He is an example and can hardly lead others if he is buried under a mound of paperwork in some dusty old library or if he is so out of touch with his peers that he doesn't know one from the other."

"I don't think that sounds so terrible," Lavinia said. "Not the paperwork part, but I'd quite enjoy getting lost in some dusty old library."

Kitty giggled again. "You would say that. I'm sure you would walk out of there with an entire stack full of books in which to stick your nose."

Lavinia plopped down on the bed and sighed dreamily. "That would be magnificent.

Though the duke's office is at the Oxford Library, and I hardly think they would just let anyone walk out with an entire stack of books."

Kitty shrugged. "They probably would if you were his duchess."

"Do you think so?" she asked, perking up.

Harriet rolled her eyes. "Trust you to find the most exciting thing about marrying a duke is his ability to provide you with books."

That wasn't the only thing about a possible match between them that excited her. The memory of those deep brown eyes raking over her sparked more than a little interest. She couldn't deny that a library was a powerful enticement, though.

Still, she sighed. "As wonderful as new books would be, I don't think he will choose me."

"Of course not," Harriet said, finally laying down the brush so she could braid Kitty's hair.

She glanced up, and Lavinia caught her gaze in the mirror, and for once Harriet seemed to realize that she had said something boorish. She even looked slightly shamed by it.

"I don't mean it to be unkind," she said. "But he can only marry one of us, and as socially awkward as he is, he's going to need a woman who can navigate the often-treacherous waters of society. And forgive me, Livy, but not only are you not the type to flourish in such surroundings, you've never shown the slightest interest in it, let alone a proclivity for it. You would be miserable married to him."

Would she, though? There was truth in her sister's words. Lavinia *was* usually miserable at societal events. But it wasn't because she didn't find pleasure in them for their own sake. She actually quite enjoyed the music and the decorations and the atmosphere. It was more that she didn't really have anyone to converse with. What fun was a party when she did nothing but sit in a corner by herself and watch everyone else have fun?

She'd enjoyed talking to the duke for the few minutes it had lasted. And they did seem to have a great deal in common. At least from what she could piece together from what her sisters and Nigel had told her. Perhaps if she were able to arrive on the duke's arm to every party, she'd enjoy them more.

She didn't say any of that to Harriet, though. It wouldn't change her sister's thinking. Nothing ever did, once she had her mind set to something, and her mind was set on becoming the next Duchess of Beaubrooke. And Lavinia couldn't argue that Harriet was infinitely well-suited for it.

So she simply gave her sister a gentle smile. "Perhaps you are right," she said.

Harriet, having gotten her way yet again,

smiled benignly and turned back to Kitty's hair.

Kitty had apparently ignored the conversation altogether, whether it was because she didn't hear it, as engrossed in her own world as she was at that moment, or because she just didn't care, Lavinia didn't know. But she envied her ability to do so. Lavinia often wished she could block out Harriet's words. Even more, she wished she could carve out the ache that they caused in her heart. She didn't love the duke, obviously. One didn't fall in love on the basis of a brief conversation in which the man had barely spoken.

But she *had* enjoyed his company, fleeting though it may have been. And there seemed to be at least the possibility of a greater connection. It was so easy to imagine that developing into something more in the future. He had been polite and seemed actually interested in her and what she had to say. She couldn't remember a time anyone other than Nigel had been so.

And yes, his well-known to the point of being legendary obsession with plants was a little...much. But to her mind it was rather sweet. At least he'd found something that he cared about enough to devote his life to it. Which was more than most of the wealthy young suitors that she had seen traipsing through their house could say.

Most of them spent their time on frivolous pursuits, not bothering to do anything worthwhile with their lives except attend party after party. At least the duke spent his time on something that could be so helpful to so many. She found it terribly interesting. *He* was interesting. And that was much more than she could say for anyone else she had met.

And far too much to say to Harriet. Lavinia wouldn't betray her interest in the duke. The humiliation when he chose someone else would be too great. And the daily reminder for the rest of her life would make everyone uncomfortable. So she kept her thoughts to herself.

It would have made it much easier to sleep that night if she'd been able to keep her thoughts *from* herself as well. Instead, she slept restlessly, thoughts of intense brown eyes, full lips smiling down at her, and a tiny dimple that made her heart skip invading her dreams.

CHAPTER FOUR

Alex arrived in the parlor drawing room at the Wynnburns' London home to find the entire family already gathered and waiting, along with more than one rival suitor. And his own mother, of course. He shouldn't be surprised.

Their mothers had been discussing this wedding for quite some time, meeting bimonthly for nigh on two years now. Since before Charles had died, even though he had barely begun to make the Wynnburn ladies' acquaintance at the time. The plans were well underway. Anyone who was anyone knew about the upcoming nuptials.

The wedding, of course, would be kept relatively intimate. By his mother's standards, that is. Just friends and family. Though, with the families involved, there were still far too many people for Alex's liking. And St. George's Church itself was far too accessible to the public. There were sure to be onlookers.

But it would be nothing compared to the wedding ball that evening, which would be a grand affair. An event of this undertaking didn't happen overnight, so it was really more practical than anything else to keep all the arrangements that had already been made in place. Only the marital couple had changed.

Really, there was only one detail left: which bride would be walking down the aisle?

He wished he knew.

Alex clenched his jaw and turned to the rest of the crowd, who had stopped speaking and turned in his direction at the announcement of his arrival. Lovely. He gave a perfunctory nod to the room in general. This was one of the parts he always hated about his new position in life. All eyes on him, no matter where he went. As the second son, he'd been mostly overlooked. Well, perhaps not overlooked. He was still the son of a duke. But overshadowed, certainly, by his much more charming older brother. Now that he'd stepped into the role, he wasn't quite sure what to do with his newfound popularity.

He glanced about, taking note of both Harriet and Kitty surrounded by several eligible gentlemen. They each made sure to graciously acknowledge him without slighting their other callers. Diplomatic indeed. And wily. Both managing to show interest in him while ensuring he saw the other men's interest in them.

He held in his sigh. He was truly unequipped for these parlor games. All the more reason, perhaps, to marry a woman adept at them. Then he could let his wife deal with the niceties he had little time for or interest in.

Their mother, Lady Abberforth, held court in the center of the room with their father, the earl, looking on indulgently.

Lady Abberforth hurried up to him. "Your Grace, welcome to our home."

He bowed his head, mentally discarding several awkward responses before settling on, "Thank you."

If Lady Abberforth expected a more effusive salutation, she did not let it show. Instead, she turned to her daughters, who each came to stand beside their mother. "We're delighted to see you again so soon," she said, her two daughters nodding in agreement.

He wasn't sure how to respond to that, either, since everyone involved had known he'd be calling on them this very morning. They likely expected him to respond with some sort of charming quip, but nothing presented itself. He was no good at these niceties. So instead, he merely nodded with what he hoped was a polite smile in the direction of each of the ladies.

"Lady Harriet, Lady Katherine."

He glanced around. He had yet to meet the third daughter. In fact, he was beginning to wonder if she even existed.

Lady Abberforth glanced about as well, belatedly realizing her other offspring was not in attendance. Her gaze finally stopped on a young woman who sat curled up on the window seat, a book in her lap. His eyes widened slightly, and he nearly took a step forward before he stopped himself.

"Lavinia, dear," her mother called.

The young woman's head shot up, her brown eyes appearing large behind a pair of thin-wired spectacles perched on her nose. "Come greet His Grace," her mother admonished.

Lavinia? It was her! The lady from the wedding. The one who'd spent the evening conversing with the potted palm. She was the third daughter?

Lavinia clambered to her feet, quickly pulling the glasses from her face as she hurried over. Socially adept, she was not. At least, not compared to her sisters. Lavinia's cheeks flamed red, but he suspected it was due more to everyone's disapproving gazes rather than his own perusal of her.

"Your Grace," she said, dropping a small curtsy.

He was too stunned to do more than jerk his head in a sharp nod and stare. He was vaguely aware that Lady Abberforth continued to speak, saying lovely things about him and his cousin's wedding and celebration ball the previous day.

But he wished he'd had more than a day to ponder. Time to decide which woman to make his wife. Which would be the best fit, for him and his situation. Time to come to terms with the fact that the one he'd been most interested in getting to know was a mystery woman he'd never find again.

Yet here she was.

Up until a few weeks earlier, adding a wife and family to his life had seemed the absolute worst thing that could happen to him. Harriet was the obvious choice. He knew that. Stunningly beautiful, poised, sophisticated, already connected to the most advantageous people, not only able and willing but thrilled to join the wives of the upper echelon. She was everything any man could ask for in a wife.

And Alex had little to no interest in spending another moment with her.

Katherine—Kitty—seemed very sweet, beautiful, charmingly droll, and full of life. She would keep him on his toes for certain. He could tell even from the one dance they'd had he would never have a dull moment with her. He would also never have a *quiet* moment with her in his life. She was so full of erratic energy that being around her had worn him out within minutes.

He enjoyed being around people—some

people, at least—and could be quite social when the mood struck him. But such instances inevitably left him drained and craving the quiet solitude of his office or greenhouse. Quiet solitude and Lady Katherine Wynnburn were not words that belonged together in a sentence. Any more than he and Kitty belonged together. Kitty was a force of nature, and she deserved someone who would allow her to be that. Too much time in his sorry company and he feared that bright, burning ball of energy within her would be extinguished. He would never want to be responsible for that.

And then there was Lavinia. His mystery lady. Despite their brief encounter at the wedding, she'd made a favorable impact upon him. And if the blush of her cheeks just now meant anything, she wasn't totally averse to him, either.

She seemed to match him in all the ways that mattered to him. She had been raised by the same mother as her sisters, so he had no doubt that she would be able to run his estates just as efficiently as Kitty or Harriet. She may not be as connected or canny as Harriet or as effervescent as Kitty, but with time he had no doubt she would manage just fine.

More importantly, she seemed to share many of his interests or was at least interested enough that being his wife wouldn't be too much of a burden. He hoped. They didn't know each other well, true. But he knew she enjoyed reading and solitude enough that she sought out quiet corners to hide with a book, even at a wedding that many would have committed crimes to attend. Such a woman wouldn't waste his time with balls and galas and social events. She'd understand his desire for research and study and would leave him to them. Or perhaps even join him.

She may not be what the Duke of Beaubrooke needed, but she could be what *he*, Alex, needed.

Lady Harriet's and Lady Katherine's eyes widened as he walked past them and went straight to Lavinia. He bowed.

"Lady Lavinia, I would be grateful for a tour of your lovely gardens."

Her eyes widened and flickered to her mother who, while obviously surprised, nodded with a smile, waving at one of the maids to accompany them.

Once outdoors, they walked in awkward silence for a few moments, Lavinia holding up her quizzing glass every few minutes.

"Lovely day for a walk," he finally said, immediately cursing himself for the inane comment.

Her eyes widened slightly, but she nodded.

"It is. Thankfully the weather is cooperating."

"Indeed."

They walked a few more moments in silence, and Alex searched for something else to say. What did one say to the woman one intended to marry when they'd met a grand total of twice?

"Definite chill in the air, though," he finally said.

"A bit. Though we'll no doubt long for it when the summer heat arrives."

"Indubitably. Though"—his fingers trailed over the petals of a camellia—"your gardener should be sure to cover these beauties if the temperature drops."

"I'll be sure he does," she said, her lips twitching, and he cleared his throat.

"My apologies. My skills lie more with my hands than my speech, I'm afraid."

Her eyebrows shot straight up at that, and he quickly tried to smooth over his inadvertent innuendo. "That is, I'm a botanist, an academic. I could easier write you a veritable tome of hopeless nonsense on that potted palm in the corner than engage in entertaining conversation for more than a quarter hour."

She laughed softly. "I have not had much experience in the art of diverting conversation myself. That is much more Harriet's or Kitty's forte."

"Ah, yes, your formidable sisters."

Her mouth dropped slightly open. "I have heard them called many things, but formidable is not one of them." She tilted her head slightly in thought. "Though the description does fit Harriet, I'll admit. Just...do not tell her I said so."

He leaned a bit closer. "Your secret is safe with me."

She smiled up at him, and his stomach somersaulted. He pressed a hand to it, frowning, slightly at the curious sensation.

"Kitty, however, is very sweet," she continued, oblivious to his sudden physiological distress. "A bit effusive, perhaps. But a joy to be around in most circumstances."

That might depend on one's definition of joy, but he wouldn't argue her sentiment.

Alex glanced down and watched a bee settle on a beautiful patch of snapdragons that were such a vibrant shade of orangey-red that he couldn't tear his eyes from them. He'd rarely seen such a color. In fact, in his own garden, his snapdragons were a deep burgundy. A color he loved, to be sure. But the mix of orange and red was truly a stunning combination. Perhaps Lord Abberforth would be willing to part with a few cuttings that Alex could take back to his own garden and—

He was not in this garden to admire the flora.

He wrenched his eyes from the snapdragons to where Lavinia was carefully walking ahead of him a few steps, just as she paused to look behind her. She brought her quizzing glass to her eye for a moment and then smiled when her gaze met his. A sight every bit as lovely, and possibly more so, than the exquisite flowers at his feet.

She stood and waited for him to catch up. Their eyes again met and held, and he could have sworn the world paused to take a deep breath along with him.

Her lips parted slightly, and she looked up at him with her brow faintly creased. Though whether it was due to emotion, confusion, or if she was squinting to see him better, he didn't know.

A slight cough from the maid behind them reminded him they were not alone. Not that anything untoward had occurred, but from the faint blush on Lady Lavinia's cheeks, it was clear he wasn't the only one who had felt something.

The moment broken, he continued their conversation. "I know enough about your sisters. Tell me about yourself."

She gave him a little half shrug. "There isn't much to tell. I'm afraid I'm not all that interesting."

"The fact that I'm asking negates that opinion. I find you immensely interesting."

She blinked at him a bit shyly, but her smile seemed pleased. "You hardly know me, Your Grace."

"Agreed. Hence, the questions."

She regarded him with another soft smile. "I'm afraid my answer must still be the same. You know the important things. I enjoy reading. I love my home and family. And plants," she said, her smile growing wider. She paused a moment, her eyes narrowing briefly as though she was thinking, and then added with a faint blush, "I do not always enjoy social occasions, but I am willing and able to carry out whatever duties may be required of me. I would not disgrace my future husband… should I ever marry."

A bold statement. And a courageous one for a woman to say to a near stranger. He admired her mettle. And her honesty.

More than that, of the three sisters, Lavinia was by far the most who suited him personally. He had no doubt that when the unavoidable occasion arose that they must venture into society that she would be more than capable of performing the duties of his duchess. But from what he knew of her so far, she didn't seem the type to crave such diversions. She would be happy spending the evening in his library, quietly reading, while he continued with his research. She wouldn't begrudge him his time in his greenhouse.

He took a deep breath of the late summer air. The sooner he chose a wife, the sooner he could get back to his manuscripts and beloved plants.

Only it wasn't green leaves and growth rates that had been running unchecked through his head these last several hours since the wedding.

It was laughing eyes, a shy smile, and the unfamiliar but growing desire to spend time with something…someone…other than his plants.

And that was enough to decide him.

"Lady Lavinia. I find you most acceptable."

Lavinia's mouth dropped open, and she stared at him, stunned, for several moments before a small frown formed between her brows.

That wasn't quite what he'd meant to say. "I…" He grimaced. Damn. He was bungling this horribly.

"Would you like to start again?" she asked.

He gave her a sharp nod and then cleared his throat. "You are the least objectionable—"

She cocked an eyebrow, and he pursed his lips together. Why was this so difficult?

He took a deep breath and blew it out, taking a brief second to center himself.

"Lady Lavinia." He straightened to his full height, hands clasped behind his back. "As you are aware of my intentions in calling upon your family today, and as our families are both impatient for an announcement, I needn't expound upon all of that. I *will* say, the choice has not been easy. But I have found you to be auspicious in nature, intelligence, and appearance, and find your company most agreeable. Therefore I would be honored if you would consent to becoming my wife."

She sucked in a sharp breath. Each second that she withheld her answer made it more and more difficult to draw a steady breath. She could be assured of his intentions, yet he could not say the same of her. He must marry a Wynnburn. But she had no such compulsion. She could just as well deny him.

It suddenly occurred to him that perhaps he should have waited until he could be sure of her response *before* he proposed.

Her sisters would have said yes, he had no doubt. But would she? He hadn't realized until this moment just how much he wanted her to.

She finally blinked, a little life returning to her face. And then she smiled, and hope blossomed in his chest.

"I thank you for your kind words and faith in me, Your Grace. I find your company most pleasing as well. I am honored to accept."

And just like that, he could breathe again.

CHAPTER FIVE

Lavinia's heart nearly beat from her chest as they reentered the parlor. The other suitors had gone, and both of their families were sitting on the sofas in the center of the room, waiting for them to return.

"There you are," the dowager duchess said. "Really, Alex, there is so much to get done before the wedding. I do wish you would spend a little less time galivanting about gardens and greenhouses."

Lavinia thought she detected a quiet sigh from the duke, and truly, she understood. Her own mother, no matter how good her intentions, made her want to tear her ringlets out on a weekly basis.

"Lavinia, dear," the dowager duchess said, "I do hope His Grace hasn't taxed you overmuch. His love of all things green and growing really is out of hand. Sometimes I wonder if he was truly born or if he simply sprouted from the carrot patch."

Lavinia didn't join in the good-natured laughing that emanated from the room. Her nerves were too taut to do much more than smile amiably.

The duke had just asked her to be his wife. And in a matter of moments, he would either come to his senses and run from the room or he'd inform their families of his decision.

Her heart couldn't seem to remember if it should beat or skip about her chest. No one would be expecting the announcement that was coming. Lavinia's stomach was close to rioting at the realization that she couldn't be sure what everyone's reactions would be.

However, the duke's mother was waiting for a response, so she took a deep breath and smiled again. "I didn't find it taxing at all, Your Grace. I've always been one to love a good walk around the garden. I quite enjoyed myself."

The dowager's eyes widened slightly, but she nodded with a congenial smile. "Wonderful to hear, my dear."

It suddenly struck Lavinia that in just a few weeks' time, this woman would be her mother-in-law. She would not only have her own mother watching her every move with a critical, if loving, eye, but she would now have a second mother. The woman who'd been the Duchess of Beaubrooke for decades until the death of her husband. The woman who would be judging her, not only as a daughter-in-law but as the new duchess.

She took a deep breath and slowly blew it out, moving ever so slightly closer to the duke, as if he'd shield her from whatever might come her way.

A movement everyone seemed to have missed…except Harriet. Her eyes had focused on the excited flush in Lavinia's cheeks and the pleased look in the duke's eyes the moment they'd cleared the threshold. A flash of shock was all the emotion Harriet betrayed before she'd steeled her features into the stoic mask she often wore.

No one else seemed at all concerned or even curious as to why the duke had asked Lavinia, of all people, to walk. Could they really have thought, even in the midst of all this wedding talk, that he'd really only wanted to see the gardens?

Lavinia wasn't sure if it was amusing or rage-inducing.

"Now, Alex," his mother said, "I realize the wedding hasn't been foremost on your mind. But the banns must be read beginning this Sunday in order for them to be read for the three weeks prior to the wedding. As the date has been set for months, it really would have been preferable to have started them last week at the latest. I'm afraid you can't delay any longer, my son. You must make your choice."

"I already have, Mother," he said, his face not betraying anything that he might be thinking, though his tone sounded pleased enough.

His mother blinked at him in surprise,

obviously having been expecting an argument. "Have you now? My, that is exciting, I must say. Well?"

The dowager duchess now noticed that her son hadn't yet moved away from Lavinia. Dawning realization and outright surprise were fairly evident on everyone else's faces from what Lavinia could tell. It was moments such as these when she was thankful for her poor eyesight. Their disappointment wouldn't change, but at least for her it was a bit blurry around the edges. Her father, the dear man, smiled on, blissfully indulgent and unaware of the tension in the room.

Lavinia expected that the duke might excuse himself to speak with her father in private, but instead he offered her his arm and clasped his hand over hers where it rested before bowing in her father's direction.

"Lord Wynnburn, I know this is merely a formality, since our families have already worked out all the details. But I would be honored if you would grant me your permission to take your daughter Lavinia as my wife."

The mothers and Kitty gasped, sat in stunned silence for half a heartbeat, and then rallied admirably and rushed toward them with smiles and congratulations. Even Kitty, after a moment of shock, seemed happy for her. Harriet's face showed no emotion whatsoever, nor did she offer congratulations. Which, considering she always acted in the most perfect way possible in any situation, made Lavinia more than a little anxious.

But not enough to regret saying yes to the duke. He might have been the first person in her life, ever, to choose her first. Not because he had to but because he actually wanted to. And even if it hadn't been the most romantic declaration, Lavinia would treasure the moment forever.

Lady Abberforth bustled forward, her skirts swinging widely. Her movements were no doubt designed to cover the marked silence from Harriet. She clasped Lavinia in her embrace.

"Lavinia, dear, I'm so pleased for you." She pulled back and cupped Lavinia's face. "You will make a beautiful duchess."

Lavinia smiled back at her mother, who was doing an admirable job at hiding her shock. She had no reason to be unhappy, of course, as long as *one* of her daughters was the next duchess, and Lavinia didn't detect anything but genuine happiness for her in her mother's eyes. Surprise, perhaps. But happiness all the same. Kitty grinned and clapped and came to kiss Lavinia on the cheek.

"I'm so glad for you, Livy," she said before turning her smile to the duke. "And for you, Your Grace. I hadn't thought of it before, but you and Livy will make a grand couple. You with your plants and she with her books. It's a perfect match."

The duke nodded his thanks, but Lavinia pulled her sister into a hug, touched by what seemed to be Kitty's genuine happiness for her.

"Thank you, Kitty," she said.

Kitty just kissed her cheek and went back to sit at the table next to Harriet's now-empty seat.

Lavinia sighed. She hadn't expected her eldest sister to take the news well. But it hurt, nonetheless. Lavinia had spent her entire life as the moon to her sister's sun. Often to her detriment. The least Harriet could have done was feign congratulations for a few moments before pouting and stomping off.

"Congratulations, my dear," the dowager duchess said, pulling her in for a quick hug.

"Thank you, Your Grace," Lavinia said with a shy smile.

"I can't tell you how pleased I am to welcome you to the family." There was sincere warmth in her eyes when she patted Lavinia's cheek before going back to her seat.

Lavinia looked up at an ostensibly bemused duke. He didn't seem to know what to do now that his choice had been made and everything else was in motion. The feeling was decidedly mutual.

"Wait a minute, wait a minute," her father said. "I haven't given my approval yet."

Everyone in the room froze and stared at her father, who blinked at them all innocently. "I have no intention of withholding my approval, naturally," he said, "but a man likes to get the words out before congratulations are spread about."

"Oh," her mother said with an exasperated wave while everyone else laughed.

"Thankfully, all the contract details have already been worked out. And the rest, I'll leave to your mother."

"Oh!" her mother said again. "That's right. We'll have to change a few things…"

She frowned, belatedly realizing, Lavinia supposed, that Harriet had been the one picking out all the details a bride would want for her wedding with occasional input from Kitty. Lavinia hadn't been consulted at all.

"No matter, we'll get it all sorted. Come along." She went back to the table in the corner of the room that was piled high with swatches of fabric, pieces of dinnerware, and dozens of other items that suddenly sent a wave of trepidation through Lavinia. She had known this wedding celebration would be enormous. After all, it was the marriage of the Duke of Beaubrooke.

Their wedding ceremony would be a smaller affair as befitted such a solemn occasion.

But the celebration ball...that was another matter. The last time a duke had wed in London, people had lined the streets to see the guests in all their glittering finery. She couldn't imagine anyone lining up anywhere to try and get a glimpse of her. If they did, she only hoped she didn't make a total fool of herself.

The duke frowned. "We have discussed this before, but now that a bride has actually been chosen, shouldn't we bow to her wishes when it comes to the size of our wedding?"

Both mothers looked up as though he had spoken in gibberish.

"What do you mean, dear?" the duchess said.

"Is it really necessary to have such an extravagant affair? Dozens of guests at the ceremony? A grandiose ball?"

Both mothers again stared at him as though they didn't understand a word of what he was saying. The duchess finally broke the silence.

"These plans have been in place for almost two years now. Dukes of Beaubrooke have always wed at St. George's and hosted a spectacular wedding ball. It is tradition. Everyone is expecting it."

They all looked at Lavinia, who took a small step back under their intense gazes.

"What do you think, my lady?" the duke asked.

"What do I think?"

"Of course. It's your wedding. And I don't believe you've been able to give any input as of yet." His gaze flicked to her mother for a quick moment before moving back to Lavinia. But it had been enough to make her mother flush.

What did she want? She had no idea.

On the one hand, an enormous wedding seemed terrifying. She wasn't used to being the center of anyone's attention, and the prospect of it was daunting. On the other hand, she was going to be the Duchess of Beaubrooke. Crowds and attention would be part of her life from now on, and she needed to get used to it.

And if she were honest…a small part of her wanted that attention. Was it vain that the thought of being the one everyone wanted to see made her feel…special?

The duke gently squeezed her arm. "You can disagree with me if you'd like."

She glanced up at him in surprise. "What?"

He raised a brow. "If you'd prefer a big wedding, I understand."

Lavinia had to blink away a few stray tears while she nodded. There weren't many men who would willingly tell their wives to disagree with them. In fact, she couldn't think of any at all.

"It's not that I prefer it necessarily," she

said. "But they've already done so much work. Changing things now wouldn't make much sense. And...well, it does sound quite lovely."

"I think you and I have different ideas of lovely, my dear," he said flatly.

Even so, Lavinia's stomach fluttered with delight at the endearment that had slipped from his lips. Goodness. She'd never be able to breathe reliably again, let alone eat, if the man kept that up.

"I know it'll likely be overwhelming, and truthfully, it's a bit frightening," she said, trying to think coherently. "But I had never thought to be part of something so grand before. I can't deny that the idea is a bit appealing."

He sighed. "I can't fight all three of you."

"Four," Kitty called. "I say the bigger the better."

"Five," the duke's sister, Georgina, said as she bustled in seconds before a footman, who had obviously been trying to beat her to the parlor so she could be announced.

"Lady Georgina Reddington," the poor lad gasped, then bowed and wheezed his way back out.

"Georgina, my dear, I didn't realize you wished to come, or I would have waited for you," the duchess said.

Georgina waved her mother off and

turned back to Lavinia and the duke. "You should absolutely be showing your bride off to the whole of London."

He groaned lightly. "Very well. I shall keep my protestations to myself and leave the planning to the women."

Lord Abberforth nodded. "Wise choice, my boy."

The duke blinked in surprise at her father, and Lavinia laughed.

"In truth, I really must leave you to it, at least for today," he said, drawing her to the door. "I have work that must be done before the wedding festivities get too far underway."

Lavinia smiled up at him, glad she was near enough to clearly see his warm brown eyes. "I will escort you out, Your Grace."

They paused in the front hall as the duke pulled on his hat and gloves.

"I apologize for leaving so soon," he said. "But I'm afraid I really must attend to some work that I've been neglecting."

"I understand," Lavinia said, tapping down her disappointment at his hasty retreat. "I confess, I am a bit envious."

He raised an eyebrow in question and glanced over her shoulder before responding. "I have no doubt, now that they have a definitive answer, our mothers will be shortly taking over our lives."

His lips pulled into a half smile that

deepened the tiny dimple in his cheek and sent her stomach careening. "Another reason to get our wedding said and done sooner than later, I suppose. At least we can be grateful that most of the details are already in place."

She nodded, and while a small part of her wished that he wanted their wedding accomplished quickly for more romantic reasons, the pragmatic part knew how unfair that wish was. Besides, she *did* agree with him. The sooner they were wed, the sooner they could begin their new lives together. She had no idea what to expect. It hadn't even been in her realm of fantasy. But she was a fast learner.

And despite the fact that she hadn't been consulted on any of the details of her wedding, she *was* very thankful everything was already in place. Having to suffer through a year or longer engagement as the duke's cousin Lady Elizabeth had would be more than she could stomach. Lavinia much preferred to get the preliminaries over and done with instead of listening to gossip and speculation for an entire year. Not to mention, living with Harriet from now on would likely not be the most pleasant of experiences. Lavinia would be happy to put it behind her.

The duke finished putting on his hat and gloves, and paused, regarding her with an expression she couldn't read. His eyes narrowed, but then he leaned down to press a chaste kiss upon her cheek. When his lips met her skin, they both froze, and what he'd probably intended to be a quick peck turned instead to a lingering caress that left her blood pounding and her lungs breathless.

When he straightened, his eyes meeting hers again, there was renewed interest in their depths. Her hand trembled in his as he took his leave.

"I shall call on you soon. Lavinia."

How did just hearing her name on his lips send such a thrill through her? Her breath caught in the back of her throat. "Until then," she managed to whisper.

He gave her a slow grin that had her sucking in a sharp breath, and then he tipped his hat. She watched him until he stepped inside his carriage and one of the footmen closed the door. Somehow in the last several hours, she'd gone from a girl who spent most of her time hiding in corners and talking to plants to a future duchess who was already infatuated with her soon-to-be husband.

And they still had an entire month until the wedding.

She needed to compose herself or she'd never survive the next four weeks.

CHAPTER SIX

If someone had told Lavinia a month ago that she would be betrothed, to a duke no less, and on her way to visit her grand new country estate, she would have summoned the physician. The duke had invited her family for a visit to his country estate for a few days, both so they could get better acquainted and so Lavinia could see the home where they would live when they weren't in London.

Arrival at Wrothlake Park was a flurry of activity that had Lavinia's head spinning with excitement. Along with a healthy dose of worry. This new reality was one of which she'd hardly let herself dream. To say it was intimidating would be an understatement.

But he'd chosen *her*. And the thrill that sent through her, knowing that someone wanted *her* for who she was...the happiness that beckoned was almost frightening. As if any moment she'd wake and find that none of it was real. That she was still as invisible as always and the handsome duke had chosen another. As everyone had expected.

She sighed. Perhaps once they were married, it would stop feeling like a dream that would fade away once she woke.

For now, she had to get through this visit.

From the moment they stepped out of the carriage to the moment she collapsed in bed, it seemed there had barely been time to just breathe.

The servants had apparently all been made keenly aware that their next mistress was arriving to tour her new home. The constant attention from someone making sure she didn't need anything was both unusual and unwelcome. She appreciated the sentiment, certainly. But she wasn't used to so many people shadowing her every movement. Harriet, of course, smiled and took the attention as her due, much more comfortable with acting the part of mistress of the manor. Which was more castle than any manor Lavinia had ever seen.

Dinner had been a grand affair that had lasted long into the evening. By the time they had retired to their lavish rooms, Lavinia was almost asleep on her feet. Until the moment she laid in the grand bed and stared at the ornate bed hangings. And kept staring until the house settled around her and the only sound she heard was the occasional hoot of an owl beyond her window.

Sleep would not come. There was far too much running through her mind. From the sight of this extravagant house to wondering where the duke had vanished to. His mother had made his apologies upon their arrival.

And while he had joined them for dinner, he'd seemed preoccupied. Though, when she entered the room, he'd given her a small smile that had melted her insides every time their eyes met.

She took a deep breath and threw off her thick blankets. She was never going to sleep. But perhaps she could do a little exploring now that the castle was still. The dowager duchess had given them a tour of the main areas of the house when they'd arrived, and the library she'd only glimpsed before called to her now.

She tugged on her robe and slippers and put on her spectacles, as no one should be about to see her in them. Before she stepped into the hallway, she poked her head out of her door to be sure there was no one about. Then she crept out of her room and down the stairs, her single candle sputtering as she walked.

No one had told her she wasn't permitted to go to the library unattended, but there was something about wandering around in the dark that made her feel like she was breaking some clandestine rule. And if she was, it was absolutely worth it. There were still some candles lit and a fire going in the ornately carved fireplace that nearly filled one wall.

Lavinia stood in the middle of the library, closed her eyes, and took a deep breath, allowing the slightly musty scent of parchment and leather to wash over her before letting it out slowly. That unmistakable aroma of books never failed to relax her. She tilted her head back, smiling as she luxuriated in it for a moment longer.

She finally opened her eyes and looked around in awe at the plethora of books stacked in floor-to-ceiling dark-wood cases that lined both floors. She'd been around books her whole life. Her father's estates held fairly impressive libraries of their own. Even still, she had never seen so many in one place.

Though how many of those would be the romance novels she preferred, she didn't know. Likely very few. Still, there were bound to be many books on many subjects that she would find very entertaining.

"Do you like it?" a voice said behind her.

A startled squeak erupted from her, and she turned and hurled her candlestick at whoever had snuck up behind her.

The duke—*the duke!*—grunted and dodged the projectile, hurrying after it as it clanged to the floor. He stomped out the small flames that lit as soon as it touched the rug, and Lavinia hurried over.

"Oh! Your Grace, I'm so sorry. Oh, that beautiful rug." She pressed her hands to her cheeks in horror.

"It's all right," he assured her, but she

shook her head.

"I nearly took your head off and burned your rug in the process."

"It is not the first time someone has lobbed something at me, my lady, I assure you. Though I will commend you on your accuracy. As for the rug…" He grabbed the armchair that sat nearby and repositioned it right atop the small burn mark. "Good as new."

She kept shaking her head, her hands pressing harder to her face, as if she could squish herself out of existence. Her fingers brushed against the rim of her spectacles, belatedly reminding her she wore them, and she made to pull them off.

The duke took her hands, and she stilled immediately. "Leave them," he said. "There's no one here but me, and I don't mind them."

"You don't?" she asked, risking a glance up at him.

He shook his head. "I far prefer for you to be able to comfortably see than worry about offending some society harridan who isn't here to know otherwise. Although with your apparent penchant for flinging heavy objects at my head, perhaps I shouldn't encourage anything which might make your aim more precise."

Lavinia ducked her head with a smile, her eyes focusing on where her bare hands rested in the duke's.

She had never touched a man without at least one layer of material between them. She should pull her hand away.

But then his warm hands enveloped hers and his thumbs, gently moving across the backs of her hands, sent shockwaves through her arms directly to her heart. Which shuddered in giddy delight.

"Better?" he asked.

She nodded, her gaze fixed to his. His slow smile sent her heartrate reeling, and she took a deep breath and slowly released it, trying to calm the furious pounding. She could only hope that he assumed her reaction to him was due to her fright. Not due to the fact that she wanted nothing more than for those thumbs of his to keep drawing lazy circles on the backs of her hands.

"Good." He gave her hands a gentle squeeze and released them.

She stifled her sigh and followed him to the group of comfortable, overstuffed chairs set before the fireplace, and then he gestured for her to sit. As she did, she pulled her robe more tightly about her. Her mother would be mortified if they were to be caught. The duke, in a state of undress, clad only in his trousers and braces, his white linen shirt nearly untucked, the neck untied. And her, sitting there in her nightgown and robe, her hair in a simple braid down her back. It was indecent. Unseemly.

A little bit naughty.

And that thought shouldn't send the thrill through her that it did.

"Now that you're aware of my presence," the duke said with that little half smile that sent her heart skittering about her chest, "what do you think?" He waved his hand, encompassing the room.

"It's incredible," she said, tearing her eyes from him to look back at the fireplace. "Beautiful."

"Yes," he said, his voice pulling her gaze back to him. "It is."

But he wasn't looking at the fireplace.

She met his gaze and held it until her cheeks grew warm, and she had to resist the urge to shift in her chair. "I...I should show my sisters this room in the morning."

He shrugged. "You could. But...having met them..."

She raised her brow. "Yes?" She knew what he was implying, of course, but had the wicked urge to see if he would say it.

"Well. Have you ever known your sisters to be intrigued by old books?"

Lavinia bit her bottom lip to keep from laughing. "Fair point, Your Grace. My sisters, in fact, have never been intrigued by anything resembling a book. Old or new."

"As I suspected."

"Do you spend much time here?" she asked.

"In the library?"

"No," she said with a quiet chuckle. "At Wrothlake."

He nodded. "I do, as much as I can manage. My greenhouse is here, and all my special projects. In fact, I have a very special project that should be coming to fruition at mid-summer, so I hope you will not mind returning here perhaps a bit before the conclusion of the Season."

Her stomach flipped again at the reminder that this would soon be her home and the duke her husband. It seemed incongruous to be sitting in the candlelight, discussing where they would reside. Yet here they were. About to be wed and planning their lives together.

"No, I wouldn't mind at all," she finally managed to say.

"Wonderful," he said, his eyes lingering on her.

She sat for a few seconds longer and then reluctantly got to her feet. "I should perhaps return to my room. The hour grows late."

"That it does," the duke said, rising with her. "I'll see you to your door."

"No!" she said, then laughed at his startled expression. "That is, I will manage on my own. It wouldn't do for…for you…for a man…"

His eyebrow raised a bit more with every word she stuttered out, and she closed her eyes and tried again. "As the lord of the manor, it would hardly do for you to be escorting mere guests about the place."

"There is nothing mere about you, Lady Lavinia, I assure you. And I'd remind you that you will soon be the lady of this manor. As such, it is my honor and duty to escort you."

She glanced up at him, not sure if air still moved in and out of her lungs, and not caring much, either, as long as he kept gazing down at her like he was doing now.

He finally reached out and rubbed the end of her braid between his fingers before letting his hand fall with a sigh.

"But I suppose the sight of me standing outside your bedroom door in the dead of the night, before you are, in fact, mistress here could set a few tongues wagging."

Her mouth opened and closed a few times while she struggled for words. His implied compliment (he couldn't have meant what she thought he meant, could he?), the thought of him standing outside her bedroom door at night (her heart would never recover), and the thought of someone actually *seeing* him there (good Lord, she'd perish on the spot) left her momentarily speechless.

She finally gathered enough wits together

to nod. "Quite right, Your Grace."

He gave her a little bow, those dark eyes boring into hers.

"Take this," he said, retrieving the candlestick she'd tried to embed in his skull and relighting her candle from a candelabra on the table. "Until tomorrow then, Lady Lavinia."

Oh…her name on his lips…

She sucked in a breath. "Until tomorrow, Your Grace."

She managed to make it out of the library without disgracing herself and even made it up the stairs, though her legs trembled enough it was a near thing. The moment the door was closed behind her, she slid to the floor in a boneless heap and whispered to herself, "What just happened?"

CHAPTER SEVEN

Lavinia stood on a stool while the dressmaker buzzed around her with a mouthful of pins, wishing she were back in the duke's library at Wrothlake. Ever since they'd returned to London, life had been a whirlwind of wedding preparations, fittings for her trousseau and wedding gown, and packing the belongings she'd be taking with her to her new home. She'd had barely a minute to breathe.

Still, while the unfamiliar attention was, at times, overwhelming, it was also a bit exhilarating. The wedding was turning into much more of a spectacle than she'd ever thought she'd enjoy. But perhaps that was because she'd always felt excluded from such occasions in the past. If her new status afforded her the acceptance she'd always craved, perhaps such events would be much more pleasurable going forward.

In the meantime, she stood decked out from head to toe in heavy silk so luxurious that Lavinia was afraid to touch it. The pale-blue silk gown would be covered by an overlay of sheer muslin edged with Brussels lace. She'd never worn anything so beautiful.

Her mother stood surveying the gown with a critical eye. "We need something along the border."

Madame Lalande nodded. "I thought so as well."

"Orchids are lovely," Kitty suggested. "And symbolize fertility."

Madame Lalande, Lady Abberforth, and Lavinia gasped in unison though the modiste and her mother almost immediately began to smile and nod at each other. Lavinia's cheeks burned, and she glared daggers at her sister, who grinned mischievously.

Yes, an heir or two were of course both needed and expected of this union. But that didn't mean Lavinia wished to announce the fact on her actual gown. Especially since her botanist groom would surely know the symbolism behind the decoration.

"Perhaps roses or camellias?" Lavinia said.

They both seemed safe, and symbolized love. And while *she* would remember the delicious way the duke had stroked the camellia's petals in their garden the day he'd proposed until the day she died, no one else would know that.

"Hmm, yes," Madame Lalande said. "Perhaps this…" She hurried to a basket on her worktable and pulled out a large rosette made of silver tissue.

"Oh, wonderful," her mother said, clapping her hands.

Lavinia smiled, both relieved and happy that they'd taken her suggestion. Her opinion hadn't been asked on much else, but that was to be expected. She'd learned rather quickly this was her mother's wedding more than hers. Her mother was likely aware that if left up to her, Lavinia would hold the wedding in a library with nary a guest there to witness. And truth be told, her mother had exquisite taste, and everything she'd chosen so far had Lavinia's complete stamp of approval.

"Should they be gold tissue, do you think?" her mother asked as they held the silver roses to the bodice and along the hemline, determining where best to put them.

"Hmm, no. For the other, perhaps, but for Lady Lavinia, with her darker coloring…"

"Ah yes, I agree. Silver is much better."

Lavinia squashed the pang of guilt that threatened to dampen her happiness when the dressmaker had mentioned "the other." Harriet. The one they'd been so certain of being the bride that they'd already begun her dress.

Luckily, with Harriet being the sister of the future Duchess of Beaubrooke, she was still in need of a new gown for the wedding. However, instead of the heavy brocaded silk, her gown would be made of a lighter silk in a beautiful shade of buttercup yellow. Not quite the gold tissue and embellished netting they had planned, but a stunning gown, nonetheless. And of course, she looked wonderful in it, despite the persistence of her sour expressions.

Lavinia had hoped that Harriet had come to terms with her engagement. But it seemed the closer the wedding drew, the more her sister's resentment manifested. She had been more and more irritable by the day, and Lavinia wasn't quite sure what to do about it. It wasn't as if she'd stolen the duke from Harriet. She could only hope that her sister would get over her disappointment once the wedding was over and done with.

"The silver roses are lovely, but I think it still needs a touch of something more," Kitty said.

"More?" Lavinia asked. "If we add too much more, I won't be able to walk."

Kitty waved that concern away. "You only marry once, after all. And you'll be able to repurpose the trim for other gowns in the future. You might as well ensure you have plenty with which to work."

Lavinia opened her mouth to protest again, but Kitty pressed on.

"What about pearls?" she suggested. "Along the bottom, and maybe smaller seed pearls sprinkled in with the roses and along the train?"

"Wonderful idea, Kitty. What do you think, madame?" her mother asked.

Lavinia stared at her sister in shock, but

Kitty only smiled up at her. "You'll be the most beautiful duchess to ever walk down the aisle," she said.

Lavinia swallowed hard past the sudden lump in her throat. Kitty was lovely to everyone, but it wasn't often that Lavinia had her attention long enough for Kitty to really focus on her.

She stepped down from the stool, given momentary permission to sit and rest while her mother and the modiste discussed options for the train. Kitty followed her to the chaise with a handful of ribbons and feathers.

Lavinia sat quietly while Kitty held a white velvet ribbon to her hair, quickly discarding it in favor of a glorious peacock feather that she tucked in amongst Lavinia's curls.

"This would look quite fetching," Kitty said. "But I already heard Mother telling Father he needed to get the family tiara out for the occasion." She tilted her head, studying it this way and that. "Though it would still look quite beautiful with the tiara."

Kitty jumped up and pulled Lavinia to her feet. "Let's see what Mother thinks. I'd wager we can get them to add diamonds to your bodice. Shall we ask? Mother!" she called.

"What?" Lavinia laughed, startled, and reached out to try and grab her sister. "No. Kitty, where are you going? No diamonds, Kitty. Oof!"

She tripped over her unhemmed skirts in her attempt to catch her sister before they could cover her in yet more *frou frou*.

"Careful there," a woman said as she grabbed Lavinia's elbow and kept her upright.

"Oh, thank—" Lavinia paused to brush the peacock feather out of her face. "Thank you," she finally got out. She aimed a smile at a fashionable young woman who had apparently just arrived at the modiste's with her maid in tow.

Not just any fashionable woman, though. Claudette Peregrine, Lady Asterly, had been one of the most sought-after young women on the marriage mart several seasons ago. And she'd made the most advantageous match to the ancient but wealthy Earl of Asterly. Who had apparently not expired quite as soon as his young bride had hoped, as she was not yet a dowager countess.

Her sister had just debuted this season and was expected to make an equally brilliant match. Would likely have set her eyes on Alexander had he not already been spoken for, for all intents and purposes. Lady Asterly was also the leader of a small band of women who set the tone for most social events. If you were in their good graces, you received the most coveted invitations, were accepted into any party, and were showered with attention upon arriving at any particular event.

If you were not in their good graces…well, you didn't want to be on the outs with them.

Lavinia, thankfully, had never been either. She'd managed to avoid their notice altogether. Apparently, that was no longer an option. The realization suddenly hit her that her life as she had known it was over. She'd already known that in theory. But to see Lady Asterly's eyes light up with friendly interest upon seeing her instead of passing over her as if she were not there drove the point home in a way that merely knowing the fact did not.

"Lady Asterly, my thanks," Lavinia said, gathering her skirts about her to prevent another awkward spill.

"My pleasure, Lady Lavinia."

Lavinia glanced up in surprise, both at the fact that Lady Asterly knew her name and that she'd said it with such warmth and friendliness.

"I apologize that I am probably one of the last to offer you my congratulations on your upcoming wedding," Lady Asterly said.

"Oh, yes, thank you." She was actually one of the first and was probably aware of that fact. Very little that went on in society escaped the notice of Lady Asterly. But it was hardly something one called a lady out on in the middle of the modiste's.

"I am sure you are simply swamped with wedding preparations, but I wanted to be sure that you'd received the invitation to my little party tomorrow evening. I had my man bring the invitation by earlier this morning."

"Lady Asterly, what a pleasant surprise," her mother said, finally reappearing with Madame Lalande in tow.

"Lady Abberforth," she said. "Good afternoon. I was congratulating our lovely Lady Lavinia on her upcoming wedding and did so hope she, and of course you and your other daughters, would be able to attend my soiree tomorrow evening."

"Oh, that would be lovely," Lavinia's mother said, her voice coolly polite. "I'll consult our calendar and respond as soon as possible."

Lady Asterly's smile was slightly less friendly, at least toward her mother, but she fairly beamed at Lavinia.

"I do hope you can come, my lady. It will be such fun. Well," she said, glancing at her maidservant to ensure that whatever purchase she'd come to make had been obtained, "I must be off. I hope to see you again, my dear Lady Lavinia. Until tomorrow."

She gave them a little wave of her fingers and marched back out the door, her servants following her like ducklings.

Lavinia glanced at her mother, her eyes wide with shock. But her mother showed no surprise, only a smug and knowing smile.

"Prepare yourself, my dear. You have become the most desirable connection in town."

"What? Why?"

Harriet let out an exasperated sigh. "Because, Lavinia, you are two weeks from becoming the Duchess of Beaubrooke. You'll be the wife of one of the most powerful and influential men in the country. Or at least he could be if he pulled his nose from his plants. Which means *you'll* be one of the most powerful and influential *women* in the country."

Lavinia understood how society worked. She understood who Alex was and what his social position afforded him. And she'd known that influence would extend to her when they wed. But knowing something and experiencing it was two entirely different things.

"I'll be waiting in the carriage, Mother," Harriet muttered, not bothering to hide her annoyance.

"Very well, dear," her mother said, sighing when the door closed behind her eldest daughter. "Give her some time, Lavinia. Harriet is happy for you—"

"Obviously," Lavinia muttered.

"But," her mother said, pinning her with a do-not-interrupt-me-again look, "she's been dealt a cruel blow and must come to terms with it. I'm sure if you apologize later, it will all blow over soon enough."

Lavinia blinked at her, knowing she should keep her mouth shut. And usually, she would. Usually, she did what she could to keep the peace. To make everyone else happy. To make sure no one else felt uncomfortable. But no one had ever felt compelled to extend the same courtesy to her. And for once, Lavinia had had enough.

"For what am I to apologize?"

"What?" her mother said, turning shocked eyes to her. Lavinia had never once in her life spoken back to her mother. But she had to start somewhere.

"I am asking what offense I have committed that requires an apology. Harriet is behaving as though she were betrothed to the duke in truth. But the only understanding between them was in her own head. She decided she wanted to be the duchess and that was the end of it. But he didn't choose her. He chose me. And I will not apologize for that. To her or anyone."

"Nor should you," Kitty chimed in, ignoring her mother's glare.

"I do feel sorry for Harriet," Lavinia said, trying to bring her temper back under control. "But her disappointment is of her own making. And I will no longer let her mistreat me because she didn't get her way." She flung her hands out. "We are in a dress shop having my trousseau and wedding gown fitted. A moment that has, I'm sure, featured in many a little girl's dreams. Not mine, necessarily, but that's beside the point," she added.

"Then what *is* your point?" her mother asked, her arms folded at her daughter's uncharacteristic indignation.

Lavinia took a deep breath and blew it out. If her mother didn't understand it now, she never would. She didn't know how to explain it to her.

"I am standing here in my wedding gown. And yet with one petulant remark, Harriet has made the moment all about her. I will not apologize to her because she's not the one getting the attention for once."

Her mother moved slowly toward her, and Lavinia braced herself for the tirade. Instead, her mother wrapped her in a quick hug and then stepped back, nodding her head.

"You are right," she said, patting her cheek. "And I'm sorry if you felt like your day has been ruined. But," she said, her smile brightening, "we'll fix that right up. We've got a beautiful design to show you."

She took Lavinia's hand and dragged her over to where the modiste had drawn a quick sketch of her dress's bodice. On it, there was a beautiful motif of vines, trees, and flowers.

"In honor of His Grace," her mother said. "What do you think?"

"Oh, Mother," Lavinia said, clasping her

hands together. "It's simply beautiful. I love it. I'm sure the duke will love it as well."

"Excellent!" her mother said. "We're going to do it in diamonds."

Kitty beamed and Lavinia slapped a hand to her face. She would be more jewel than person by the time they were finished. She'd feel more confident about the wedding if she were walking down the aisle covered in fig leaves and potting soil. At least then, she'd be assured of His Grace's interest.

"He will love you, Livy," Kitty whispered to her.

Lavinia glanced at her sister, eyes brimming with questions she was too afraid to ask. "Will he?"

"Of course! The duke is...well, he's unique, isn't he?" she said with a giggle.

Lavinia grinned. "That he is."

Kitty settled back against the chaise with a shrug. "You are as well. And that is a compliment, dear sister, so don't you dare take it any other way."

"I promise," Lavinia said, touched.

"Your uniqueness complements his," Kitty continued with a shrug, as though that were that and she'd brook no argument over it.

Lavinia took a deep breath and let it out slowly. She hoped her sister was right. Though there seemed to be a lot of uniqueness that would soon be bound together until death parted it. She'd have to pray that it wasn't too much of a good thing. Though it was too late to do anything about it now.

For better or worse, she and the duke were about to find out if they complement each other in truth. Or not...

CHAPTER EIGHT

Their wedding day finally dawned, and Alex was up with the sun, anxiously looking out the window at the skies. The blue, clear skies. Thanks be to heaven. If it had rained and ruined the wedding, Alex never would have heard the end of it from their mothers. It didn't matter a fig that he couldn't control the weather. He was just going to thank whatever gods had smiled upon him that the early spring day promised to be cool but dry.

He dressed carefully for his nuptials and left for Hanover Square early. Timothy waited for him in the carriage, his hat balanced on his knee and his gloves crumpled in his hands. And it wasn't just his gloves. The man had probably just finished dressing minutes before and had done nothing but sat waiting in the carriage. Yet he was already rumpled, as if he'd balled up his clothing, stomped on them a few times for good measure, and put them back on. Everything Timothy wore looked like that. Alex was pretty sure clothing crumpled at first sight of the formidable Timothy Lambert.

"It's bloody early, Beaubrooke."

"And good morning to you as well, Mr. Lambert. Why, thank you for the compliment.

I took extra care with my appearance this morning. It is my wedding day, after all."

Timothy snorted. "You look fine."

"High praise indeed coming from you. I'm flattered."

"You should be."

Timothy sighed and leaned his head against the carriage window as they departed. "Why are we leaving so early again? The wedding isn't for three hours yet."

Alex nodded to the window as they turned up the main road leading to St. George's. "That's why," he said, gesturing to the crowd milling about along the road near the church.

"Good God," Timothy muttered. He pulled a silver flask out of his vest pocket, took a quick swig, and then passed it to Alex.

"Keep it," he said when Alex tried to pass it back. "You'll need it."

Alex snorted, took another small mouthful, and tossed it back to his friend.

He'd hoped to miss the largest crowds, but people were already lined up around the steps leading to St. George's. Good God, indeed.

The wedding of his distant cousin, the Duchess of Devonshire, a few decades earlier, had been expected to draw similar crowds. Only unlike the Devonshires, Alex and Lavinia's parents wouldn't consider secretly moving the wedding date to avoid such a happenstance.

No help for it now.

Timothy grumbled again. "I suppose being this season's most eligible bachelor has its drawbacks, eh?"

Alex rolled his eyes and opened the carriage door. "Come along. If we make haste, we may gain the entrance before too many people notice who we are."

Of course, when the season's most talked about event was about to get underway and one of the leading players arrived, trying to do so unnoticed was not possible. Alex had known there would be onlookers. Commoners were always curious about the nobility. Especially on occasions such as a marriage between two prominent families.

Timothy seemed rather amused by it all, and an uncharacteristic grin graced his face before they made it up the steps between the Corinthian columns and into the church. Guests had also started arriving already, wanting to grab the best seats.

Alex, however, marched as quickly as possible into the back rooms where he would wait until the ceremony began. He slumped into a chair, closed his eyes, and rested his head on the back of the chair.

Timothy sat beside him, thankfully silent. Timothy had always been good at that. Yes, he never missed an opportunity to annoy, insult, or otherwise aggravate his friend. But he also knew when Alex needed to be left in peace. And he would sit beside him for as long as needed, offering his silent support.

Alex's mother and sister would be arriving shortly. He had many other relatives and acquaintances that would be in the crowd, and he had a good friend in Timothy. But Alex could not stop the ache in his heart. His father should be beside his mother, watching him wed. His brother should be there.

Though if his brother still lived, would Alex even be there?

It was possible, of course. Charles would almost certainly have chosen Harriet as his bride. Which would have brought Lavinia into Alex's sphere. In fact, if not before, they would certainly have met on this very day. As their siblings wed.

Would he have noticed her? Would he have approached her? If he had, would she have welcomed his attentions?

So much of their interactions were ruled by their parents' arrangements. Without those in place, with Charles alive to fulfill their father's promise and Harriet more than willing to be his wife, would Alex and Lavinia have ever spoken more than a few words to each other?

He liked to think so. Perhaps their reason for meeting would have changed. But the pressure to start a relationship would not exist. For most, the removal of pressure was a help to the situation. But to the preoccupied Alex and the neglected Lavinia…he just didn't know.

Timothy shook his arm what felt like minutes later. But he must have dozed off, because the sun now shone strongly through the window and the noise from those filling the church filtered in even through the doors of the back rooms.

"It's time," Timothy said.

Alex looked up to see his mother smiling down at him and hurried to stand.

She straightened his jacket and smoothed his hair with an air of sad pride.

"I wish your father and brother were here," she said, her voice choked with emotion.

"As do I." He leaned down and gave her a gentle kiss on the cheek.

"Oh," she said, yanking a handkerchief from her reticule. She quickly dabbed at her eyes and then waved the handkerchief at him. "Come take your places. Your bride will be arriving any moment."

He nodded and then looked at Timothy. "Best to get it over with, then."

Alex grimaced but followed his friend out to the altar.

The pews were filled with family and friends, all dressed in their finest. He recognized a few faces. Though the farther out the seats, the less he knew the guests. No matter. As long as his bride made an appearance, the rest didn't matter.

The rector stood before him and adjusted his robes, preparing everything he'd need for the ceremony. They said a few words, but Alex was strung like an overtight bow, his attention focused, waiting for the slightest noise that would indicate that Lavinia had arrived.

Her mother and sisters had made their way inside the chapel moments earlier and taken their seats directly in front. He'd nodded politely at them. Lady Abberforth and Lady Kitty had given him broad, happy grins. Lady Harriet had given him a cool nod and had been staring into nothingness since she'd slipped into her seat.

For his future wife's sake, he hoped her sister could move on. Perhaps he should make it a priority to find Harriet a husband as soon as possible. Just to ensure they all had some peace.

A dull roar sounded from outside the chapel doors, and everyone turned toward it.

It was against tradition to watch as his bride approached him. But he didn't care. From the moment he caught sight of her, he didn't see anyone else.

She was dressed in a beautiful blue silk gown covered in netting and lace. And when the sun struck her, a thousand tiny rainbows erupted from her bodice, hair, and throat. She was a princess. A beautiful, ethereal princess who floated down the aisle to him on the arm of her father.

She glanced somewhat shyly from side to side, but he could see her gaining confidence the farther into the church she came. Perhaps she saw what he did. Awe, and perhaps envy, on the faces of all who saw her. How many of them had seen her at parties and balls yet hadn't truly *seen* her? Well, let them look now. Because she only looked at him.

Or…squinted at him, more like. Though the closer she drew, the less pronounced her squint. He pursed his lips as she took her careful steps toward him, her hand tight on her father's arm. He'd have to have a discussion with her over her use of spectacles in public. Fashionable or not, he'd prefer his wife could see well enough to walk unaided at his side.

Though the fact that her eyes remained fixed on him, as if he were her beacon in the fog, filled his chest with warm pride. His heart thundered with it. Emotion clogged the back of his throat as she drew nearer. Until her father finally handed her over and left her standing at the altar beside him.

They spoke their vows. Hers rang out just as strong and sure as his own, and once again he was filled with a thankful wonder that he'd been lucky enough to find her. Many of his friends' marriages were arranged. It was what families often did when bloodlines, bank accounts, and business or land mergers were on the line. His marriage was really no different. Their parents had chosen each other because a union between their families would unite a great deal of wealth and property and would be greatly advantageous for all involved.

At least that's the way it started.

But no marriage contract made his heart hammer when she gazed up at him. No land merger made his blood sing when her cheeks flushed as his fingers brushed across hers when he put the gold band on her finger. No dowry or settlement had his breath punching from his lungs when their hands brushed as they signed the register.

It was *she* who affected him so. Them, together.

And it was only the beginning.

CHAPTER NINE

Once the register was signed, the rector and their witnesses, Timothy and Lord Abberforth, left them alone briefly so they could spend their first few minutes together as man and wife in private.

Lavinia gazed up at the duke, *her husband*, and drew in a tremulous breath. "I can't believe we've actually done it," she said with a slight laugh.

He raised a brow as if he couldn't quite believe it, either. "Yes, we have. Your Grace," he added.

She laughed. "That will take some getting used to."

"You look wonderful," he said, lightly cupping her cheek. "So beautiful."

She smiled up at him shyly. "Thank you, Your Grace."

He drew her closer, leaning down as if he would kiss her, though he left enough distance between them that it was clear he was leaving it up to her if she wanted his kiss or not. She moved closer and rose onto her toes, resting her hands on his chest as she turned her face up to meet his.

Lavinia meant only to press her lips to his in a quick, chaste kiss. They were in church, after all. It was hardly the place for passion, or the place where she wanted to explore their first true kiss.

Perhaps it would have been easier if he hadn't been standing there, looking as resplendent as a king on his coronation day. Or if he hadn't watched her walking up the aisle like she was his angel come to guide him to salvation. Or if he hadn't cupped her face and brushed his thumbs across her cheeks, looking into her eyes as if she were the greatest prize a man had ever won.

Whatever it was, the moment his lips met hers, everything else ceased to exist. There were no other people. No rector. No crowd waiting for them to exit. No parents or friends or guests waiting just a few feet away.

It was just him. Just them.

Just his lips finally, *finally* moving over hers the way she'd imagined it a thousand times. The way she'd tried to imagine it.

Only it was nothing like she'd imagined. It was so much better.

His warm, soft lips pressed against hers gently at first, then with more pressure. His hand slipped around the back of her neck, grazing her hairline though he was careful not to disturb her carefully coiffed hair. But the brush of his fingers against her neck while his mouth moved hungrily against hers sent a shiver through her that had her clutching at him.

The music started up again, startling them apart. Lavinia's eyes flew open, and she bit her lip, her cheeks flushing so hotly her eyes watered.

The duke leaned down to whisper in her ear. "We'll be truly alone soon."

She exhaled and gripped his arm as he led her back into the main chapel and up the aisle, smiling and waving at those offering them congratulations as they went. A ball of anxiety and anticipation settled in her stomach, warring with each other until she didn't know if she was more frightened or excited about being alone with her new husband. But she was fairly sure she was going to be sick before they ever got that far.

As soon as they reached the doors, she sucked in a deep breath of fresh air and tried to focus on calming her jittery nerves. An endeavor made all the more difficult by the cheers that went up as soon as they stepped into the sun. She had forgotten about the crowds. It was like the duke's kiss had erased everything from her mind but him.

They smiled and waved for a moment before the duke carefully led her down the stairs and into their waiting carriage. Which was festooned and beribboned...and thankfully enclosed.

He helped her get settled, closed the door,

and rapped on the ceiling to let their driver know they were ready. The crowds could still somewhat see them through the windows, so they waved a bit more until the people thinned out and they could finally relax.

They both slumped back against the seats.

"I thought our mothers had chosen an open carriage for our ride to the celebration."

He grunted. "They did. I made a last-minute adjustment to the plans. Do you mind?"

"Not at all. It was a relief, thank you."

His expression softened. "My pleasure," he said, taking her hand and pressing a quick kiss to the back of it.

The gesture was probably meant to be chivalrous. Friendly. Courteous.

He'd probably not meant her to gasp at the sudden warmth of his lips that permeated through to her skin even through the glove she wore. He'd probably not expected the fine tremble that went through her body at the brief contact. Or the way she leaned just a bit closer to him, tilting her face up as he closed the distance between them.

His lips descended again. Only this time, they weren't in a church with all their friends and family waiting. They were alone. And they were man and wife.

His lips moved over hers, silently asking, then demanding, that she yield. And she did so willingly. Gladly. Slanting her head farther back and leaning in closer to give him better access.

He wrapped one arm around her and drew her close. His other hand cupped her face, his thumb stroking across her cheek and pressing gently on her chin. She yielded further, her mouth opening under his seeking lips. And when his tongue dipped inside, she leaned into him with a little whimper that seemed to break whatever control he'd been maintaining.

His hand slipped around the back of her neck, and he drew her even closer, their mouths moving almost feverishly together until...

The carriage pulled to a stop, and they both came up for air, looking around, a bit dazed.

The duke groaned. "It appears that we have arrived at our wedding breakfast, Your Grace."

Lavinia glanced out the window with a small frown. They were at her parents' home. Their respective mothers had finally relented on a few of their extravagant plans and allowed the couple to choose the locations for their wedding celebrations. As well as limit the guest list. If they'd had their way, the breakfast and ball later that evening would have been held at one of the palaces with hundreds in attendance.

They'd relented somewhat on the ball. That would be held at the Beaubrookes' home, which housed a much larger ballroom than did the Wynnburns' and would still keep the guest list to a manageable size.

But for this, their first meal together as husband and wife, they wanted a more traditional, simple celebration. Only family and close friends. Which, given who their families were, still numbered over two dozen. But it was a vast improvement over the original plan.

Lavinia sighed. "Must we go inside? What if we told the coachman to keep driving?"

The duke rested his forehead against hers. "Our mothers would have the constables after us before we'd made it a mile. In fact, I'm fairly sure they are about to send someone out now to hurry us along."

Lavinia looked out the window and laughed. Just as he'd predicted, both of their mothers stood at the top of the stairs leading into the house. Waiting.

Impatiently.

"I suppose we must go then."

He kissed her cheek, and Lavinia leaned into it, her body unconsciously seeking more contact with his.

"We need only get through this breakfast. And then we'll have the rest of the day to ourselves."

Lavinia glanced up at him, her eyebrows raised. "Do you really think our mothers will let us out of their sights?"

His grumbling exhale made her stomach do a curious little flip. "I have a plan, never fear."

She wanted to demand he tell her what it was, but before she could, the door to the carriage opened to reveal the disgruntled face of Timothy.

"Your mothers request the honor of your presence at your wedding breakfast, Your Grace," he said in his monotoned voice that somehow managed to convey both utter disinterest and supreme annoyance all at once.

The duke glowered, and Lavinia bit her lip to keep from laughing. "Very well, Timothy. Inform our dear mamas that we are on the way."

Timothy rolled his eyes and turned away, muttering something about insufferable something or others and having better things to do.

Lavinia laughed again. "I like him," she said, and Alex snorted.

"That's wonderful to hear, my dear. Because like it or not, you'll be seeing a great deal more of him. He's a right surly sort when he's of a mind to it, but he's a wonderful research assistant. And friend."

She nodded. "I am glad he is your ally. I'd

hate to have him as an enemy."

"Hmm, so would I." The duke held out his hand. "Shall we?"

She released a deep sigh. "If we must."

"We must."

"Then lead the way, husband."

His hand tightened on hers, and he leaned in quickly to growl in her ear. "That word is unexpectedly delightful on your lips, my wife." He pressed a quick kiss to her neck and stepped down from the carriage, reaching back to help her down.

She placed her shaking hand in his and descended. He led her into the house, past their exasperated mothers, and into the parlor, where they would receive their guests until everyone had arrived. Lavinia took several deep breaths, trying to regain her equilibrium.

She'd anticipated being somewhat affected by her new husband. The small caresses they'd shared leading up to the wedding had been enough to show her that she enjoyed his touch. Desired it, even. But she had never expected her reaction to be this strong.

She'd assumed kissing him would be pleasant. She'd experienced the tingling and breathlessness that had come from him touching her. And she knew the basics of what to expect once they'd wed. Her mother had sat her down and given her a few perfunctory instructions. Lavinia still wasn't sure entirely what to expect that night, other than in a clinical sense.

But if a mere kiss had sent her senses careening and her body trembling, aching for more, then she had a hard time wrapping her mind around how it would feel if his lips and hands were to touch something other than her face. Would he do that? Her mother hadn't really gotten into specifics. She'd explained the final…act…and what went where, though that all seemed a bit fantastical as well. But…well, frankly, Lavinia was having a difficult time imagining it all.

A little less difficult than just that morning, though. If the sensations she just experienced had been wrought from a simple kiss, then…

"Your Grace," an amused voice said in front of her.

She blinked, and Nigel's face came into focus. "Nigel," she said with a smile, offering her hand to him. "I'm so glad you came."

"Of course I came. Although I'm afraid I cannot stay. But I wanted to convey my congratulations."

"Thank you, Nigel. Will you be at the ball this evening?"

"Certainly. But I have a few unavoidable meetings this morning, I'm afraid."

"You will be missed."

"Naturally." He grinned and left her with another bow and a wink.

The duke, who had been greeting other guests, returned to her side, his brows raised. She followed his glance and frowned. Harriet sat in a corner of the room, a corner that Lavinia had often frequented, in point of fact. She didn't seem upset, exactly. More…sad, if Lavinia had to put a name to it. And despite Harriet's disappointment in how things had transpired, Lavinia couldn't help but feel that there was something else afoot.

She pursed her lips, still undecided on what to do about her sister. If she should do anything at all. All she did know was that she wasn't going to worry about it just then. Harriet still had every eligible young man in the room attempting to pull her into conversation. She might be indulging in some mulish behavior for a moment, but Lavinia had no doubt her pride wouldn't let her wallow for too long. And if there were something more serious going on, then Lavinia would do her best to help. But she couldn't do anything just then.

Nor did she have much time to think about it during their breakfast. Or afternoon tea. And certainly not through the ball where she danced with her duke…when she wasn't being introduced to seemingly every member of society who had previously ignored her existence.

She certainly had no intention of being

churlish or holding any grudges. It was, however, very overwhelming to suddenly have so much attention focused upon her. When really, she only wanted the attention of one person.

Toward midnight, the duke excused himself from the group he'd been conversing with and made his way to Lavinia, and she swallowed hard against the sudden nausea rising in her stomach.

It was merely nerves. She'd thought of little else but this moment for the last couple weeks. The closer the wedding night approached, the more anxious she became. Both with anticipation and trepidation. The anticipation had been the strongest leading up to this moment. Though now that it was here…

Her husband wrapped his arm lightly around her waist as he stopped at her side.

"While I absolutely agree that congratulations are in order on this auspicious occasion, if I hear it from one more person, I cannot be held accountable for my reaction."

Lavinia smiled, though it was perhaps a bit more subdued than before. "I completely understand."

"Well then. As the bride and groom, I think we'd be forgiven if we were to disappear a bit early. I believe we have put in enough of an appearance, don't you?"

Her gaze shot to his. "I do, Your Grace."

He held out his hand. "Shall we retire?"

She swallowed against a suddenly dry mouth. "If you wish, Your Grace."

A slight frown creased his brow, but he took her hand, and they quietly slipped out of the room and up the stairs to their bedchamber. If they were seen by anyone, no one remarked on it. Thankfully. It was expected, of course, that at some point the bride and groom would disappear and the rest of the guests could carry on as they'd like. But it was another matter entirely to be the one slipping away. When everyone knew exactly *why* you were doing so.

The moment the door closed behind them, Lavinia's heart pounded. She pressed a hand to her chest, trying to quiet the mutiny that seemed to be taking place inside. Why she was having a sudden attack of nerves, she wasn't sure. Well, that wasn't completely the truth. Of course she knew. Just because she'd been anticipating this moment, eagerly, especially since their shared kisses after their wedding, didn't mean she wasn't also more than a little terrified.

"Lavinia," he said, apparently not for the first time.

His frown had deepened, and he looked at her with concern. "Are you well?"

She nodded, though the rushing in her ears made the movement sharper than she intended. "Merely a bit tired, I think," she said, her voice sounding raspy, even to her ears.

He regarded her a moment, then seemed to come to a decision as he straightened and clasped his hands behind his back.

"It has been a very long day," he agreed. "I find I am quite weary myself. I will bid you good night," he said, turning to go.

"Wait," Lavinia said, taking a step forward to stop him. It was their wedding night. Where was he going?

He glanced back at her.

"I thought...I assumed..." She stumbled over the words, not prepared for or accustomed to asking a man to stay the night with her.

"You needn't worry, my dear," he said with a strained smile. "We needn't rush anything for which you are not ready. The last few weeks have been quite overwhelming, and at the end of it, we still do not know each other very well. After the carriage, I had thought..."

He frowned again and shook his head a little. "It's no matter. A few passing kisses are inconsequential, I'm sure, to..." He cleared his throat. "I am content to wait to further any relations between us until we are better acquainted, and you are comfortable."

She glanced up at him. Every ounce of her being wanted to scream, *I am!* But her husband was already bowing and pressing a quick kiss to her cheek.

"But—" she managed to get out.

And then he was gone, and she was alone.

Well…that hadn't gone as planned.

CHAPTER TEN

Lavinia awoke the next day to the sounds of a bustling London morning. Alone. She had thought to relish being with her husband, just the two of them, with nothing else to do but enjoy each other. She hadn't expected the need to convince her new husband that his patience was appreciated but unnecessary. Yet convince him she must. At least she would not have to do so with an audience.

Her new mother- and sister-in-law had gone to visit friends to give the newlyweds some time to settle into the house. Not that it had really been needed—there was more than enough room in the enormous house for four people—but she appreciated the sentiment.

She glanced at her husband's empty side of the bed. His pillow was cool, so he must have been up for some time. She stretched and attempted to feel guilty for lying in bed while her husband was up and about being industrious. But she just couldn't find it in her.

She did need to get up, though. They would be leaving soon for a brief honeymoon at Wrothlake, and there was no doubt much to be done before they departed. Before she could think too much on the matter, there was a knock at the door. Lavinia quickly rose and donned her robe before calling out, "Enter."

Mrs. Bugsley, the housekeeper, bustled in, holding the door open for one of the maids who carried a silver tray with a small teapot, cup, and accessories. The maid was dismissed after setting the tray down on a small table, and Lavinia sat down to a piping-hot cup of tea.

"I'm not sure how you'll be wanting to do things, Your Grace, but the dowager duchess always takes her morning tea in her room, bright and early, while we go over the menu for the day and get everything settled. Once you are dressed, breakfast is served in the dining room where we can go over the invitations and messages that need to be answered. Unless you wish to change how things are done?"

"Not at all. That will be just fine, thank you, Mrs. Bugsley," she said. "No need to change things if they worked."

For a moment, she wondered how her mother-in-law felt, if she was relieved to pass the responsibilities of running the household over or if she resented someone taking her place. Lavinia would have wished to ask for her direction. But she would do as best she could until her mother-in-law returned.

Lavinia liked Mrs. Bugsley, and thankfully,

it seemed they'd get on well. From what she'd seen so far, Mrs. Bugsley was a no-nonsense woman who ran the house with an iron fist. They quickly arranged the menu for the day—easy enough, as Lavinia just approved everything Mrs. Bugsley said. She had no strong feelings on the matter, really, so unless a dish was presented that Lavinia disliked, it was much easier to approve it all.

In short order, she was dressed and downstairs in the small family dining room with a steaming plate of eggs and fresh bread with butter. She hadn't gotten halfway through it when Mrs. Bugsley entered with an overflowing tray of mail.

"These are the invitations that came in while you were away," Mrs. Bugsley explained. "If it suits, we can go through them quickly and you can decide which you'd like to accept and which to send your regrets to."

Lavinia nodded and took another bracing sip of tea. She was beginning to wonder if she needed something stronger. There must be over two dozen invitations there.

Mrs. Bugsley had just picked up the first one when the butler entered, her sisters on his heels. "Lady Harriet Wynnburn and Lady Katherine Wynnburn," he announced.

"I hope we're not disturbing you," Kitty said, sliding into a seat near Lavinia.

"Of course we aren't," Harriet said before

Lavinia could answer. "We are family, after all." She headed straight for the sideboard and poured herself a cup of tea before sitting down opposite Lavinia.

Mrs. Bugsley glowered at them but didn't say anything when she glanced at Lavinia, who merely shrugged.

"Sorry for barging in," Kitty said. "But we did see His Grace on the way in, and he told us we could come on up and get your lazy-bones from bed."

Lavinia's mouth dropped. "He did not."

Kitty giggled. "Not quite in those words, but the sentiment was the same."

Lavinia pursed her lips together but was smiling behind it. "Well, I am already up, as you can see."

"Hmm, unfortunately. I was looking forward to pulling you from your bed," Kitty said with a laugh.

Harriet ignored their playful banter. "We brought the invitations that came in this morning," she said, adding to the pile on the tray. Another dozen, at least.

Lavinia shook her head. "I don't even know this many people."

Harriet snorted. "That hardly matters. They know you. You are the new Duchess of Beaubrooke. Everyone will want you at their event."

"Oh. Goodness," she said faintly.

She'd known, of course, that her new status would bring with it a great deal of social notoriety, for lack of a better word. Her mother, as the Countess of Abberforth, had received stacks of invitations every morning as well. Though never quite so many. And Lavinia knew that her position as a duchess would bring her a great deal more attention than as the overlooked middle daughter of an earl.

But still. Being faced with the reality was quite overwhelming. Especially as she hadn't expected it to start quite so soon. The marriage was barely twenty-four hours old.

"I'm not sure where to begin," she confessed. "I can't possibly attend them all."

Harriet shook her head. "Of course not. Most of these you won't want to waste your time with. But you need to be strategic about who you choose and who you snub. Choosing incorrectly can have repercussions that might be difficult to recover from, no matter who you are. You don't want to offend or encourage the wrong people."

Lavinia nodded. She knew that much.

Mrs. Bugsley looked at Harriet with newfound respect and gave her a sharp nod. "I'll leave you in your sister's capable hands, Your Grace. Once you've decided which invitations to accept, let me know and we'll get your responses delivered. And I'm sure you'll be wanting to plan your own event soon. I will handle your social calendar until we can engage a social secretary for you."

"Thank you, Mrs. Bugsley. That would be wonderful."

The woman gave her a sharp nod and swept from the room.

She hadn't considered a need for a social secretary before, but she certainly did now. It would be a great help to have someone take care of all this for her.

And…

"My own event?"

"Of course," Kitty said. "Everyone will want to meet you. Once you and the duke have returned from your honeymoon, people will be expecting some sort of party. Perhaps a grand ball," she said, her eyes lighting with excitement.

"Yes, but first, we must deal with this," Harriet said, gesturing to the massive pile in front of her. "This one for instance," she said, holding up an invitation to a musical gathering at the home of someone or other. Harriet pulled it away before she could read the name.

"That one sounds lovely. I'd enjoy attending a musical evening," Lavinia said.

Harriet stared at her, and even Kitty shook her head before standing to get herself a cup of tea and some toast.

"What is wrong with attending that one?" Lavinia asked.

"It's being thrown by Mrs. Cranston," Kitty said, as if that explained anything.

When Lavinia just stared blankly at them, Harriet rolled her eyes. "Mr. Cranston was embroiled in a scandal last year involving trade routes and shipping merchant loads and several other issues that I won't get into. Since then, their fortunes, and those of the people they swindled into investing, have been greatly reduced. As you can well imagine, they are desperate to get back into society's good graces and seem to be hopeful to use you to do so. If you attend, particularly if you bring your new husband along with you, it gives them legitimacy again. Or at least gets their foot in the door."

"Is that such a bad thing? Everyone makes mistakes."

Both Harriet and Kitty gaped at her, but it was Harriet who answered. "Not everyone makes the kinds of mistakes that bankrupts multiple people because of your lies and cover-ups. If you still feel badly for them, let me point out that while Mrs. Cranston is desperate to be accepted back into the bosom of society, Mr. Cranston seems wholly focused on rebuilding his fortunes and has new schemes lined up to do so. And for those schemes to work, he needs investors. If you and the duke arrive at their home for their little soiree, who do you think will be the first person he asks?"

"Ah," Lavinia said.

"Exactly. Even if you were to say no, just the fact that you were there will open the door for others. And that wouldn't end well for anyone but the Cranstons. And likely not even them in the long run."

She held up the invitation and waved it about for a moment before dropping it on the rejection pile.

They went through each invitation, rejecting or accepting depending on Harriet's social savviness. When they'd finally gotten down to the last one, Lavinia dropped her face in her hands.

"Perhaps His Grace should have married you," she said to Harriet. "At least you'd have been able to open your mail without a support team to make sure you weren't inadvertently starting a small war or bankrupting half the *ton*."

Harriet froze for a second, staring at her, and then shook her head. "This is part of being the Duchess of Beaubrooke. You wanted to be the duchess, didn't you?"

Lavinia shook her head. "No. I just wanted the duke."

Harriet nodded slowly. "And that is why he married you. And why he made the right choice," she said with a long sigh.

Lavinia blinked at her in surprise. Kitty did the same.

"Are you admitting that you were... wrong?" Kitty asked.

Harriet scoffed. "Don't be absurd. I still would have made an excellent duchess." She leaned forward and squeezed Lavinia's hand. "But I would have made him a terrible wife."

She stood and began pulling on her gloves. "Now, you have your invitations for when you return. When you get back, we'll go over the others that will have arrived. Generally speaking, you don't want to accept last-minute invitations. If they didn't care enough to invite you the first time, they shouldn't have the pleasure of your company. But there are exceptions. Don't accept or reject anything without me."

Lavinia chuckled. "I won't." And she meant it. Harriet had been more than helpful. She'd been invaluable.

"You will be gone a week?"

Lavinia gave her a dazed nod, and Harriet continued on. "I'll see you when you return then, and we can begin planning your welcome home party," Harriet said.

"Oh, perhaps a card night," Kitty suggested. "Those are always entertaining."

"I'm throwing a welcome home party?" Lavinia asked.

Harriet and Kitty exchanged exasperated looks.

"Really, Livy, you were raised right

alongside us," Kitty said. "We have the same mother. She taught you the same social skills. How did you manage to not learn a single thing?"

Lavinia gave them a sheepish grin. "I wasn't paying attention?"

And she hadn't been. Yes, it was true that she'd often been forgotten and overlooked, but she was beginning to wonder how much of that had started with her. It was probably difficult to pay too much attention to someone who took every opportunity to disappear. She wouldn't accept total responsibility. Her family bore a good deal of that. But she could admit that when it came to certain things, she hadn't learned them because she'd chosen not to.

"Well, I hope you're paying attention now," Harriet said. "What you do in this home can make or break your husband's fortunes. And I won't have a sister of mine being a complete social disaster."

That was the last thing Lavinia wanted. The duke had chosen her. *Her*. The first person in her life to have done so. And she didn't want him to regret that decision. He needed her. Needed her to handle this aspect of their lives so he could focus on his research. She had quite literally been bred for this, for all that she'd rejected that part of her upbringing until this moment.

However, she was a quick study and had the steadfast desire to be the partner her husband needed. It was a bit daunting, but the growing ember of hope in her soul thrilled at the fact that someone needed her. She'd never felt like her presence made a difference one way or another before. But she'd always craved that. To have someone want her, need her, the way her husband did now. It was an almost heady rush, filling her with a sense of responsibility and purpose. She would not fail him.

"Understood," Lavinia said, giving her a mock salute that had Harriet rolling her eyes heavenward again.

She jested, but she did truly understand. And if the life of a social icon hadn't been exactly what she'd wanted for herself, she had no doubt she'd learn to enjoy it. Surely, her entire life wouldn't be filled with balls and soirees. She'd still be able to find quiet moments for herself to indulge in the things she loved. But she needed to get her bearings first, establish her place in society. Ensure her husband's needs were met. And truth be told, she'd quite enjoyed their wedding ball, far more than she'd anticipated. It had helped that the other people in attendance had been aware of her presence. Perhaps becoming a little more social wouldn't be so terrible after all. She might even be looking forward to it.

"Your homecoming party will be smaller, more intimate. No more than fifty people."

"That's small?" Lavinia asked.

"Yes. These will be your closest friends and acquaintances. Family. The duke's business contacts, etcetera. People who are important, personally, or who have a direct effect on the fortunes of the family. This will not only introduce you to everyone—and no, your wedding celebrations did not count—it will also let them know they are important, thereby cementing your ties. Then, later this year, perhaps in a month or two, you'll throw a grand ball."

"Oh, yes," Kitty said, clapping her hands before stopping with a gasp.

Her sisters' gazes shot to hers, Lavinia's in concern, Harriet's with mild interest.

"You should throw an end-of-the-Season ball."

Harriet nodded, a touch of pride in her eyes. "That is an excellent idea, Kitty. A grand ball to bid farewell to another successful Season would be perfect."

"That would be lovely," Lavinia said, excitement finally building in her chest. Most of the social events sounded dull as dirt, and throwing her own party terrified her somewhat. Although, with Harriet's help, she did feel a great deal more confident. But a grand ball would be wonderful.

"Oh, but…"

Harriet glanced at her. "What's wrong?"

"I believe the duke was planning on spending the summer at Wrothlake Park. His greenhouse is there, and he has a particular project that should be coming to fruition in mid-summer. Perhaps before the end of the Season."

"Well, he'll have to reschedule," Harriet said. "Or move his plants here. Unless it's a tree, I'm sure that would be possible. Country balls are a wonderful way to spend an evening, but to get the attendance you want, you need to be in London."

Lavinia nodded. "I will speak with him and see what I can do."

"Good," Harriet said, leaning in to kiss her cheek. "Until next week, then," she said before marching out of the room, Kitty on her heels.

Lavinia looked back at the stack of invitations in front of her. The rejection pile was much larger than the accepted pile. But it was still intimidating. She had the sudden urge to crawl back into bed.

Perhaps this time she could convince her husband to join her.

· · ·

"You simply cannot disappear for an entire week," Timothy said as Alex stacked another manuscript on top of his pile. "You have already been neglecting your work as it is of late."

"Timothy, my friend, you fret too much," he said. "I need to gather a few manuscripts that I left at the estate, and as I'll soon be staying more in the country in any case, it is a better place to start the new grafts we discussed. Besides, I am wed now. I would like to spend at least a few days with my new wife so she does not think that I abhor the arrangement. And frankly, after the whirlwind of the last few weeks, I could use a couple days in the country."

Timothy grunted. "Unless the girl is covered in leaves and enjoys being stuck in the dirt and watered once a day, I don't see this working out well. You'll probably forget she's even there within a day of arriving unless you set her up in your greenhouse."

Alex glowered at his friend, but Timothy wasn't far off. He didn't think he would be *that* bad with his wife. Though considering he'd left her alone on their wedding night and had left the house this morning before she'd awoken, he wasn't making an auspicious start. He would need to put some effort into ensuring he didn't ignore her entirely.

But there were definitely times when he got immersed in his research and the rest of the world just slipped away for days and sometimes weeks at a time. There had been

more than one occasion where his mother
had had to send servants to track him down,
sometimes to entirely different cities (and
once to a different continent) because he had
been chasing some exotic plant or another.

He couldn't help it. The plants were in his
blood. If he were cut open, he would probably bleed pure chlorophyll.

He'd always been interested in plants, especially useful plants. And he'd discovered so
much already. But not enough. There was
more out there. More to learn. More to discover. More to create. And he would do it all.

But first he had a bride to woo.

"Well, while you're off courting your
bride—a useless notion as you're already
married, let me remind you—try to keep in
mind that we are running out of time,"
Timothy reminded him. "The Royal Society
won't wait for you to finish a grand honeymoon trip."

Alex sighed. "I know, Timothy. Trust me, I
will be working. And like I said, I need to get
to my greenhouse to set up the new grafts, so
I would have had to go at some point."

"You have a greenhouse here," he grumbled.

That was true. He had a greenhouse, or at
least a conservatory, at every home he spent
any length of time in. But the greenhouse at
Wrothlake Park was special.

"We both know that these grafts will be safer at Wrothlake than here in London. Less chance of anything untoward happening to them. Or prying eyes seeing what they aren't meant to."

Like Lord Nigel Bainbridge's.

Bainbridge, who always seemed to be cropping up where Alex least expected, or wanted, him. Bainbridge, who had been the bane of his existence since their childhood. Bainbridge, who was the most likely person to beat him to the discovery of a lifetime.

And even with his rival looming, for a second, the image that flashed through his mind wasn't of the newly grafted plants in his greenhouse and the urgent Royal Society deadline, but of a laughing woman standing in her parents' garden, her beautiful brown eyes alight with joy. And burning with a newly stoked fire as she lifted her face for his kiss.

He cleared his throat and shoved another manuscript in his satchel before closing it up.

"It will be fine, Timothy. I promise. I will be back in a week's time."

"I hope so," Timothy muttered before heading back to his office, grumbling under his breath about women and potting soil.

Alex just shook his head and took his leave. Though he understood his friend's concern and confusion. While Timothy was correct in that it wasn't the most ideal time to be traipsing about the countryside, it was unavoidable. So he might as well make the best of the situation. And hope that his new bride would be happy there as well.

While he was a patient man, he had no wish to prolong his self-imposed isolation from his wife. There were some definite advantages to marriage, and he was eager to partake. But he would abide by his wife's wishes in the matter. He could but hope spending more time alone together would spark her interest as well.

There was only one way to find out.

CHAPTER ELEVEN

Lavinia stood by the large French doors that led out to the gardens and watched the birds bathing in the fountain. She adjusted her spectacles on her nose, glad to be away from the judging eyes of the society darlings so she could enjoy the gift of adequate sight for a few days.

She already loved Wrothlake. Hopefully, they'd be able to spend a great deal of time here. In fact, she'd be happy to live here all year. Though she would prefer to wake with her husband instead of alone. She'd been a wife for several days now, yet she didn't feel much changed. That needed to be remedied.

Movement caught her eye near the green-house, and her heart caught in her throat.

Dare she seek him out?

If she didn't do it now, she might never work up her nerve again. So she took a deep breath and hurried outside and into the gardens. She headed directly to the massive greenhouse that sparkled in the sun not far from the house. That wicked little spark in the duke's eyes on their wedding night had engrossed her since the moment his lips had first touched hers. She'd barely slept a wink since their wedding, and when she did, she dreamed of the moment he'd left her on their wedding night…and what might have occurred had he remained, over and over, until she'd dragged herself out of bed with the sun.

She wanted more. His willingness to wait until she was comfortable with a physical relationship was much appreciated. Not every husband would be so considerate. But she didn't want to wait. She wanted to explore those feelings he ignited when he touched her. Now she just needed to find the words—and the courage—to let him know.

The butterflies in her stomach grew the closer she came to the greenhouse. Peeking through the windows didn't reveal anyone inside, though the building was large enough and stuffed so full of greenery she wouldn't be able to see anyone unless they were pressed against the glass.

Only one way to solve her little mystery. She took a deep breath and cautiously pushed the door open. The humid heat of the place brushed across her chilled skin and welcomed her inside. The decided coolness of the spring morning would be sorely missed when the summer brought its heat. But at the moment, with her shawl still on the back of her chair in the library, the heat of the greenhouse was welcome.

A noise, what sounded like a clay pot clattering on the stone floor, emanated from farther back in the greenhouse and she tried to peer over the dozens of potted plants to see who it was.

"Your Grace?" she called out.

The greenhouse was quite large, the biggest she'd ever been in, with rows upon rows of flowering plants and greenery. It was quite lovely, actually, and smelled of dirt and foliage and other earthy things.

"Hello?" he called back.

She went to the end of the aisle and glanced up the next aisle.

"Your Grace?" Where was he? The place was a veritable jungle.

He popped his head up from a spot three or four rows in, his head peering over the tops of his plants.

"Lavinia?" he called.

"Where are you?"

"I'm back here. Three more rows up and make a right," he said.

She followed the sound of his voice and found him on one knee, next to a couple of rather sad-looking little plants. One had several brown and wilted leaves and looked on the brink of death. Which she'd know, because most plants she attempted to look after herself took on that appearance before too long.

The other seemed rather odd, as if it had mismatched branches and stems, and it looked as though it was tied together with little bits of string. He leaned his elbow on his knee and watched her draw nearer, his gaze focused. Every step she took. From the tip of her toe when it appeared from beneath her skirts to the bonnet she patted to see if it was still in place.

It wasn't. She'd forgotten the blasted thing in her haste to see him.

And her husband was still watching her with a concentrated attention that sent a pleasant shiver along her spine.

He seemed to realize he was staring and turned his attention back to his plants. "Good morning, Lavinia," he said. "Did you need something?"

"No, Your Grace. I simply wished for your company."

"Ah," he said. "Well, if you should need anything, you have only to ask."

"Thank you," she said, trying to smile past the veritable circus in her belly.

"Did you sleep well?" he asked.

The question seemed innocent enough, but there was a wicked gleam in his eyes that flustered her to no end.

"No, actually, I didn't sleep at all."

"Hmm, neither did I." His gaze moved over her before locking with hers, and the air inside the greenhouse suddenly seemed too thin.

She finally tore her eyes from his and sucked in a shaky breath. "Is there something wrong with them?" she asked, pointing down at the plants by their feet.

He followed her gaze and gently touched a brown leaf from the wilted plant. "I rescued this poor thing from my sister. She had it up in her room but has been dreadfully neglecting it. So I intervened."

Lavinia grinned. "You mean you stole it."

His lips twitched. "Well, now you sound like Georgie."

Then he ran a finger lightly along one of the leaves of the other plant, and that shiver tripped down her spine again. She could all too easily imagine that finger caressing her skin.

"This one is one of my grafting projects. But it's not doing too well, I'm afraid."

"Oh."

Nigel was always going on about grafting, but it had been difficult to envision exactly what was happening. She dropped to her knees beside it, fascinated to see what she'd heard of for so long.

"Is this where you attach them?"

She pointed to part of a stem that had been split so the stem of a different plant could be placed inside. It was tied together with bits of twine to keep the split stem pressed together around the new shoot. What looked like bits of melted wax sealed it all together.

"Does that keep the exposed bits from drying out?" she asked.

His face lit up as though she'd just declared him King of England. It only lasted a second, but the sight of his obvious delight made her feel like the sun had come out to shine just for her. "Yes, exactly. Well done, you."

"It wasn't too difficult to surmise."

He snorted. "You'd be surprised at how many would disagree with you."

She watched him in comfortable silence for a moment while he continued to pat at the soil at the base of the plant. But there was a question burning in her mind that she couldn't ignore. Many questions, actually. But she'd take them one at a time.

Finally, she took a deep breath and decided to get it over with. "May I ask you a question, Your Grace?"

"Alex," he said.

"Pardon?"

"My name is Alexander, but my family calls me Alex. You are my wife, after all. Call me by my given name." His gaze flickered briefly to her face before glancing back down. "If you wouldn't mind," he added, softening the demand to a request.

Why did the word "wife" affect her so?

Every time he said that word, her knees went weak. "If that is what you prefer," she said, sucking in a breath for her suddenly air-deprived lungs. "Alex."

The slow smile he gave her made her stomach drop to her toes and bounce right up again. It seemed unfair that such a small expression could affect her so strongly.

"What was your question, Lavinia?"

She steeled her spine against the sudden desire to swoon. Oh, that was even better than "wife." What was wrong with her? It was just her name. A name she'd never been particularly fond of, either. Though on his lips… she loved it more each time he said it.

He raised a brow, and she realized she hadn't said anything yet.

This was the moment. Her chance to tell him she wished to be his wife in truth. She just needed to open her mouth and say the words.

"I…uh…I wished to tell you—"

Lavinia stepped back, gasping when her heel caught the edge of a dip in the flooring and sent her tumbling backward into a large clay pot.

It didn't break, she was pretty sure. She was also pretty sure she wasn't broken, other than her pride, which was irreparable at this point. She was, however, wedged tightly in the pot, her hind end firmly inside while her feet dangled uselessly over the edge.

Alex hurried over to peer down at her, eyes wide as they roamed over her, assessing the damage. His mouth opened and closed for a moment, and she sighed. She didn't know quite what to say, either.

His eyebrow quirked up. "Do you require some assistance, my lady?"

She slapped a hand over her eyes, though shutting out the sight of him did nothing to appease her humiliation. Of all the moments to make an utter fool of herself. Not that there were any good moments to do so. But whilst attempting to seduce her husband... she squeezed her eyes tighter, all thoughts of seduction abandoned. Just then, her only wish was to depart with her dignity intact.

"Lavinia."

"Yes?" she muttered, wishing the pot would just finish swallowing her whole.

His quiet laugh had her peeking through her fingers at him.

He opened his mouth again and then shook his head, rubbing his hand over his face as if he was trying to scrub the amusement from it. It didn't work.

"Hold on to me," he said, bending over so she could wrap an arm about his neck.

She hesitated only a second before doing as he commanded. He tucked one of his arms behind her knees and the other under her arms and around her waist and pulled.

She exited the pot with a slight popping noise that had her wanting to bury her face against the duke's—Alex's—chest.

"What did you wish to tell me?" he asked, setting her on her feet.

So many words flew through her mind. *Take me back inside. Make me your wife. Touch me like you did before. I don't wish to wait any longer.*

But what came out was, "I…you…I…" She pushed at her spectacles and then realized she still wore them and had meant to take them off before embarking on this pathetic attempt at seduction.

But when she tried to pull them off, Alex stopped her, his hands coming up to grasp hers.

"Leave them on."

Her eyes flickered to him in surprise. "You…you don't mind them?"

"You need them to see. Of course I do not mind them."

She ducked her head. "They are hardly fashionable. I can make do with the quizzing glass. But…"

"But?"

She gave him a small smile. "It is nice to be able to see clearly from both eyes at once."

He reached up to adjust the spectacles. "Wear them from now on if it makes you more comfortable to do so. Even in public."

"Truly? My mother finds them unflattering."

He grunted. "As your husband, mine is the only opinion that should matter to you."

She looked up at him, her eyes searching his.

"And I find you incredibly beautiful," he said.

She swallowed hard. "You do?"

His eyes raised and pinned hers. "Very much so."

She sucked in a deep breath, her stomach in a riot. "I…I thought, since we still haven't…"

He took her chin between his fingers and lifted her face so she could not look away. "I wish only to ensure you are ready to take that step. Don't ever think that I am not looking forward to becoming your husband in truth, Lavinia."

Her breath stuck in her throat, her heart pounding so furiously her head spun.

"When you are ready," he added. "Though it comes to me that you may never be ready. And if that is the case—"

"No," she interrupted, not wanting any doubt in his mind. "I find you quite agreeable," she insisted.

His eyebrow quirked up. "High praise, indeed."

She tilted her head as she looked up at him

and squinted her eyes just a bit. "Your love of plants may be a bit obsessive."

That surprised a laugh out of him. "You would not be the first to believe so. One of few to say so directly to me. But certainly not the first to think it."

She looked down at her toes, another question swirling in her mind that she was hesitant to ask. But there was no time but the present. "May I ask you something more personal?"

He took her hand and kissed it, letting his lips not only touch her skin but also linger. She tried to gather her thoughts, but she had a difficult time concentrating on anything other than the warm press of his lips and how it stole her breath.

"Ask me anything you wish, Lavinia. You needn't ask permission."

"I wondered…" Her breath hitched when his fingers skimmed her palm. "If perhaps we should…"

She trailed off. She couldn't say it. Oh, she wanted to. But it was too much. How did a wife go about seducing her husband? She had no experience with even talking to men, much less enticing them to…do more than talk.

"We should what?" he asked, his finger brushing against the pulse thundering in her wrist.

An idea occurred to her and that maddening finger caressing her skin finally decided her. "As a scientific man," she said, "this would be purely in the interest of research, mind you."

His eyebrow quirked up, but if he knew where she was going with this, he apparently wasn't going to rescue her. Maybe he wanted to see how far she'd go with her suggestion. She wondered that herself.

"I do enjoy a good bit of research," he said, his eyes narrowing as he studied her.

Just spit it out, girl! Or drop the matter entirely.

"As we are now wed…"

"We are," he added, and she swallowed hard.

"We are, and will be expected to provide an heir or two for the estate, I assume…"

He nodded slowly. "Fair to assume that would be expected of us, yes." His expression was unreadable, though surely, he knew what she was trying, and failing, to imply. She squared her shoulders.

"Then perhaps it would be best to see if we are compatible…in that way."

His eyebrows hit his hairline, his eyes wide. And interested.

CHAPTER TWELVE

Oh, this woman! She had no idea how tantalizing that offer was. But he would be an absolute cad to agree. Tempting though it may be. Though the fact that she was asking meant she was at least ready to explore their marital relationship. Would he not then be a bigger cad to refuse?

"We have already kissed," she added. "And I, at least, found the experience…quite pleasant."

"Pleasant?" Well now, that was downright insulting. "I would hope it would have been a great deal more than pleasant."

She smiled shyly. "Then perhaps we should try it again."

Little minx. He might have his hands fuller than he expected.

"Do you not want to kiss me?" she asked, a slight frown furrowing her brow. She tried to pull her hands from his, but he held on, his eyes focusing on the full lips she was asking him to claim.

"What I want is irrelevant. It would be exceedingly wicked of me to agree."

She pursed her lips. "Have you not ever wanted to be exceedingly wicked?"

He grunted. "That implies that I have not

ever been. And you do not know me well enough to make that assumption."

Her grin widened, and she looked so surprised and delighted—and possibly intrigued—with that declaration that he nearly laughed. He shook his head. "You've gone rogue on me."

She took a deep breath and released it in a rush. "I have always been assured of my place in the world, Your Grace. I had no expectations for that to ever change. And now, suddenly, I find that everything has changed. And I think I find it…freeing."

He nodded. "I can understand," he said. Even though the change in his own fortunes had actually led to less freedom, he could certainly see that becoming a duchess would offer Lavinia a whole new world of freedom she hadn't experienced before.

She tilted her head to look at him. "Do you not want to kiss me?"

He pulled her closer, his hands sliding up to lightly grip her upper arms. But he shook his head. "What a man wants and what a man should do are often two entirely different things."

She stepped closer, reducing the space between them to a mere breath.

"And what am I, then?" she asked, her voice hardly more than a whisper. "Something you want or something you must do?"

He pulled her closer and wrapped an arm around her waist. Her breath came more quickly as he brought his hand up to drag his thumb over her bottom lip. Her mouth opened slightly with a silent gasp.

"I think you'll find," he said, gently brushing the tip of his nose over her own, "that sometimes duty and desire go hand-in-hand."

"Do they?" she asked, her voice faint.

He cupped her cheek, and a faint shiver ran through her, igniting a heat in his blood that he hadn't felt in a long time.

"Oh yes. I am the Duke of Beaubrooke. I have a great many responsibilities, including a duty to sire an heir and propagate my family line. However," he said, taking her chin between his fingers to tilt her face up when her eyes fell, "just because it is my duty doesn't mean it's not also something I am very much looking forward to."

Her eyes flicked back to his. "Are you?"

"Oh yes, Lavinia. Never doubt that."

It was all he could do not to bend her over the potting table and show her just how wild and wicked he could be. She rose on her toes, her hands moving to his chest as she pressed herself closer.

But with her trembling against him, her eyes closing while she lifted her lips to his, his sense of honor warred with his baser nature that demanded he claim her.

"Lavinia," he whispered, and she dragged in a shuddering breath.

"Yes, Your Grace."

"If you are certain you are ready…"

"I am," she said, pressing even closer to him. Close enough she could undoubtedly feel how ready he was.

"Then I think we should retire to our bedchamber."

· · ·

They stood looking at each other in the privacy of their room, neither one talking. Or making a move toward the other. And since she had no idea what she was doing, he was going to have to show her. She sincerely hoped she wouldn't need to tell him so, because she had no idea how to go about being so forward.

Maybe it would help if she just…let it be known that she wasn't afraid.

Right.

She pulled off her earrings and laid them carefully on the table by the window. And then she kicked off her slippers, which were making her feet ache. She near groaned in relief to have them gone. And then…she could no longer go it alone.

"Can you help with the hooks and ties, Your Grace, or would you prefer I call Marta?"

That finally snapped him out of his trance, and he crossed over to her. "No need. I can help."

Before she could turn, though, he stopped in front of her, his eyes moving over from her head on down. She couldn't tell if he liked what he saw, but she hoped so. Because she was who she was. There was no changing anything now.

He leaned forward and kissed her forehead, an achingly sweet gesture that somehow settled the nerves rioting in her stomach. Or settled some of them, she should say. Her body was a mass of sensation, and he'd barely touched her yet. Though whether it was from him or the anticipation of what was about to happen…not that she was entirely sure what that was…she didn't know.

He took her hair down, pulling the pins out one at a time. And then he turned her around so he could start working on the ties and fasteners at her back.

"Did your mother tell you at all what to expect?" he asked.

"Not much," she admitted. "The basics of…the act. I think. But…the details were exceedingly vague."

He snorted softly but shook his head. "I will never understand why women don't discuss this more. It seems like it would be a good thing to know before the moment arrives."

She heartily agreed.

His fingers made quick work of her fasteners and he had her dress carefully removed and draped over the chair in far less time than it had taken to put it on. He continued with her petticoats and stays, even down to her stockings, until she stood before him in nothing but her thin shift.

By the time he was finished, her breaths were coming in short bursts and her head was nearly spinning with the blood rushing through her veins. And he hadn't even touched her yet.

Then he started taking off his own clothing, and…she wanted to help him as he had her. She wanted to remove everything, take the opportunity to let her fingers skim over his skin. But she was frozen in place, watching him remove his simple waistcoat and cravat. And then pull his shirt over his head. Until he was in nothing but his trousers.

He came toward her and brushed a finger across her cheek.

"If there's anything I do that you don't like, tell me. Having said that, as it is your first time…I don't know if your mother explained…"

She took pity on him and nodded. "I know enough to know what to expect. I know there will be some pain and discomfort, and yes, I am nervous about that. But my mother said that it could feel good as well. If the man knew what he was doing."

Alex barked out a laugh, and the sound broke the tension in the room, bringing a shy smile to her own lips.

"Your mother is a wise woman," he said, still smiling as he pulled her into his arms.

Then he looked down at her, smoothing her hair out of her face. "And you are a very beautiful one."

He finally closed the distance between them and tilted her face up for his kiss. She'd anticipated this. They'd had their kiss after the ceremony, of course. And that moment in the carriage. But this. This melding of their mouths while there was almost nothing else between them, *this* she hadn't expected.

Her body was already shaking, seeking something more. She pressed closer to him, rising up on her toes. The heat of him seeped through her thin gown and into her skin, and she shivered, wanting more. He kissed up the column of her neck, his lips grazing the sensitive spot near her ear. Her hands moved over his chest, and he groaned. A rush of excitement and power crashed through her at the reaction she was able to draw from him with such a simple touch.

His tongue traced a trail down the gentle slope of her neck, and she tilted her head to give him better access. When his teeth nibbled at her neck, her eyes fluttered closed, and her mouth dropped open in a silent gasp.

And this time when his lips closed over hers, she immediately opened to him, moaning in the back of her throat when his tongue swept over hers. He pressed her against him, and she shivered again at the evidence of his desire for her.

It was a very strange thing to be told one's whole life that to even touch a man was so forbidden, it could ruin one's entire life. And then, one day, after a few words from a clergyman, she could stand in this room with this man and do whatever she wanted with him. To him. It was a bit hard to reconcile, and she was sure at least some of the anxiety fluttering in her chest was latent guilt for engaging in activities she'd always been taught were sinful. That were now, somehow, the actions of a good and dutiful wife.

Alex's hand brushed the side of her breast as he gripped her shift, and the molten heat that shot to her core had her gasping out loud. Duty be damned. Nothing about what had occurred so far could ever be described in her mind as a duty. Everything was an exquisite pleasure.

Alex slowly drew her shift up until he pulled it over her head, and she stood before him, trembling, in nothing at all. His breath left him in a rush, like someone had punched all the air from his lungs, and the reverence on his face soothed her nerves.

"You are so lovely, Lavinia. Perfection."

He looked at her, his hungry gaze roving over her until she couldn't stand it anymore. She reached out for him. If he could look his fill at her, she wanted the same courtesy. Her hands found the top of his trousers, and she started to undo the buttons. She thought perhaps he'd stop her, but he didn't. He stood still and let her get them open and then pushed them from his hips.

He…didn't look as she'd expected. But there was also a strange mix of excitement and trepidation as she gazed at him. Surely, he…that…wouldn't fit where it's supposed to. But it must or humans would have died out long ago. Silly, perhaps, but that bit of logic calmed her. And while she was still nervous, there was an aching emptiness in her that was longing to be filled.

This time when he pulled her to him, bare skin met bare skin, and that sensation alone had her knees weakening. Alex scooped her into his arms and laid her gently on the bed, crawling up to lay beside her. He kissed her again, his mouth moving against hers with increasing urgency. And when his leg came between hers and moved against her, she threw back her head and gasped.

Suddenly his hands and mouth were

everywhere, and she couldn't get enough. It was somehow too much and not enough all at once, and she whimpered, clinging to him.

When his hand slipped between her legs, she jumped. And then melted into his touch. She had never imagined anything could feel like this. Until he slipped a finger inside her. He took his time, not only making her feel good but also showing her what to expect, letting her get used to the sensation.

She bucked under his hand, trying to draw him deeper. And when he finally covered her, she opened for him eagerly, wanting more.

He moved slowly, working himself more inside with each thrust, trying to let her become accustomed to him. The stretch and burn took her breath away, and then there was a moment of sharp pain that had her clinging to him.

"Sorry," he murmured. "That was the worst of it. I've got you. Hold on to me." He kept murmuring to her until she relaxed beneath him again, though he shook with the effort of holding still.

Then his lips and hands began moving over her again. Touching and licking and stroking until the pain of her body learning to accept his ebbed into something else. Something that made her start to move with him.

His hands gripped her waist, keeping her

movements slow and steady until she was half frantic with the need to increase the tempo. She could feel him shaking against her, and she arched up under him, trying to draw him in deeper. Something built deep within her, a yearning ache that increased with intensity and desire. She didn't know what it was she chased; she just knew her body needed something desperately. The long, deep strokes filled her over and over until she grasped his shoulders and held on tight while a wave of devastating pleasure crashed over her. He was two strokes behind her, his arms tightening around her as he reached his own climax.

He held her tight, pressing kisses to her lips and forehead. "Are you well?" he asked.

Well? That wasn't the word for it. She wasn't in pain. Yes, there was a decided ache, and she had a feeling she'd be sore in the morning. But it wasn't a bad sore necessarily.

But well? She was…shattered. Changed. Her heart clenched when he kissed the tip of her nose and gazed down at her, concern for her in his eyes. As well as something else. He looked at her as if he finally saw her. The real her. It felt as though he were looking into her very soul.

For the first time in her life, the thought didn't terrify her. She didn't want to hide away from him. She wanted him to see it all. Because for the first time, she felt as though she was…accepted. Wanted. That he saw her and liked what he saw.

And at that moment, the hope in her chest blossomed into a burning fire that she couldn't extinguish if she wanted. A hope that this new connection between them would someday turn into something deeper. Something she'd never dared dream of until then.

She couldn't tell him all of that just yet. She could barely comprehend what she was feeling herself.

So she lifted her face for another kiss. "Yes, I'm well," she assured him. "That was…that was…wonderful."

He smiled down at her and then kissed her again before slipping off the bed. He went to the dresser and poured cool water over a cloth in the basin, then brought it back and tenderly cleaned her, pressing kisses along her stomach and thighs while he did.

• • •

Alex had meant only to care for his new wife, make her more comfortable. He'd certainly not planned to begin anything anew as she was likely sore from their activities. But when her breath hitched and she began to arch into his touch, his plans changed.

He laid the cloth to the side, letting his fingers move up the silky-soft skin of her inner thighs instead.

"Alex," she said with a gasp, reaching down for him.

"Shh," he said. "Just lie back."

This time would be just for her. He wanted to show her how much pleasure they could bring each other. How good it could be. And that there were activities in which they could indulge that had nothing to do with duty to his bloodline.

When his lips brushed against her core, she sat up with a sharp inhale, her legs trying to close.

He chuckled and held them open, meeting her startled eyes as he dipped back down and trailed his tongue along the seam of her sex.

Lavinia threw her head back, and her hand grasped at his hair. He'd thought she meant to pull him away. Instead, her grip tightened, pressing him closer, and he obeyed his lady's silent command with rapturous delight.

She'd intrigued him from the moment he'd seen her surreptitiously reading at a royal wedding. And he'd suspected she hid great passions within her every time he saw her eyes flash with an inner fire when they spoke. He'd hoped they would be compatible. That they'd find a harmony together, companionship perhaps. A great many marriages had less.

But now, as his beautiful wife came

exquisitely apart under his ministrations, her taste sweet on his tongue, he had a new desire. A new dream for a future filled with passion and…possibly even love. He'd never dared hope for such a marriage before. But this incredible woman had an intellect as bright and curious as his own, a sweet spirit that warmed his soul, and a beauty that stole his breath.

He'd spend every night of their lives worshipping her if she allowed it.

Lavinia came with a cry that marked his very soul. He'd never be the same again, no matter what the future held for them. The thought brought a touch of fear. He didn't like the unknown. Had no faith in anything but science.

Until now.

"Rest now," he said, giving her one more lingering kiss as he pulled the blankets up around her.

She closed her eyes but didn't settle until he had climbed in beside her and wrapped her in his arms. Only then did the tension leave her body enough to fully relax. She cuddled in against him, and he thanked the heavens for the day that he'd sat beside her at that wedding.

CHAPTER THIRTEEN

Alex set aside the manuscript he'd been going through and checked his pocket watch with a sigh.

"I must get going," he said, standing up and removing the soft gloves he wore to protect the ancient manuscripts he'd been looking through.

"Already?" Timothy looked at him through his spectacles from the other side of the table.

Alex grimaced. He'd been back in the city for all of two days and Timothy was not reacting well to having to share Alex with a new wife.

"I'm frankly amazed I managed to escape at all." Managed to tear himself away from his new bride while she was lying naked in his bed would be more accurate. But hardly an appropriate sentiment to share. He cleared his throat and tried to banish that alluring thought. "My absence won't go unnoticed for long."

Timothy muttered something about attention-hungry women, and Alex smiled at him fondly.

Timothy had been a dear friend of his since their early days at Oxford. Timothy's family was in the shipping business and had done very well for itself. While some families might try to take advantage of their son having a close friendship with the son of the Duke of Beaubrooke, Timothy's family had been nothing but kind to him, treating him as one of their own rather than as one of the heirs to the Beaubrooke estate. So much so that Alex had tried to spend most of his holidays with Timothy's family.

While Alex's own parents had been fairly affectionate with their children and kept a happy home for the most part, there was something about the less formal atmosphere at Timothy's home that Alex couldn't help but crave. He was just Alex there, not Lord Alexander, and certainly not Your Grace, even now that he'd inherited the title.

He hadn't an inkling that he would be the duke in those years, but as the second son of the Duke of Beaubrooke, he was still afforded a great deal of prestige. Something that he hadn't had to worry about at Timothy's home. It was both refreshing and relaxing to just be Alex. He missed those days. So he treasured his time with Timothy even more as he was one of the few people who still treated Alex as they always had.

Not to mention, he was one of the best research assistants that Alex could hope to have on his team. He had a knack for finding manuscripts buried in piles and piles of random stacks and extracting just the right one that would get them the information they needed. There was no way he'd be able to complete his research without Timothy's help.

"Well, I can't say that I am thrilled that you are leaving just as we are beginning to make some progress. Then again," Timothy said with a shrug, "if I had a pretty wife who wished to spend time with me, I certainly wouldn't be burying myself in old manuscripts, either."

"You *do* have a pretty wife," Alex reminded him.

"'Who wished to spend time with me,' I said. Anne is quite content to have me out from under her heels most of the day."

Alex snorted. "I do wish to spend more time with Lavinia, I'll grant you that. Though I am still reluctant to leave. I just began combing through a particularly promising manuscript, the one you found yesterday."

Timothy nodded, listening, though his eyes were on his own manuscript.

"I've already found quite a bit of information on a few obscure species that I believe might prove to be hardier than the variety we have here in England."

"Truly?" Timothy asked, perking up.

"Absolutely. If I could get my hands on a few shoots, we might make some real progress in this project."

"That would be excellent. And I'm assuming from that excited gleam in your eye you know a person or two that might help?"

Alex raised his brows. "I know a few I can contact, yes."

Timothy wasn't wrong about the excitement, either. Being this close to realizing his dream overrode nearly everything else.

While he truly did look forward to his new life with Lavinia, he was not happy that his marriage was already interrupting his research.

"All in all, it sounds as though we have excellent prospects all around, then."

"Indeed. And hopefully, once we are more settled, I'll be able to get back to my research without too much interruption."

"You're expecting a new bride not to interrupt your research?" Timothy said with an indelicate snort. "I wish you luck with that."

"My thanks," Alex said with a wry smile.

"Of course," Timothy continued, "even if your marriage doesn't prove distracting, you'll still have your estates to preside over and the interminable social calendar to navigate."

Alex sighed. "I'm aware. But I'm hoping Lavinia will be able to rise to the occasion and help with much of that. She's not as gregarious as her sisters, but she no doubt will be able to handle the social aspect of our lives quite nicely."

Hopefully keeping him out of it as much as possible. The more she could take on, the more time he would have for his research.

Timothy arched an eyebrow. "Are you marrying a wife or a social secretary?"

Alex opened his mouth to respond and then snapped it shut again. "My mother was always a great help to my father. I simply have hope that Lavinia can be the same for me."

Timothy made a noncommittal grunt and turned back to his work, and Alex took the opportunity to escape, hurrying up the stairs to the second level of this section of the library. And nearly running into Lavinia when he reached the top.

"Lavinia," he said, pleasant surprise running through him. "I didn't expect to see you until this evening."

He raised her hand to his lips and pressed a quick kiss to it before turning to their mothers, who had taken a bit longer to catch up.

"Yes, well, we thought it best to come fetch you," his mother said as he leaned over to kiss her cheek. "It seems the most expeditious way to ensure you are not late to your engagements. In case you'd forgotten, the archbishop is due for supper this evening. You absolutely cannot be late."

"You needn't worry, Mother. I hadn't forgotten."

He held out his elbow to Lavinia, who took it with a subdued smile that concerned him. Then again, if she'd spent the afternoon in the company of both their mothers, he could understand her demeanor. Just the thought of it started a headache forming.

He patted her hand and escorted her out into the late afternoon sun.

Timothy had raised some understandable concerns, but Alex wouldn't truly know how his life would be affected by his marriage until they'd been married for longer than a week. Though, with a dinner guest so soon after their return and the overflowing stack of invitations on their sideboard, perhaps Timothy's concerns were more apt than he realized.

He took a deep breath. They simply needed to settle into their new lives. Once a routine was established, he could hopefully get back to focusing on his research.

• • •

"I cannot believe you married that dolt," Nigel said.

Lavinia stopped with the teapot in midair and gaped at him. "Nigel, that is a horrible thing to say. His Grace is not a dolt. In fact, I find him to be very intelligent and charming."

Nigel snorted. "I never took you for one of those sensible ladies with no thought in her head but handsome men, yet here you are. Thoroughly wed and absurdly happy. I scarcely recognize you. You're beginning to concern me."

"You find the duke handsome?" she asked, laughing when he scowled at her.

"Oh, come now, Nigel," Kitty said, reaching over to take another biscuit. "You knew she would marry someone at some point."

Nigel took his cup of tea from Lavinia and sat back with a frown. "I knew that in theory, yes. But she seemed so opposed to the idea that I held out hope."

Lavinia didn't say anything while she poured out another cup for Kitty and herself. Harriet had taken to avoiding them since their return from Wrothlake Park. A sad surprise, as Harriet had not only seemed to come to terms with the duke's choice but had been determined to help Lavinia in her new duties. But something had changed over the week she'd been gone.

Harriet's withdrawal saddened her, but Lavinia was also determined to not let it ruin her happiness. She had no doubt Harriet would find a much better match that would bring her joy once she got over her disappointment. If that, indeed, was the issue at hand.

In the meantime, while Lavinia knew that Nigel didn't mean any harm by his comments, she couldn't help but be a little hurt. As her closest friend, he should know better than anyone that one of the reasons she'd seemed so opposed to marriage was because she never thought anyone would be interested enough to want to marry her. And it was much easier to pretend she wasn't interested rather than admit how much that hurt. So he should surely understand how much it meant to her to not only marry, but marry a man who, so far at least, suited her so well. No matter how that man and Nigel felt about each other personally.

Something they'd need to work on or the only time she'd be able to spend time with her lifelong friend would be occasional chats and teas when Alex was otherwise occupied. Not to hide anything from him. But to keep the peace.

Though surely Nigel exaggerated their feud. He *was* prone to exaggeration.

She dropped a few lumps of sugar into her sister's tea and passed her cup over.

"You're just upset over who I've chosen," she pointed out.

"Yes! Exactly. You could have married anyone in England, Livy, and I would have celebrated from the rooftops. But you had to choose my sworn enemy."

"Oh." Lavinia shook her head. "Stop being so dramatic."

Nigel sputtered. "What? What? Me? Dramatic?"

Kitty giggled into her cup, and Lavinia rolled her eyes. "I don't know why I put up with you some days."

Nigel let out a long-suffering sigh. "Because you love me."

Lavinia snorted. "Yes, well, let's not test how far that will take you, hm?"

Nigel squinted one eye and glared at her through the other while taking a fat, slurping sip from his cup. Kitty almost snorted her own tea.

"Lord, save me from this man," Lavinia muttered.

"You do realize," Nigel said, grabbing a biscuit to dunk in his cup, "now that *His Grace* has you, he's sure to have an even greater advantage when it comes to our research."

Lavinia frowned. "I don't see how so."

"Well, what am I going to do without you to help me transcribe my notes and organize my research and inspire my greatest ideas? You know I cannot do this without you."

"Sounds like she was doing it entirely without *you*," Kitty pointed out, and Lavinia snickered into her teacup.

"Oh, hush, you," Nigel said, glowering at Kitty. "No one asked you to go pointing out inconvenient facts."

"Nigel, you are being ridiculous," Lavinia said. "I don't truly help you do much of anything. The transcribing can be done by anyone. In fact, you employ a secretary to do exactly this kind of thing for you. The poor man is quite put out whenever I come over because he is out of a job for the day and must sit and twiddle his thumbs while you insist on me doing his work."

"Well, your penmanship is so much nicer."

Lavinia just stared at him over the lip of her cup while she took a sip. There were some comments that didn't deserve to be acknowledged.

Nigel pouted. "I should've married you first is what I should have done."

She raised a brow. "I didn't think you thought of me romantically."

Nigel shrugged again. "I don't, but it would keep you away from His Gracelessness."

Lavinia rubbed at her forehead. "Nigel, you are beginning to make my head ache."

"Drink more tea," he said before popping another full biscuit into his mouth. "Have you thought that perhaps he is marrying you to spite me?"

"What?" she asked, her cup freezing in midair. "He doesn't yet know of our friendship that I'm aware of."

Not that she'd been keeping it from him. They just hadn't spoken of such things as childhood friendships yet. And as for his supposed rivalry with Nigel…it was difficult to tell when Nigel was in earnest or not. She knew that the men were researching similar subjects, but surely experiments involving bits of shrubbery weren't really the basis of a blood feud. But if that were truly the case…

Lavinia swallowed past the sudden lump in her throat. "Do you think he will mind when he finds out?" She was fairly sure Nigel was joking, or at least exaggerating. Yet she couldn't help but wonder if there was some truth to that.

Nigel nudged her foot with the toe of his boot. "Come on, Ninny. I didn't mean anything by that comment. I have no doubt our delectable Alexander, Duke of something or other, took one look at you and fell head over heels in love and his desire to marry you has nothing whatsoever to do with me. Mostly."

"Joking or not, Nigel, you are most certainly wrong," Kitty said. "I've seen the way the duke looks at her. Like he wants to put her in his pocket and carry her around. He's quite taken with her."

Nigel gestured to Kitty. "There, see?"

Lavinia nodded, slightly mollified. "I'm sure you're right," she said, willing it to be so. "After all, choosing a spouse based solely on a desire to best one's rival seems a poor way to go about selecting a mate."

"Agreed," he said, raising his cup of tea to her.

She raised her own in a mutual salute, and they both drank and carried on about their conversation, but Lavinia couldn't stop the little bit of unease that crept in Nigel's words.

Before she could dwell on the thought too much, Barnes entered. "Your Grace, Lady Harriet is here to see you."

Lavinia frowned. "Harriet?"

"Yes, Your Grace. With a man she says is her husband."

CHAPTER FOURTEEN

Lavinia went straight to the drawing room where Barnes had put her sister. "Harriet?"

Her sister stood, her back ramrod straight, the same haughty expression on her face that she usually had. But for the first time, Lavinia could see the cracks in the facade.

"What is amiss? Barnes said you're here with your…husband?"

The man who'd been sitting beside Harriet stood, his hat in his hands. He seemed vaguely familiar, but Lavinia couldn't place where she'd seen him. He was handsome, but with a ruggedness to him that was nothing like the gentlemen that Harriet typically courted. His suit was good quality but well-worn, and his shoes were polished but had seen better days. Better years.

And Lavinia suddenly understood why her sister would come to her. She didn't have any other choice. Her parents, though they loved their daughters and wanted them to be happy, would never accept a penniless son-in-law, no matter how much the daughter in question loved him.

Lavinia wasn't quite sure how to go about asking the obvious question, but it had to be asked. She stepped closer so only Harriet could hear her.

Her gaze flicked to the man and back to her sister. "Are you…"

She couldn't quite get the words out, but she didn't have to. Harriet stepped back with an exasperated huff. "Don't be absurd."

Lavinia let out a sigh of relief. "Then…why did you come to me?"

Harriet's lips were pinched and closed, looking like she wanted to say something, but she just couldn't force the words out.

"If you'll allow me?" the man said. "Maybe I can explain."

Lavinia glanced at her sister, but she didn't argue, which concerned her more than anything.

"Please," she said, gesturing to the sofa where they'd been sitting.

"Thank you, Your Grace."

Lavinia nodded and then waited for them to tell her why they were there. Harriet perched stiff and obviously uncomfortable on the edge of the sofa, but the man leaned forward, resting his elbows on his knees and turning his hat in his hands as he spoke.

"My name is John Riley. I'm an artist."

Lavinia's eyebrows rose at that, and she glanced again at her sister, who wouldn't meet her gaze.

"Harriet and I met when I was hired to paint some portraits of an acquaintance of hers. She called while I was there. I've been hired by several prominent families in the area."

"I thought you looked familiar," Lavinia said. "I must have seen you at some point."

Harriet looked pained, and Lavinia nodded at John to continue. Probably best to get it all out before Harriet expired on the spot.

"There's not really much to tell," John said. "We met that day and got to talking. And then we met again. And again." He shrugged. "The truth of the matter is that we fell in love. And would like to marry."

Lavinia's eyes flashed again to her sister. "Then you are not already married?"

Harriet did look at her at that, obviously hearing the relief in her voice. "We will be, just as soon as I can convince his stubborn hide to run away with me."

Lavinia's mouth dropped open, and it took her a few seconds to regain her composure. That Harriet was the one who seemed to be instigating all this was at once both confusing and made perfect sense. Harriet would never allow anyone to be in charge of any part of her life if she could help it. But the Harriet that Lavinia had known would also never suggest running away with a poor artist. The Harriet that Lavinia had grown up with had planned on marrying soon and marrying well and had spent their entire young adulthood with that end in mind. Lavinia had never seen Harriet so much as look at a man who was less than a baron, let alone entertain thoughts of marriage.

Though this did perhaps explain Harriet's anxiety and sadness over the past few weeks. Lavinia had thought it was because of Alex. But it was due to another man.

"I knew this was a mistake," Harriet said to John. "We should have just gone straight to Gretna Green like I wanted."

"Give her a moment to take it all in, Harriet. It's a lot to absorb all at once," John said, patting her sister's hand.

Lavinia nodded. "Thank you, Mr. Riley."

And it was a lot to take in. Of all the people who might have done something like this, Harriet would have been the last that Lavinia would guess. Kitty, on the other hand…impetuous, passionate, Kitty, yes. But not Harriet. Harriet was far too responsible, far too aware of how the consequences of her actions affected not only her but the rest of the family. Kitty in particular, who would have a dreadful time finding her own match if Harriet were to besmirch the family's reputation with such a disastrous match.

Though perhaps the situation was not quite so dire now that Lavinia had made such a brilliant match. Still, it wasn't like Harriet to be so impulsive. She must truly be in love.

Lavinia rubbed her forehead. "So, what is it that you would like for me to do?" she asked. "Intervene with our parents?"

Harriet looked at her, her face finally showing a little of what she was hiding beneath the surface. "Help us," she said simply. "Help me."

And how could Lavinia deny her?

She nodded, slowly at first and then with more conviction as relief crossed Harriet's face.

"All right. I will do what I can. You may stay here until we get this figured out. I will," she said, interrupting Harriet's silent rejoicing, "need to let Mother know you are here."

Harriet looked like she was going to protest, but John took her hand. "You can't hide from them forever. And Her Grace said she'd help."

"Call me Lavinia, please. You'll soon be family, after all."

He smiled gratefully and nodded.

"I will speak with the duke and see what we can do to help. In the meantime…I don't suppose you'd agree to return home?" she asked Harriet.

Harriet's stubborn expression was all the answer Lavinia needed, but she answered anyway. "Not until we are wedded and bedded and there is nothing they can do about it."

Lavinia bit her lip to keep her shocked gasp from escaping, and even John's face flushed. But he just quietly took Harriet's hand and looked back at Lavinia. A united front. Lovely.

"Then I shall have rooms made ready for you. And I'll send word to our parents that you are safe."

She held up a hand to forestall Harriet's objections. "I know you do not wish for them to know where you are, but they are our parents and are likely worried beyond reason for you. I promise you that I will not let them take you away. But it is cruel to make them worry."

Harriet's tough demeanor cracked a little at that, and she gave a sharp nod of her head.

"Good." Lavinia rang the little bell that would summon Barnes. Thankfully, Alex's staff was well trained and prompt, and Barnes entered almost immediately.

"Oh, Barnes. My sister and her…fiancé will be staying with us for a while. Could you show them to the guest rooms in the east wing?"

Barnes, the professional that he was, didn't even blink. "Of course, Your Grace." His gaze briefly flickered to Harriet and John. "If you'll follow me."

They stood, and Harriet paused on the way out.

"Why are you helping me?"

Lavinia frowned. "Why wouldn't I? You're my sister."

"Yes, but…" Her lips pinched together for a second before continuing. "I wasn't always kind to you. Especially during your wedding."

Lavinia sucked in a breath and sighed. "I know. And while I wish things had been different, I do understand. It doesn't matter now. That was the past. No sense in dwelling on it."

Harriet pressed her lips together again before slowly nodding. They walked toward the doors together, just reaching them when Harriet stopped again.

"Just how do you plan on helping us?"

Lavinia huffed out a laugh. "I'm not entirely sure. I suppose the best, or at least the fastest, way to handle this is to bribe a vicar into marrying you as soon as possible so the deed is done and cannot be undone no matter who protests. And then we'll need to find your artist some form of employment so he can support a wife. He doesn't appear penniless but…"

Harriet nodded and looked after her soon-to-be husband with a look so tender Lavinia nearly cried. If Harriet had said nothing else, that look alone would have convinced her to help them.

"He's not completely without means. His father is a fairly successful merchant, and he was raised comfortably. But he's also the third of four sons." She shrugged. "His mother did leave him a bit, though. Not a lot, but enough to survive on."

"Well, we'll see what we can do to improve his circumstances," Lavinia promised. "Now go get settled. I have to have a discussion with Alex and…" She shook her head. "For a fairly unconventional man himself, he does have some backward notions at times."

Harriet nodded and then surprised Lavinia again by pulling her into a hug. "Thank you, Livy."

Lavinia's heart clenched, and for a moment the two sisters clung together.

"Right. Off you go," she said, sending Harriet after Barnes with a slightly less than steady smile.

Then Lavinia sucked in a breath and prepared to convince her husband to go against everything he'd been raised to accept.

• • •

Alex rubbed his hand over his face for what felt like the thousandth time. He wouldn't have any skin left at the rate he was going.

"Lavinia," he said, trying for a reasonable tone. "I do not think you are aware of just how difficult it is to rush a marriage. A legal one, at any rate. There is a reason people go to Gretna Green."

"Yes," she said. "Because they don't have money. Luckily, we do."

He gritted his teeth and tried again. "Lavinia, we cannot simply—"

She rounded on him, and he stuttered to a halt. "Yes, we can, Alex, so please refrain from being an ass."

Alex's jaw dropped. He wouldn't have been more shocked if she'd grabbed him by the balls and declared him ripe for plucking. He wasn't sure if he should laugh, applaud, or put her over his knee. Perhaps all three. And from the look on her face, she was just as surprised.

She sucked in a deep breath through her nose and let it out slowly. "Leave us," she said to the servants who were milling about, barely pretending to do their jobs. Some didn't bother to hide their disappointment in being kicked out right before things got really interesting.

As soon as they were alone, she turned to him, and he crossed his arms, waiting for the onslaught.

"I realize that it is your duty to be frugal with money so that we'll have plenty if a disaster strikes. And I respect that. But I also suspect that you'll spend any amount of time and money on your precious research. Which I also understand and respect. It's your life's work, and it's also your money, and what you choose to spend it on is your business.

"However, I am your wife. I have no desire for new dresses, or jewels, or any other sorts of gifts of any kind, so you will not have to worry about added expenses because of me. I brought a truly ridiculous trousseau and will doubtless need nothing for the foreseeable future."

He wisely refrained from pointing out the fortune in flowers and frippery that was even now being spent, albeit by their mothers for the most part, on their grand, Season's End ball.

"This is important, Alex. You told me if I ever wanted for anything at all, I need only ask. Well, I am asking for something."

"You're right, and I wouldn't be fighting it if you were asking for a new dress. But you are asking me to bribe the Archbishop of Canterbury into granting a special license for your sister and her pauper to wed in haste and secret."

She just folded her arms and stared at him. "Yes. What of it? People do it all the time."

"Only if they have the money and prestige to do so."

"Yes! Exactly. And thankfully, we have both."

He threw his hands up. There was no arguing with her.

"Look," she said, rubbing her temples. "I

know you don't understand why I want to do this for her. But I do. She's my sister. I want her to be happy. And John may be poor, by some standards, but from what I've observed he's a good man who loves my sister. And frankly, if they truly wish to wed, there won't be any stopping them. You've met Harriet. Do you really think she'll let a little thing like the entire world being against her stop her from what she wants?"

Alex snorted. "No, I don't."

Lavinia nodded. "So. We can either let her run away to Gretna Green and live in poverty with the stigma of having run off with a man well beneath her station for the rest of her days. And poverty it will be, because once word gets around that Mr. Riley absconded with the daughter of one of society's most illustrious families, he'll never find work in London again."

Alex sighed, knowing she spoke the truth.

"Or we can help them. Pay for the special license. Have a small but elegant wedding here," she said. "Find our new brother-in-law a patronage somewhere or set up enough commissions that they'll never want for anything and let them live out their days happily in love."

Alex let out a deep sigh. She would argue him into the grave. And he wasn't so churlish that he didn't wish for her sister to be happy.

His only sincere wish was that he wasn't an integral cog in the plan for her happiness. He much preferred to be in his office surrounded by stacks of nice, quiet manuscripts, not arguing with his surprisingly tenacious wife about her sister's unfortunate nuptial plans.

But this was what Lavinia wanted. And what Alex wanted was for Lavinia to be happy.

"Very well," he said, conceding defeat. "You've convinced me."

She looked up at him with a smile so sweetly brilliant it took his breath away. "You'll help her, then?"

"I'll help."

"Oh, Alex!" She threw her arms around him and pulled him down for a kiss so exuberant he nearly vowed to do whatever she wished from that moment forward as long as this was his reward.

"I still don't approve," he admitted. "But I'll help. In fact…"

He tried to recall the conversation he'd had not too long ago with a particular artist friend of his, Mrs. Clara Pope, about a position. "I believe I might know of a position for Mr. Riley. The King of Prussia has been searching for a court painter. It's not permanent, but he would be employed for several years. The pay is excellent and, if I put in a word, could probably be made more so. And our Mr. Riley would be making the acquaintance with all of the best artists on the continent. And their clients. It should afford him plenty of opportunities."

"Oh, Alex, that sounds wonderful."

He nodded. "Yes, it should do nicely. I'll inquire about it today. After I pay a visit to the archbishop."

She kissed him again. "Thank you."

"Hmm," he grumbled. "Don't thank me yet. I haven't actually accomplished any of this."

Lavinia giggled, and that sound alone made helping Harriet worth it.

CHAPTER FIFTEEN

The day of Harriet's wedding dawned bright and beautiful. The spring air was still a bit chilly, but the skies were clear and would hopefully remain so.

Alex had done as he'd promised and not only gotten the special license from the archbishop so Harriet and John could wed at home, and without waiting for the banns to be read, but had also secured John the position of court artist with the King of Prussia. It would mean they would be out of the country for several years. But the position paid very well along with all their expenses covered and was prestigious enough that news of the wedding was being considered by most of the gossips as eccentric and romantic rather than tragic.

Their parents, of course, had not been happy about their daughter's choice. But the outcome with Alex's help was far preferrable to what could have been. Besides, there were appearances to be maintained. For the bride's parents to appear in any way unhappy about the occasion would be to admit that their daughter wasn't making the wisest choice. Also admitting that they hadn't had any choice in the matter at all.

And that wouldn't do.

So, while their smiles were a touch strained, their voices a little too shrill, Lord and Lady Abberforth were presenting a united front with their eldest child and by all accounts had welcomed Mr. John Riley into the family with open arms. After all, as Lavinia had wed so brilliantly, it gave Harriet a little more freedom in her choice. Who needed more than one duke in the family?

Everything was ready; the cake was baked, the wedding breakfast was cooked, and the family was gathered. The only thing left to do was make sure the bride was ready. Lavinia hurried upstairs to Harriet's room and knocked gently. Her mother opened the door, her eyes already suspiciously wet.

"Oh, Lavinia darling, come in. Come see how beautiful your sister looks."

Harriet stood in front of the mirror, absolutely resplendent in her pale pink silk gown. Lavinia had given her one of the gowns that had been created for her trousseau that she'd had yet to wear, and they'd had it hastily altered to fit Harriet's taller, leaner frame. They'd also used some of the lace from Lavinia's wedding gown to embellish the sleeves and hem of the gown. And the crowning touch was the Wynnburn family tiara.

"Oh Harriet," Lavinia breathed when she got close enough to see her clearly. She clasped her hands in front of her. "You are exquisite."

"She puts all other brides to shame, doesn't she?" Kitty asked, looking lovely herself in her wedding finery.

Harriet beamed at her in the mirror and then turned to pull her into a hug.

"Thank you so much," she whispered. "For everything."

Lavinia was too overcome to do more than nod and hug her sister back.

"Are you ready?"

Harriet nodded, but before they left, their mother drew them all into a hug and then kissed them each on their foreheads. "My girls," she said, her voice choked with emotion.

Lavinia swallowed hard and waved her hands. "All right, no more of that or we'll all be unfit to be seen."

They laughed, and then Lady Abberforth opened the door and led her daughters down to the waiting assembly.

Lavinia took her seat in the front row, between Nigel and Alex. Only Alex had not yet arrived.

"Where is he?" Lavinia asked Nigel in a strained whisper.

He leaned in, his shoulder touching hers. "I'm sure he'll be here soon," he said, reaching down to squeeze her hand.

"Lavinia," Alex said, slipping into the chair beside her just as the vicar stood to signal the beginning of the ceremony. "Bainbridge," he said, scowling at Nigel. "What are you doing here? I thought only family was attending the ceremony."

"He *is* family, Alex. Oh, there she is," she said, lifting her quizzing glass to watch her father and sister walk up the aisle they'd created in the parlor. She didn't know why Alex would make a scene at her sister's wedding, rivalry or no, but they would discuss it later.

The ceremony was beautiful, as most were when the couple was truly in love. Harriet fairly beamed at John, who gazed at her with an adoration that almost hurt to watch. The clergyman declared them husband and wife, and they marched back up the aisle to cheers and congratulations.

Alex turned to her, sparing a scowl for Nigel, and began to say something, but a footman interrupted and handed him a message that had just arrived.

He heaved a deep sigh. "I will be there in a moment."

The footman bowed and left.

"If you'll excuse me," he said to Lavinia. "I'll return shortly."

She opened her mouth to protest, but he'd already hurried from the room.

Alex had taken to disappearing more and

more often of late. And while she knew he
was at a critical point in his research and that
he was running out of time before his deadline with the Royal Society, she still couldn't
help but be upset by how often he left her to
her own devices. She'd known before they
wed that he'd planned to spend much of his
time with his projects. She just hadn't realized
how much time he'd meant.

Everyone gathered for a few minutes in
the main drawing room to wait until the
guests who would attend the wedding breakfast arrived. They hadn't invited many people,
of course. But there were several of the couple's especial friends, some of John's extended
family, some of Harriet's particular friends.

People seemed genuinely happy for the
couple. Perhaps it was too difficult to be
churlish in the face of true happiness. Or perhaps they were still too afraid of the
formidable Harriet Wynnburn to dare utter a
word about her.

The wedding breakfast was nearly ready.
Servants came in a steady stream to and from
the kitchens getting everything set up. The
formal dining room had been bedecked with
seasonal sprays of greenery and ribbons that
Lavinia had arranged herself, and she had in-
structed the staff to use their finest china and
glassware. Harriet deserved the best, and she
was going to get it. They were going to treat

this wedding as they would any other. Harriet's reputation remained intact. A small miracle, really, considering the reality of her marriage.

Lavinia stopped before a spray of holly and bit her lip. She'd been so proud to show it to Alexander. Not because it was pretty, though it was that, but because she'd learned the whole history of the plant and why it was used in decorations. It had been fun to learn about something he was interested in and show off her knowledge. She'd wanted him to be proud of her, wanted to make him happy.

Now she felt so foolish.

"Your Grace?"

She blinked back tears and turned to find Barnes waiting. "Yes, Barnes?"

"Everything is ready, Your Grace."

"Thank you, Barnes. Please call them in."

He bowed his head and left to do her bidding.

Nigel came and offered her his arm. "As you seem to be missing a host, might I escort you in?" he asked, giving her a sympathetic smile that nearly unraveled her carefully held emotions.

"Thank you, Nigel," she said, taking his forearm, for comfort as much as for the help she could use in navigating to her seat. "I can always count on you."

She held up her head and walked proudly

to her seat, ignoring the murmurs she heard about the missing duke. He surely had a good reason to step out and would hopefully return quickly. In the meantime, she took a deep breath and pulled herself together. She would deal with this all later. For now, she was going to ensure her sister's wedding breakfast went flawlessly. And then she'd see her on her way to her new life.

Then…then she'd figure out what the hell was going on with her own.

. . .

Alex finished composing his response to the Royal Society and sent it off with the messenger who had arrived before hurrying back to the dining room where the guests would now be seated enjoying the wedding breakfast.

The Royal Society apparently had some concerns about the similarities between his research and that of Lord Nigel Bainbridge. While there, so far, hadn't been anything submitted that was a direct copy, their focuses were similar enough that the Royal Society was starting to wonder if they were either working together or had done so in the past or if something more nefarious might be afoot.

Hopefully Alex's response explaining their similar interests and backgrounds would explain any possible overlaps in their submitted research. But he was beginning to wonder if it was more than that.

He and Bainbridge had always been friendly rivals, going back to their school days, though the friendliness had grown less and less the older they got. Perhaps because the stakes had grown as well. But while Bainbridge had always seemed to enjoy the competition between them, and relished winning to the point of lunacy, Alex had never known him to cheat.

Though that did not mean it had never happened. Simply that it had not happened to Alex's knowledge.

The timing of this incident was of the utmost concern. The fact that there seemed to be an issue with a possible duplication of research, now, when the stakes were the highest, was more than a little suspicious. Alex had always been meticulous with his research, secretive nearly to the point of paranoia with this particular project. No one had even seen his grafts aside from Timothy.

And Lavinia.

He stopped short in the doorway of the dining hall, his eyes riveted on where his wife sat at the head of the table, her new brother-in-law in the place of honor at her right, and one of her dearest friends in the world on her left.

Bainbridge.

Who was leaning toward Lavinia as they whispered together. She smiled softly at him, and he reached over and patted her hand.

Alex clenched his jaw as what felt like a lead ball dropped into his stomach. He steeled himself against it and took his seat, nodding at the guests and Harriet, who was seated in the other place of honor on his right.

Bainbridge glanced his way and then whispered to Lavinia, who held up her quizzing glass to glance at him. He wished she'd simply wear her spectacles, fashion be damned. He'd rather his wife could comfortably see.

Lavinia smiled, lifting her wineglass slightly to him. He gave her a look that he hoped conveyed his apologies for having left momentarily. She was obviously upset, to his eyes at least. And to Bainbridge's, if the way he hovered over her meant anything. But to everyone else, she likely appeared in high spirits.

He met Bainbridge's gaze and the two stared at each other, neither willing to concede and look away first. Lavinia leaned over and whispered something to Bainbridge and his lips pursed for a second before he raised his glass in a miniature salute. Alex gave him a cool nod, only acknowledging him to keep the peace with his wife. He had to swallow back his irritation when Bainbridge returned the gesture with a smile.

That one...always smiling. Alex swore Bainbridge only did it to get under his skin. Or to see if he could make him smile back which was occasionally hard to stop himself from doing. Damn the man. He was too likeable for his own good. Certainly for Alex's own good. He'd let his guard down over the years, and he might be paying for that now.

Throughout the meal, he kept an eye on Bainbridge and his wife. There didn't seem to be anything outwardly untoward. They were affectionate toward one another in the way one would be with a sibling with whom one was close. Though that thought alone was enough to make his stomach roil with indigestion. He hadn't realized just how close Bainbridge and Lavinia were.

Bainbridge was noticeably protective over her. He'd whisper to her now and then, obviously pointing out when someone who was too far for her to see clearly spoke. His face near glowed with affection whenever he looked her way. Same when she looked at him.

Alex didn't fear that there was anything more than sibling affection between them. He knew what a man looked like when he desired a woman, and that was not how Bainbridge looked at his wife. More importantly, he knew what Lavinia looked like when she desired a man. Had seen that look aimed at him more times than he could now count. Even in the midst of her current disappointment in him, there was a look in her eye when she aimed her gaze his way that set his blood afire.

But it was evident that Lavinia did greatly care for Bainbridge. Just how much she'd do for someone she cared for so greatly, Alex didn't know. And that thought was what gave him pause. There was too much riding on this research.

Alex didn't need the grant money. In fact, if he was awarded it, he'd turn it down. What he needed was the credibility and resources that winning the grant brought. It would validate his research, his years of hard work. And would allow him to continue doing what he loved, opening the doors to working with the best minds in the field. Allowing him to perhaps, finally, discover the correct grafting combination for the plant for which he'd been searching for years.

Years that would mean nothing if his research were to be shared, intentionally or otherwise, with his greatest rival.

His eyes locked back on where his wife and her lifelong friend sat chatting at the other end of the table, trying, and failing, to banish the suspicion that ate at him.

He took a deep drink of his wine and tried to put the matter from his mind. What were his choices, after all? Accuse his wife of something for which he had no proof? A move that would irreparably damage their fledgling relationship. Or become even more secretive over his research and spend more time working for the information he sought? The sooner he completed his experiments, the sooner he could present his research to the Royal Society, cementing his name with his work.

Yet again, a move that could damage his relationship with his wife. She was already beginning to gaze at him with mournful eyes when he'd disappear into his greenhouse or run off to his office yet again. If he stopped talking to her about what he was doing while he was off working, he didn't imagine that would be well received.

So what was a man to do?

Damn if he bloody well knew.

CHAPTER SIXTEEN

Lavinia raised a gloved hand to her mouth to hide yet another smile from breaking free. She'd been watching Alex play, and lose, at whist for an hour now. And with each passing minute, he looked more and more…tortured. Even Kitty's smile seemed strained. Then again, she was usually paired with more lively partners. And typically did not lose.

Lady Georgina looked as though she was having fun, at least. Especially since she and her playing partner had won nearly every hand.

"Our illustrious duke is perhaps a better hand at gardening than cards, I see," Nigel said, coming up beside her.

"Oh hush. He isn't doing too badly," Lavinia admonished him. Then she cringed as Kitty and Alex lost yet another round.

Nigel chuckled. "You were saying?"

"Perhaps Kitty isn't as focused as she typically is."

Nigel quirked an eyebrow up. "Kitty is in her element, as you well know. She does not lose. If she is doing so tonight, it is due to her partner."

"Perhaps," Lavinia muttered, knowing full well he was correct. Still, admitting Alex had any weaknesses didn't sit well with her.

"Ah, it seems as though he's decided to show mercy and let her find a more suitable partner," Nigel said, leaning closer so only she could hear him.

Alex was, indeed, taking his leave of everyone at the table. Kitty watched him with an air of both disappointment and relief. Oh dear. With the whirlwind of their own wedding followed so closely by Harriet's, Lavinia was just now beginning to really entertain as she should. She needed this evening to be a success. For her husband's sake, as well as her own, even if he'd rather be in the conservatory. The man had to come out and be social sometimes or soon she wouldn't be able to distinguish him from his plants.

Besides, if she couldn't manage small evenings such as this, she had no hope of hosting something larger. And as Alex's wife, it was her job to do just that. That snippet of conversation she'd overheard between Alex and his research partner confirmed it. Mr. Lambert may have been jesting about Alex marrying a social secretary, but that was, at least in part, what her new role encompassed. Alex as much as said so himself. He was busy with important work, and he needed her to handle these things for him. So she needed to do it well.

She had endeavored to host an event he

might enjoy, though, since she was all but forcing him to attend. If he was leaving the gaming already, that wasn't a good sign.

"Perhaps I should go rescue our darling Kitty," Nigel said. "And leave you to your duke."

Before she could answer, the duke in question stopped beside her, with a cool nod to Nigel.

"Your Grace," Alex said, bowing to her. "You look lovely this evening."

Her cheeks flushed, but she kept her gaze boldly fixed to his. "Thank you, Your Grace. You are quite lovely yourself."

His mouth pulled into that slight half smile that sent her heart spinning.

"I find you lovely as well, Your Grace," Nigel said, leaning in.

Alex's amusement seemed to immediately dissipate. Well, most of it. Nigel seemed to get under his skin in the worst of ways. But Lavinia was relatively certain even he couldn't help but find the man amusing. Occasionally. And probably against his better judgment.

"Bainbridge," Alex said, with as scant a nod as he could get away with in polite society.

"Beaubrooke," Nigel said, mimicking his tone.

They stared at one another long enough

that Lavinia began to look back and forth between them with growing interest.

"Shall I leave the two of you alone for a moment?" she asked.

They both turned startled glances toward her, and she raised her brows in question.

Nigel cleared his throat. "That won't be necessary. If you'll excuse me," he said with a quick bow and a smile for Lavinia before he continued on to the gaming tables.

"You invited Bainbridge?" Alex asked her.

She glanced at him in surprise. "He's been a friend of my family's since we were children. It would be odd to host a gathering and not invite him." She frowned. "I suppose I should have considered, knowing how Nigel feels about you, that the feeling was mutual."

He raised a brow. "Oh? And how does Nigel feel about me?"

Lavinia gave him the look that question deserved. "I'm sure you could tell me as well as or better than I could tell you."

Alex grunted but didn't elaborate.

"Do you really care for him so little?"

Alex grimaced. "We have…a complicated relationship."

Her eyebrow quirked up, and he dragged in a breath through his nose, letting it out slowly.

"We saved each other from a birching a time or two back in our Eton days. Our

House Master was more sadistic than most, but he tended to leave us alone if our noses were buried in a book. It made us a little more studious than most boys endeavored to be, I suppose. But the boy with the highest marks got extra privileges."

"Ah," she said, nodding in understanding. "So you became a sort of convoluted tangle of allies and academic rivals?"

"Something like that," he said, grumbling. "Old habits die hard, I suppose."

"Indeed," she said, quirking up an eyebrow. "In that case, you were very well behaved, Your Grace."

His lip twitched. "I am not entirely without virtue."

She smiled up at him. "I'm pleased to hear it, Your Grace."

He stood silently at her side while they watched the party around them. As Lavinia didn't have many friends yet, the dowager duchess had helped her choose an invitation list, considering it an opportunity to introduce her new daughter-in-law to her inner circle. About two dozen of the dowager duchess's "closest" friends were now seated at tables of four spread around the room. Most played whist, though a few games of loo were also going on. Those not playing wandered among the rest of the guests, chatting, drinking, and availing themselves of the refreshment table with a great deal of laughter and merriment. The evening seemed to be a success…minus the underlying animosity between Nigel and Alex.

That was definitely something she should have addressed before now. But Nigel's rants were always tinged with a touch of humor, so it was ofttimes difficult to determine his seriousness. And she and Alex hadn't known each other long enough to have discovered all of each other's idiosyncrasies—strange habits, curious interests, lifelong blood feuds—just yet. She had supposed it was a harmless rivalry that at times got a little heated.

But there seemed to be more to it than that. At least on Alex's end.

She stifled a sigh. She'd need to pay closer attention before some inadvertent blunder came back like an angry dog to bite her in her overly soft posterior.

"Do you play?" Alex asked her.

She nodded. "On occasion. If one of the tables needs an extra person. I mostly watch, though."

His forehead creased with a faint frown, and he looked back over the crowd as if he were contemplating something, but he didn't say anything further.

They watched Kitty and Nigel win and then lose several rounds to Lady Georgina and her partner, Lord Edward Connolly, the son of some noble or other. Lavinia could never remember, though Harriet would not only know the man's name, but his complete genealogy, all the way back to William the Conqueror.

The pressure to say something witty and entertaining to Alex weighed on her. They hadn't spent much time together since they'd returned to London. At least in a social setting. And when they were alone, they were usually preoccupied with…other endeavors. Which just the thought of had her shifting subtly closer to her husband, suddenly wishing the party was at an end. They wouldn't be able to make their excuses for quite a while, however. A downside to being the hostess.

But it would hardly be proper to discuss all the naughty things she wished her husband to do to her as they stood in the midst of their guests. Unfortunately, no safer subjects came to her mind. Thankfully, Alex didn't seem to object to standing beside her in silence. In fact, it was the most comfortable she'd felt the entire evening.

However, when he checked his pocket watch for a second time, she couldn't help but think that he was bored. So she blurted out the first thing that came to mind. "I'm sorry I'm not more diverting entertainment, Your Grace."

He glanced down at her, startled, and she clenched her fists in her skirts to keep from slapping her hand over her face.

"On the contrary. I find your company very diverting." He leaned down to whisper in her ear. "Especially when we are alone. Which, I confess, I far prefer to these social gatherings."

Her cheeks blushed hotly, and she snapped open the fan that hung from her wrist to try and cool them. Or at least hide them from their guests.

His low chuckle had her sucking in a strangled breath and wondering how soon it would be socially acceptable to bid good night their guests so she and Alex could retire to their bedchamber.

He returned to perusing the crowd, his gaze darting about the room. "I actually find it quite refreshing to be able to enjoy a few moments of silence without feeling as if I need to fill every minute with inane chatter."

"Yes," Lavinia said, grinning so wide he could probably see her back molars. "I feel exactly the same way."

He smiled again, warming her down to her slippered toes, but before he could say anything else, Nigel called her name.

"Livy," Nigel waved over from the table. "Come play. Kitty and I need an easy team to beat." He winked at Kitty, who smiled up at them.

"Yes, please do," Kitty said. "And bring His Grace back with you."

Lavinia hesitated only a second and then nodded. While normally, she'd be quite happy to be included, she enjoyed Alex's company. And was surprisingly loathe to share him.

Still, she was the hostess, and she must keep her guests happy. So she swallowed her disappointment and glanced up at him. "It seems we've been summoned. Shall we?" she asked, holding her hand out toward the table in invitation.

"I really must return to my work." He glanced at his pocket watch again, hesitating until his sister, Georgina, pranced over to him, raising on her tiptoes to kiss his cheek. "Do come play, Alex," she said.

She turned to Lavinia with a mischievous smile. "The two of you can take the place of Edward and me. I think we've done enough damage to Lord Bainbridge's coin purse for one evening."

Lavinia returned her smile, grateful for her friendliness. "I'm happy to join in, though I believe Kitty is keen to partner His Grace again. I will make the great sacrifice and volunteer to partner Nigel."

Of course, this was less a sacrifice and more an effort to control a possible altercation. It was one thing for Alex and Nigel to attend the same event. It would be another entirely for them to partner in a game.

"I'm honored," Nigel said drily.

Alex nodded, a bit curtly. "Of course. If Lady Kitty isn't too tired of me, I'd be happy to partner her again."

Before they headed to the table, Alex caught her arm and slipped her spectacles into her hand.

She glanced up at him, shocked.

"Wear them," he said.

"But…" Her eyes darted around the room, though without her spectacles or quizzing glass, the features of the guests were hazy.

He took them back from her and unfolded the thin wire arms so he could slip them onto her nose. He took care to make sure the loops fit comfortably behind her ears and let his thumbs trail across her cheeks in a quick caress.

"It will be difficult to play cards if you are holding a quizzing glass with one hand. This is your home. You deserve to be able to comfortably see while you are in it."

She ducked her head and adjusted the glasses, quickly glancing around the room while she did so. But Alex took her chin and turned her face to him.

"You are the Duchess of Beaubrooke now," he said quietly. "You needn't care what any of these people think."

Her heart skipped and she looked up at

her husband, who gazed at her with a challenge in his eyes. She straightened her shoulders and gave him a slow smile, nodding.

"Very well," she said.

The look of pride he aimed at her sent happy little tingles darting throughout her body. And shored up her resolve to thumb her nose up at anyone who might snigger at her unfashionable accessory.

"Come along, Livy," Nigel said as she and Alex took their seats. "Let's show these two how this game is played."

He glanced at her spectacles with a bit of surprise but immediately dismissed it. As did everyone else at the table. There were a few whispers behind fans but not nearly enough to overcome the sheer wonderfulness of being able to see clearly.

"Livy?" Alex asked as they settled in.

Lavinia's cheeks flushed. "An old nickname. Nigel grew up on an estate that bordered our own."

Nigel grinned and shuffled the cards. "Luckily for the Wynnburn sisters, I didn't have many playmates my age. So I often found my way over to Branston Hall."

"Yes," Kitty added. "He's been torturing us ever since."

Kitty and Lavinia laughed, but Alex's only reaction was a brow raise and slight *harrumph* sound. She hoped it had more to do with his general dislike of social occasions rather than a true irritation with Nigel's presence.

"I'm glad you agreed to partner me again, Your Grace," Kitty said, leaning toward him and laying a hand on his arm. "Nigel is a terrible partner."

Nigel rolled his eyes. "I could say the same of you, my dear Kitty, but I'm far too much of a gentleman."

Lavinia's laughter rang out, loudly enough to draw a disapproving look from her mother, and she clamped her mouth shut, the chastisement felt from across the room. "I won't bother to dignify that with a response," she said, her mouth still twitching, though she kept her laughter under control.

Kitty giggled, and Alex managed to not glower, which Lavinia would take as a win.

"Lord Bainbridge doesn't seem to understand the meaning of the word gentleman," Alex said to Kitty. "Thankfully, I do. Though I'll admit that besting him, in anything really, is always the highlight of any evening."

Kitty laughed again, drawing a rare, genuine smile from Alex. Lavinia was happy to see it, though there was a small twinge of jealousy she hadn't been the one to spark it. But Kitty could have even the most skittish horse eating treats from her hand in under five minutes. It wasn't a surprise that even her reclusive duke would succumb to Kitty's charms.

Alex caught her eye, and his lips twitched in a barely discernable half grin that sent a delicious shiver down her spine and immediately mollified her. Kitty might have amused him this once. But there were far more things that Lavinia did to draw a smile from his lips. And she was just as eager as he for the evening to end.

CHAPTER SEVENTEEN

Alex watched the sisters as the cards were dealt out. Nigel he preferred to ignore entirely whenever possible. Though even he had to admit the man had been on his best behavior so far. A rare occurrence for him. For Alex also, if he were being honest. At least when he was in Bainbridge's vicinity.

Lavinia spread her newly dealt cards out in her hand and shuffled them about, matching up all of the suits, he supposed, as he did the same in preparation for the first trick. Alex hadn't played in a while, but whist was an easy enough game. Drop the largest card of the suit being played on the pile and you'd take the pile, scoring points for your team. Not normally something that required a great deal of his mental acuity. Especially if one had a good eye and was able to pay enough attention to the cards their partner dropped in order to give the team as a whole the best advantages.

Probably a good thing as, between his never-ending rivalry with Bainbridge and the neglected experiments that needed his attention, his focus was not exactly at his best.

Lavinia dropped her first card, the ten of Spades, which Kitty followed with the six, and

Bainbridge followed with the nine. Alex was forced to play the four of Spades as that was the only card of that suit he held, which left Lavinia winning the pot. A circumstance he wouldn't begrudge, if it weren't for her partner.

"Excellent, Livy," Bainbridge said. "Keep that up and we might find ourselves with a fair purse full of coin."

Alex cocked an eyebrow, dropping a Queen on the Jack of Hearts Bainbridge had laid down. "Better not get too boastful too soon," he warned the other man as he scooped up the pile. "It could lead to your downfall."

Bainbridge waved him off. "The cockier the better, I always say."

Alex took a deep breath and blew it out. "I know. You've been saying it for the better part of two decades."

Kitty's eyes widened. "You two have known each other that long?"

"Oh, indeed," Bainbridge said. "Ever since our school days. More to the point, he's been my greatest rival since before we needed the assistance of a razor in the mornings."

"I don't know that I'd say *greatest* rival," he said drily. "You are a superb researcher, Bainbridge. All I do is play with my plants all day."

Lavinia fumbled her cards, Kitty frowned

slightly as if she couldn't quite understand why the conversation was focused on the men in the group, and Bainbridge snorted.

"He does much more than that, Livy dear. He is, in fact, one of the most knowledgeable experts on grafting botanical species in England."

Lavinia raised her brow. "I am aware. His Grace has been most gracious in sharing his research with me. You seem quite peeved by his expertise, Nigel. Oh, and we win again," she said with a huge grin as she scooped up the last round of cards and made a note of the points she and Bainbridge had won.

"A few more hands and we win the game," Bainbridge said. "Not that I'm surprised in the least."

"Hmm, you two are entirely too attuned to each other," Kitty said before bestowing an angelic smile upon Alex. "Perhaps we should shake things up a bit, Your Grace, and swap partners."

Alex raised both brows but inclined his head. "Your wish is my command, Lady Kitty. I am always happy to partner my wife."

He sent a heated look her way, making that simple statement mean so much more, and Lavinia bit her trembling lip, understanding him perfectly.

"Chivalrous to a fault," Bainbridge muttered before shrugging. "I shall win just as easily with Kitty as I would with Lavinia. I am quite versatile."

"Um hum," Lavinia murmured, shaking her head. "Very well, Your Grace. Let's show these two what it takes to win."

"It would absolutely be my pleasure." Alex gave her that smile again, and she dropped her gaze to the cards in her hand with a blush.

Perhaps she hoped some intense perusal of numbers and suits would get her body functioning correctly again. Because if she suffered as he did, concentrating on the task at hand was growing more and more difficult. If she didn't stop responding to his glances and innuendos as she was, he might have to resort to pulling her into the nearest alcove to see just how wicked they could really get.

Bainbridge laid his card down and turned back to Lavinia. "As for your earlier statement about His Grace's expertise, you're quite right. I am mightily put out by it indeed. *I* should be the foremost expert in England. Or at least in this region."

"Should you?" Alex asked.

"Indeed!" he said before turning back to Lavinia. "His Grace had already made a name for himself at Eton and continued to do so from the moment we entered Oxford's halls. He was every professor's dream student."

Lavinia glanced at Alex, who merely

shrugged. "I take my studies seriously."

"This round goes to us!" Kitty said, beaming at them all.

"Good show," Lavinia said.

"Excellent!" Bainbridge said with a grin for Kitty before he turned back to Lavinia. "I took my studies seriously as well, as I'm sure you know. But we had the unfortunate luck to be interested in the same somewhat obscure, or at least unpopular, topic and have both been researching for years trying to discover a particular method and combination of plant graft in order to create a medicinal the likes of which the world has never seen. And we're close."

"That is very exciting," Kitty said.

Lavinia beamed at Alex, and the naked pride on her face filled him with a heady satisfaction. Having someone acknowledge how hard he worked on his projects with pride instead of derision or indifference was a new experience for him. One that could grow addicting.

"One of us will discover it, I suppose," Bainbridge said.

"True," Alex responded, pinning him with a glare that had withered lesser men. "And I am determined it will be me."

"Then you'd better do it soon, Your Grace. We've only a few months left to complete our research."

"It's not *our* research," Alex said, his tone brooking no argument.

"We are researching the same thing," Bainbridge stated. "Hence, *our* research."

"I research alone. Or...at least not with you. Hence, there is no *our*."

Lavinia ignored their bickering and frowned slightly. "Why do you only have a few months?"

They both looked at her and opened their mouths to speak, but Bainbridge gave Alex a sarcastic bow of his head and "go ahead" hand gesture when Alex glared at him.

"There is technically no time limit on the research itself. However, the Royal Society has recently received a large anonymous donation that it has earmarked for a grant to fund this research. They will make their choice on who will receive the grant money at the end of the Season. Which means whoever has the most promising data by that time will most likely receive the grant and the resources that will bring."

Bainbridge nodded, then added, "If someone can complete their research, at least so much as to successfully graft the plants in question, they'd be all but guaranteed the grant."

"And you are both working on grafting certain plants together to create a new, more potent plant?" Lavinia asked.

Alex nodded. "Yes, exactly. Though, so far, neither one of us has been entirely successful."

"Unfortunately, he is correct," Bainbridge agreed. "Though I've heard His Grace has a promising candidate or two brewing in his greenhouse as we speak."

And where would he have heard that? Suspicion spiked through him yet again.

Alex probably would have been better served feigning ignorance, but he wasn't quick enough to compose his face, and Bainbridge saw the confirmation of what he'd said in Alex's expression. And Alex saw the unrestrained interest in Bainbridge's.

"Quite fascinating," Lavinia said and looked as though she actually meant it. When he'd tried to explain it to most people, their eyes had glazed over. Not that he blamed them, actually. His chosen passion was frightfully dull to most of the population. Still, it was refreshing to have someone look at him with something more than baffled tolerance while he prattled on about plants.

Or it would have been before that messenger from the Royal Society arrived. Now every time anyone expressed interest, even Lavinia, Alex would wonder why.

"How soon will you know if your current grafts are successful?" she asked.

Alex's eyes widened. But he couldn't not

answer. He could, however, be vague.

"A few of my more promising candidates have already proved unsuccessful. Of the remaining, I should know in the next few months."

"Which is a bit too close to the deadlines for comfort," Bainbridge said.

Alex nodded grudgingly. "Agreed."

"And how do you know if a graft is successful or not?" Lavinia asked.

"It bears fruit," Bainbridge said. "In this case, a flower. Which is then tested to see if it bears the correct compounds to produce the effect desired when consumed."

Lavinia tilted her head in thought for a second before responding. "If the flower does not produce the correct effect, or if the plant produces no flower, would another part of the plant possibly hold the compounds you seek?"

Alex's heart swelled with some strange mixture of happiness, excitement, and pride. Even Bainbridge beamed at her as if she were their prize pupil.

"Possibly," he said. "The roots, leaves, and stems can also be tested."

"But the flowering of the plant typically signals its readiness. And the parent plants were both flowering plants, so it is assumed that is where the answer lies," Bainbridge said.

"Though yes," Alex added, "we may indeed need to look beyond the flower for our answers."

Lavinia nodded slowly, her intelligent eyes gleaming as she looked back and forth between the two men. "Fascinating indeed."

Bainbridge grimaced at him but then swept up the stack of cards and beamed at Kitty. "We win again!"

"You must be the good luck charm, my lord," Kitty said. "One more round and we win the game."

"Then win we shall, my dear Kitty. Deal the cards!" Bainbridge said before turning his attention back to Alex. "I very much fear, however, that while I might defeat Beaubrooke at whist, he already has the upper hand when it comes to our mutual interests."

"Oh, and how is that?" Lavinia asked.

Alex raised his brow again. "Do tell, because I'm not sure of what you speak."

Bainbridge snorted and dropped his card. "He has an inside man."

Alex laid his card down, barely noticing when Kitty happily squealed and gathered the stack to her. He was quite sure Bainbridge had an inside man...or woman...as well. But he didn't want to show that hand just yet. "Are you referring to Timothy?"

"Of course I'm referring to Timothy."

"Mr. Lambert?" Lavinia asked, her head

swiveling back and forth between the two.

Alex nodded, and Bainbridge turned to her. "Having a friend who is currently the assistant to the Keeper of the Archives means he can ferret out the most likely manuscripts and set them aside before anyone else can see them. Quite unfair if you ask me."

Alex's brow rose yet again. "Timothy was your friend in school as well. You could ask him for the same favors as me."

Bainbridge waved that off with a scoff. "Oh, Timothy doesn't like me much. Never has. I don't know why," he said with a confused frown.

Lavinia laughed. "Oh, don't you?"

Bainbridge grinned. "Well…I can think of a few things, I suppose."

Even Alex chuckled at that until Kitty jumped up and exclaimed, "We win!"

Everyone else at the table glanced at her, apparently having momentarily forgotten they were in the middle of playing a game.

"Well done," Alex said, also rising to his feet to give Kitty a jaunty bow. "And well deserved."

Kitty blushed while Lavinia and Bainbridge also rose. Alex glanced back and forth between Lavinia, Kitty, and Bainbridge before clearing his throat. He hated to break up the party. Well, he hated to leave Lavinia. Bainbridge, he didn't mind leaving in the least. But all this talk of his research had awakened his anxiety and reminded him how little time he had left to find the solutions he sought. He'd already spent more time than he'd intended at tonight's soiree.

"I'm afraid I must take my leave," he said to Lavinia with genuine disappointment.

Lavinia's head jerked up, and she looked at him with dismay.

"You are leaving your own house in the middle of a party, Your Grace?" Kitty asked.

"I'm afraid so, yes. I have a few matters to attend to that cannot wait."

It looked as though Lavinia was near biting her tongue, probably against the understandable urge to express her disappointment in front of their guests. However, she knew how important his work was and how little he enjoyed these social occasions. In general, at least. He was surprised to realize this evening hadn't been as much torture as he'd expected. Moments with Bainbridge excluded.

His gaze kept straying to Lavinia's as he said his goodbyes to her parents and withstood a blistering reprimand from his mother. Through it all, his eyes never strayed from hers. And hers never left him.

They would have to have a conversation later. Once they got a few other much more pleasurable things out of the way, that was.

CHAPTER EIGHTEEN

Alex rubbed his temples, trying to chase away the headache that was taking up residence behind his eyes. From the moment they'd arrived home from their honeymoon several weeks ago, he'd been bombarded with one disaster or another.

So far, he'd dispatched workers to repair the stone around the village well, taken care of three disputes between tenants that were severe enough his manager had sent a messenger into the city and that he felt woefully underqualified to mediate, and cleared up a miscommunication with his bank; his solicitor had sent notice that they needed to meet about some contract; several bill collectors had shown up saying they hadn't been paid and thankfully he'd had the receipts to prove otherwise; and Timothy had been berating him for nigh on twenty minutes for neglecting his work.

And while he yearned to go bury his head in his manuscripts and escape from everything else, he couldn't. People's livelihoods depended on him. The crops on his estates had not fared as well as usual this year, and if the fall crops failed to yield what was expected, he would need to do something to help his tenants and bolster his own finances. Which were not in as good of shape as he'd hoped.

His brother had started to rebuild their fortunes, which, while adequate for the moment, were not as robust as they had been in the past. And his wedding, while beautiful, had been an unnecessary extravagance. He would have to sit his mother and sister down and curb their spending for the time being. At least until he was certain this year's rents and crop yields would bring in the needed revenue to keep the estates going.

At least his wife had a good head on her shoulders.

In the meantime, he had to deal with the towering stacks of paperwork on his desk, answer all the correspondence waiting for him, send for his solicitor so he could sign the contracts waiting on his signature, and write to his estate manager with several ideas on how to increase their crop yield.

And it wasn't even lunch yet.

"Timothy," he said, interrupting him before he could gear up for yet another tirade, "I am aware that I haven't been spending as much time on our research as is needed. But I have other matters I must attend to."

"Yes, but if the new plants are not grafted by next week, we won't be able to gather enough data to prove our graft is successful before the Royal Society's deadline."

"I'm fully aware—"

"I'm aware you're aware—"

"Timothy!" he snapped, holding up his hand.

It was a measure of how shocked Timothy must have been that the man actually did stop talking and stared at him with wide eyes. In all the years they'd known each other, Alex couldn't recall ever once raising his voice. And he was more than ashamed he'd done so now.

He sighed deeply. "I am sorry, my friend. I am under a great deal of pressure at the moment and—"

"Do you think I cannot recognize that?" Timothy said, his soft voice gruff with emotion. "I know I don't have all the fancy responsibilities you do, but I have my own to shoulder as well. Including a wife of my own who I am neglecting in order to see this through."

Alex's gaze shot to Timothy's as a fresh wave of guilt hit him.

Timothy gave him a sympathetic look, though he didn't let up. "But in this precise moment, I'm trying to ensure that the project on which we've toiled for the better part of a decade now succeeds. We are so close I can taste it. To see that opportunity frittered away because you're suddenly too occupied...

Forgive me, but I had to speak."

"I know," Alex said, rubbing his forehead again. "And I am not purposely neglecting our project." Or his wife. Though he very much feared he was doing both. He sighed deeply. "I am simply endeavoring to manage everything that needs to be sorted so that I can make time to concentrate on it."

"I'll attempt to be patient with you, then. But I cannot promise more than that."

Alex grunted. "It is enough. In the interim…" He dug through his paperwork until he found the letter he sought and held it out to Timothy.

"What is this?" he asked, taking it.

"That is the address to an apothecary in London."

Timothy squinted at it. "It's not one I've ever heard of."

"Neither had I. But I had a man investigate, and they are legitimate. They also are in possession of a certain plant we have been seeking."

Timothy's shocked eyes met his, and Alex slowly smiled.

"The actual plant?" Timothy asked. "Not seeds or dried leaves, but the actual plant?"

Alex nodded. "And that is his response to my inquiry as to whether or not he would be willing to part with a clipping or two."

Timothy quickly scanned the letter, and

this time when he looked up his face was alight with excitement.

"I had hoped to be able to retrieve it myself, however…" Alex waved his hand at his desk with a sigh. "And I couldn't entrust it to just any messenger."

"Of course not!"

"So I'd hoped…"

Timothy clapped his hat on his head and gave Alex the first true smile he'd seen on the man in years. "I'll have it in my possession before supper."

"Good man," Alex said.

Timothy spun on his heels and marched for the door, letter in hand.

Lavinia was at the threshold when Timothy pulled the door open.

"Oh! Hello, Mr. Lambert."

"Your Grace," he muttered, tipping his hat before hurrying on his way.

Lavinia watched him for a second and then turned back to Alex, eyebrows raised. He waved her in. She closed the door and hurried over to him, only instead of sitting in the chair in front of his desk, she came around to his side and plopped onto his lap.

He chuckled and wrapped his arms around her.

"You weren't in bed when I woke," she said, looping her arms around his neck and squirming deliciously in his lap.

"There is always work to do," he said, pressing a kiss to her temple. "You may trust that I would have much rather stayed with you."

"Truly?" she said, tilting her face up as her hand slid up his neck to cup his cheek and guide him down to her waiting lips.

He didn't have time to dally with his wife at that moment...but he couldn't resist.

His lips met hers, and she moaned softly, arching her back so she could press more fully against him. Her fingers slipped into his hair, drawing him closer, keeping him her willing captive.

His hand trailed down her side until he gripped her thigh, drawing another moan from her.

Oh hell. Who needed to do paperwork anyway?

He dragged his hand down her leg until he reached the hem of her gown and started to ruck it up, exposing her silk-covered legs.

"Alex," she breathed, kissing a trail up to his earlobe while he licked the soft skin of her neck.

She shivered against him and—

A knock sounded at the door, and they both froze, and then Lavinia jumped from his lap, straightening her dress, her hands flying to her hair as she quickly moved to the other side of his desk and dropped into the chair.

Alex scooted his chair as close to the desk as he could manage, as anyone who cared to look could see he had been far more occupied with his wife than with correspondence.

A maid entered, carrying a tray with the tea he had asked for earlier and had completely forgotten about the moment his wife had entered the room.

"Thank you," he said when she placed it on his desk. He was happy to hear that his voice was mostly steady.

She bobbed a little curtsy to both of them and then left, closing the door behind her.

Lavinia let out a shaky laugh the moment the girl was gone, and Alex groaned and rubbed a hand over his face.

"Next time you enter with seduction on your mind, perhaps you should lock the door and then we can ignore anyone who comes knocking," he suggested.

She giggled. "The only problem is that I had no intention of seducing you. I came to talk. But you were sitting there looking so tired and lonely. I only meant to give you a moment of affection."

Alex snorted. "If that is your idea of affection, you may offer it to me whenever you'd like. Now, before I pull you back on my lap and finish what we started, what did you wish to talk about?"

"Hmm?" She blinked at him and then

snapped out of whatever internal thoughts she'd been having. Judging by the look on her face, he had no difficulty imagining the direction of her thoughts. Especially as he was likely thinking the same.

"Oh! Yes," she said. "I was speaking with Mrs. Bugsley and Harriet and Kitty while we were going over invitations, and we were discussing which gatherings I should host. I know how busy you are, so I do not wish to overwhelm you. And I will handle all the necessities, of course. I only need the honor of your presence.

"We simply must throw a grand ball. I know you were hoping to be at Wrothlake before the end of the Season, but for the ball it would really be so much better if we stayed in the city. We'll have quite a lot of guests, of course, and being in the city will ensure most of them can easily travel to us and—"

"Lavinia, stop," he said, keeping his voice calm only through a great feat of willpower.

She blinked up at him. "Yes?"

He shook his head. "We cannot host more gatherings right now, let alone an extravagant ball. It's just not possible."

Her face fell, and for a second, her dismay nearly swayed him. Her excitement had been palpable. But also surprising. It was terribly unlike her to be excited for a social event. Where was the woman who hated balls so much she hid in corners with secret books and talked to potted palms?

"What do you mean, we can't host more parties? Harriet said it is my duty to manage our social schedule. And I cannot manage a schedule that does not exist. If we want to remain in the good graces of society—which we do, naturally, not only to maintain the connections those in the upper echelon must maintain, which are certainly a great help to you with not only your estate business but also your research—I'd imagine it is imperative. But also, we both have sisters who must still wed, and we of course desire the best matches possible. To that end, Harriet says we must not only be seen at events but must host a number of them ourselves."

"Harriet says?" he asked, his irritation growing.

"Yes. And Lady Asterly agrees. As do both our mothers. Harriet also said that this ball could be the grandest of the year, all anyone would talk about until next Season. But we'd need to start preparing for it now, of course. I know you do not enjoy these things, so I shall take care of everything, as you prefer."

He frowned. "As I prefer?"

"Of course. I must admit, I had no idea all of this went into planning a ball. Oh, I've watched my mother do it dozens of times, but somehow, I managed to miss the finer details."

"Obviously. Especially the rather important detail of how much such a ball would cost."

Lavinia had the grace to flinch. "I know. From helping my mother with her parties, I know how extravagant they can get. But ours wouldn't be that bad, I promise. But as Harriet says, with us newly married, people will want to meet me and congratulate us and—"

"No, Lavinia."

"What?"

"I said no. Everyone who wanted to meet us has already done so, I assure you."

"But Harriet says—"

"If all you're going to do is spout Harriet's opinions at me, perhaps I should have married her!"

Lavinia flinched as if he'd struck her, and Alex closed his eyes. Damn it all. He hadn't meant to raise his voice, and he certainly hadn't meant to say what he said.

"Lavinia..." He stood and took a step toward her, but she slid from her seat and marched for the door.

"Lavinia, wait."

She ignored him, but he moved faster than she did, and he caught up with her just as she put her hand on the doorknob. He slapped his palm against the door to keep it shut. She didn't move, didn't speak. Just stood there with her head bowed and her hand on the doorknob, breaking his heart.

"Liv," he said, gently turning her to face him.

She let go of the door handle but wouldn't look up at him until he took her face in his hand and lifted it.

Her chest heaved with quickened breaths, but he didn't think it was from tears. Or not entirely. Oh no. Once she finally raised those deep brown eyes to his, he could see what simmered under the surface. She was hurt, yes. But it was anger that burned in her eyes. She was furious. And so beautiful it made him ache.

"I must apologize," he said, his hand moving to cup the back of her neck. "I didn't intend to snap at you." He leaned his forehead against hers, perhaps unwisely keeping himself within battle range.

"Say something," he finally said when the silence had dragged on too long.

She put her hands flat against his chest and pushed. Not enough to shove him from her, but enough so that they could look each other in the eye.

"I know we are going to have disagreements from time to time," she said, her voice low and raspy with anger. "And I know we will say things that make each other cross. But I am not a child, Alexander. If there is a reasonable explanation for why you have made the decision you've made, then tell me what it is. Do *not* just say 'because I said so' and expect me not to push for more information."

He nodded. "That's perfectly reasonable. As for what I said about Harr—"

"Don't," she said. "Just don't."

"I didn't mean it, Liv," he said anyway. "Not the way it sounded."

Her breath was still coming in fast bursts, but something had changed. It wasn't entirely anger that made her eyes flash.

Her hands curled into fists, bunching up the fabric of his shirt for a moment. Then they slipped lower. And this time when she took fistfuls of his shirt in her hands, she dragged the material upward, out of his trousers.

"We need to learn to communicate with each other," she said, her breath hitching in her throat as her hands found the bare skin of his stomach.

He hissed in a breath and tightened his grip on the back of her neck.

"Yes, we should speak," he said, and she looked up at him from under her lashes, her heated gaze scorching him. "Later."

He hauled her to him, their mouths crashing together as he spun them and pressed her back against the door. Her hand fumbled behind her for a second until she found the lock and turned it. Clever girl. No interruptions this time. Although he frankly didn't care who walked in just then. If he didn't claim her immediately, he might incinerate from the heat burning through him.

She broke away to suck down air, and he took advantage of her exposed throat to lick his way down the long column of her neck. He grabbed the neck of her gown and yanked, palming first one breast and then the other as she arched against him.

"Alex," she begged, her hands fumbling with his trouser fastenings, and he helped her free his hard length, groaning when she wrapped her trembling hands around him.

"Now, Alex. Please," she moaned.

He jerked her skirts up and hitched one of her legs over his hips, driving into her with one hard thrust. He froze, reveling in the feel of her body gripping him tightly, and then she arched under him with a soft whimper.

He bent slightly, wrapping his arm around her waist and lifting her so she could wrap both her legs around his hips. He drove into her again, and she threw her head back with a strangled gasp.

"Don't wait," she breathed, bucking against him with every thrust.

Her inner walls fluttered around him, and she clutched at him harder. He plunged in again, and again, grinding himself against her core with every thrust until she came with a strangled cry, her muscles clenching around him. He was right behind her, one more stroke and he followed her over the edge, keeping her captive against the door while they dragged in ragged breath after ragged breath.

She leaned her forehead on his shoulder and choked out a giggle. "I…" She sucked in another tortured breath and giggled again. "I hadn't realized a good, solid door could be so useful."

"Indeed." He tried to calm his own breathing, finally sucking a long, deep breath in while he lowered her to the ground. He pulled the handkerchief from his pocket and did what he could to clean her up before rearranging her skirts and putting himself to rights.

She patted futilely at her hair, and he helped her tuck in strands here and there until she was presentable enough to make it back to their room for a more thorough repair job.

She took a deep breath and blew it out, once again placing her hand on the doorknob.

"Before I go," she said, turning to look at him. "Would you like to explain to me why you don't wish to throw a ball?"

He nodded, belatedly remembering what

had started the argument in the first place. He explained the issue with the crops and the possible issue with their tenant's rents if the crops failed, along with the other expenditures they'd made recently, including their enormous and hugely expensive wedding.

She listened and then nodded. "Are our finances in dire straits?"

"No," he said. "And most likely won't be. We can weather a disaster or two. But I prefer to have needed revenue at hand in case there is need of it as it is not only our fortunes but our tenants depending on it."

She nodded again. "And if I can find a way to hold the parties but keep the costs reduced?"

He regarded her for a moment while she waited for his answer. It was a reasonable request. And as he'd admitted, their finances were not dire just yet. There was no reason they couldn't host a celebration at the end of the Season. As long as costs were kept down.

He nodded. "Then we can discuss it. But please come to with me any expenditures you wish to make before you make them."

"I will do that. Thank you," she said with a soft smile. She turned the knob.

"Oh, and Liv?"

She turned, her eyebrows raised in question.

"Come visit me again in about an hour."

The smile she flashed at him on her way out had his knees weak enough he dropped into his chair.

He dragged in a deep sigh and rubbed his hands over his face. That woman was going to be the death of him. How did they go from flirting to fighting to fornicating all in the space of a few minutes?

He was now further behind in his schedule. And he didn't care. In fact, it was all he could do not to chase her up the stairs and have a repeat performance. Before he could, though, a footman entered with yet another letter for him from the solicitors.

He sighed deeply and got back to work.

CHAPTER NINETEEN

Lavinia rolled over and reached out her arm but found nothing but cold sheets. She sat up. The candles were still extinguished, but the soft glow of the fireplace lit the room enough that she could see.

Alex sat in the window seat, one leg propped up as he gazed out into the dark city. The dull light from the streetlamps faintly illuminated his face. Downstairs the grandfather clock struck three, and she frowned.

"Alex," she called softly.

He jerked a little, as if she'd startled him, and then gave her a soft smile. "Hi," he said, getting up so he could climb back in bed with her. He sat back against the headboard and wrapped an arm around her while she cuddled on his chest.

"I didn't mean to wake you," he said, smoothing her hair back from her face.

"You didn't," she assured him. "But why are you still awake? Have you slept at all?"

He let out a sigh so deep she could feel it in the recesses of her own heart. "No."

She stroked a hand across his chest. "Still hungry?"

"No."

Her finger drew lazy patterns across his

chest. "Thirsty?"

"No," he said, his voice still quiet, though she could hear his amusement.

"Hmm. Afraid of the dark?"

He quietly chuckled, and she hid her smile in the billowy material of his shirt. "No."

She pressed a kiss to the small patch of bare skin that was exposed at his neck. "What is wrong, Alex?"

He sighed again and drew her closer. "Nothing. Everything." He kissed the top of her head. "Nothing that can be solved tonight. Just too many thoughts going through my mind."

She pressed another kiss to his chest. She could imagine what was bothering him. For days now she'd watched him dispatch letters, sign documents, pour over land grants and farm reports and investment statements. And when he had a spare second, he tried to get some bit of work done on his grafting project. But he had far too few spare seconds. The last time Timothy had come over, he'd been about apoplectic with concern.

They had at least managed to get their new plant splices set up and were anxiously waiting to see if the grafts would take and if they would produce the compound they hoped for. But she knew her husband would rather be elbow deep in soil or old parchments than dealing with all the minutiae of the estates.

"You need to get some rest," she murmured. "You're exhausted."

Even his snort sounded tired. "You know that, and I know that. But my brain seems blissfully unaware."

"I should lock you in this room and make you sleep for a week."

His amused exhale rumbled out of him, slow and sleepy. "I wish you luck with it."

"What did you use to do when you couldn't sleep?" she asked. "When you were young?"

"When I was young?"

She pulled back enough that she could see his face. "Yes. Did your nursemaid make you a special tonic?"

He blew out another breath through his nose. "No. My nurse was an old terror of a woman. No liquids of any kind after bedtime."

Lavinia settled back against him. "My mother would tell us stories sometimes."

"Would she?" he asked. He kissed her head again, letting his fingers drag across her scalp and down through her hair. "My mother was not a story reader," he said. "But sometimes, if we were afraid, she would sing to us."

Lavinia smiled. She could picture him, a young boy curled in his bed with his older brother nearby while their mother sang songs to them. "What would she sing?"

He laid his head back against the headboard and hummed out a breath while he thought.

"There was a song, something about golden slumbers and kissing my eyes. I do not remember exactly. When I couldn't sleep, she would sing that to me, over and over, until my eyes would finally close."

"All right, then. Lie down."

His eyebrows quirked up, and she smiled at him and patted her lap. "Lie down. Please."

"Liv—"

"What's the worst that could happen?" she asked. "Hmm? Either it works and you fall asleep, or it doesn't, and you are stuck with your head in my lap."

His mouth opened, and then he snapped it shut again and laid down, resting his head on her thigh.

"I thought so," she muttered.

He wrapped one arm across her legs, and she dropped her hand to his head, stroked her fingers through his hair, and began to sing.

He fidgeted at first, obviously uncomfortable about being sung to like a child. But she kept her voice low and soft, kept the movements of her fingers through his hair steady and soothing, and before too long, his movements stilled. His breathing grew steady. And finally, just before the clock chimed four, soft snores sounded from him.

She kept humming for a moment, to be sure he'd really fallen asleep. But after several minutes, she carefully leaned over and pulled a blanket up around the two of them, pressed a kiss to his head, and fell back asleep.

. . .

When Alex woke several hours later, the sun was already streaming through the window and his first reaction was to groan and jump from bed. There was so much to do and, as usual, little time.

But then he remembered the night before, when his sweet wife had woken and found that he hadn't yet been to bed. He vaguely remembered at some point during the night pulling her down to lie beside him. And wonderful woman that she was, she'd let him wrap his body around her and cuddle her the entire rest of the night. It was the best sleep he'd ever gotten.

How had he ever suspected that she might be…what? Spying on him for Bainbridge? Smuggling his research to his rival? Ludicrous. Surely, if any information had slipped, it had been inadvertent. And he could reduce the likelihood of anything of that nature occurring by keeping his research even closer to his chest than before. Just to be safe. A paranoid precaution.

He would be glad when his presentation

with the Royal Society was behind him. Maybe then these thoughts would stop torturing him. And he could finally rest and enjoy his time with Lavinia without worrying about either of them passing along information, unconsciously or otherwise.

In the meantime, he'd like to find his wife. When he found her, he was going to…what? Scold her for taking care of him? Chastise her for singing him to sleep and ensuring he got much-needed rest? He shook his head. Maybe he would just show her what a well-rested husband could do with all his new energy.

Judging by the cool sheets and undisturbed pillow, it appeared she'd been up for a few hours. What time was it?

He sat up and glanced at the mantle clock, jumping out of bed when he saw it was almost noon! Why had they let him sleep so long?

He hurried and dressed, interrogating and rushing his poor valet so hard during his morning shave that the poor man nicked him and nearly had the vapors until Alex was able to calm him down. Alex should be the one having the vapors. He was the one who had woken several hours late and was currently bleeding. Of course, being the man who cut the face of the Duke of Beaubrooke wasn't a distinction anyone wanted. So Alex forced himself to hold still until he was cleaned and shaven. Then he hastened downstairs to find his wife.

Barnes met him at the bottom of the stairs. "Good afternoon, Your Grace. I trust you slept well."

"Too well, Barnes. Why wasn't I woken at the usual time?"

"Her Grace insisted we let you sleep, Your Grace."

Alex frowned at that. On the one hand, he didn't like anyone interrupting his routine, especially when it was carefully curated to fit in everything he must do in a day and scheduled to the minute with urgent meetings and paperwork. On the other…he'd been exhausted and had obviously needed the rest. And she *had* told him she meant to keep him in that room until he got some sleep. And damn her, but he felt better than he had in weeks. Which was aggravating in the extreme. He hated being wrong.

"Where is she?" he asked.

"In the conservatory, Your Grace."

Alex's frown deepened, that sick feeling he was beginning to hate stirring in his gut. What was she doing in there? She was often gone these days, calling on one friend or another. But typically, if she was home and it was not receiving time, she was in the library.

He hurried toward the back of the house

where a set of French doors led to the conservatory. He'd installed them a couple years ago to help keep the temperature inside the room at a more constant level than when the room was open to the rest of the house. The conservatory was of course nowhere near the size of his greenhouse in the country, but it was likely more than double the size of an ordinary conservatory. Even so, it was barely adequate for his needs. But he made do with it while he was in the city.

At the moment, it housed the precious grafts of his experimental plants. He kept them right in the heart of the room, surrounded by the other plants, both for insulation and protection. An ordinary person wouldn't know what they were if they were to see them. But he didn't want to take any chances with someone accidentally knocking a pot over or causing some other catastrophe. Only a few of the servants ventured in here, and only those whom Alex had specifically approved. Lavinia hadn't been told not to go in there, but she rarely did. And for the moment, he preferred she didn't. Just in case.

"Lavinia?" he called out when he reached the conservatory.

"Alex," she said with a smile when she caught sight of him. "You look well-rested."

She stood to come to him, rising onto her toes for a kiss when she reached him.

"I am, yes," he said, obliging with a quick kiss. And then another, lingering a little longer.

"I'm glad to hear it," she murmured against his lips before turning back to the flowers she'd been tending. Nowhere near his grafts.

The episodes of suspicion followed by immediate guilt were beginning to make him seasick. He needed to get his head on straight and get his life in order. Lavinia was his wife. If he couldn't trust her, whom could he trust?

"What are you doing with them?" he asked.

She frowned down at the wilted plants. "These were going to be for…" She glanced up at him, her cheeks flushing a bit. "For a special gathering I am planning."

He raised a brow. "I haven't heard of this one." He had to bite his tongue to keep from snapping at her about yet another party for which he hadn't been consulted.

"Don't be cross," she said. "It's just something small. Your birthday is soon. I wanted to do something special."

He nearly groaned. The only thing he wanted for his birthday was to be left alone with his plants and research for an entire day. That would be heavenly. But he didn't wish to hurt her feelings. And judging from how upset she seemed over these flowers, him telling her he didn't want whatever she'd been planning would only make the hurt worse.

"They seemed to rally briefly, but now they don't seem to be doing very well."

"Hmm, no, they don't."

"Do you know what's wrong?"

He lifted the leaves and looked at them for a few more moments and then nodded. "I believe so. I think they are still salvageable."

"Truly?"

He swallowed back his sigh, helpless in the face of her hope and faith in him. He didn't deserve her. "Give me a few weeks with them."

She laughed lightly. "That's about all the time I *can* give you. The party is in just a few weeks' time."

"Surely not," he said, raising startled eyes to hers. "I hadn't realized my birthday was so soon."

She just shook her head. "The world does keep on turning even when you have your head buried in your work."

"Well, yes, but…" He blew out a deep breath. "There's so much to be done before then."

"I agree."

He frowned, wondering if she realized they were speaking of two different things.

But she shook her head again. "Do not fret, dear husband. I know you aren't referring to my little plant problem."

He pulled her in for a kiss. "I can still make time for your little plant problem," he said. "I promise."

"That would be wonderful, Alex, thank you." She gave him another quick kiss. "And I'm glad you woke before I left. I have several engagements this afternoon, and there is a soiree at Lady Asterly's this evening. I know you have work to do, but it would be wonderful if you could accompany me. People are starting to talk about my attending these functions with one of our siblings or mothers instead of with my husband."

And there went the last vestiges of his good mood. He'd expected these moments would occur had he married Harriet or Kitty. But not Lavinia. Their marriage should have been easy. Both of them focused on academics, not social niceties. Arguing with Lavinia on a daily basis about whether or not he'd attend, or worse, host, yet another social engagement was becoming exhausting. For both of them, he was sure. He felt like he was failing on all fronts. Not giving his research the time it needed. Not giving his wife the time and attention she deserved. It seemed as though he were constantly being asked to choose between his life's work and his wife's heart, and far too often it was his wife who suffered.

This couldn't continue. But until he had enough information for his presentation, he didn't know what else to do.

• • •

"Lavinia," he said, drawing her into his arms, probably to soften the words she knew were coming. "We've discussed this. My work cannot wait."

"Yes, yes, I know. It's just—"

She bumped into the table, nearly toppling one of her pots. Alex quickly leaned over, pushing it away from the edge of the table just before it fell. But in doing so, his shoulder brushed against Lavinia's side.

She sucked in a breath, just that small contact sending a bolt of heat straight to her core. He didn't miss her gasp. His gaze flashed to hers, then dropped to her lips. He moved so he was standing in front of her, an arm on each side as he leaned against the bench. His body pressed against her legs until she had to spread them to make room for him.

"Alexander," she said, her breath coming faster as he leaned in again, his breath hot against her neck. "Do people often walk by here?"

She could feel him smiling against her skin. "The servants perhaps, every now and then. But they can't see us back here. And won't enter without knocking."

She wasn't so sure about that. They were surrounded by glass walls and a glass ceiling. Though a person would have to fly in order to see into the conservatory from up there.

"Why do you ask?" His hand trailed down

her leg until he reached the hem of her dress, and she threaded her fingers into his hair, pressing him closer and tilting her head to give him better access to her neck.

"No reason," she gasped out as his teeth scraped against her tender skin.

He rucked up the bottom of her skirts just as she turned her head to meet his seeking mouth. Their lips crashed together, mouths opening, tongues thrusting together as he bent her over the table.

She didn't know how they had gone from a discussion of wilting plants to rutting on the tabletop like heathens, but she had never wanted anything so badly in her life. If he didn't touch her soon, she was going to die.

His hand finally found her bare leg, and he gripped her thigh. She moved her legs farther apart, making room and arching against him, trying to bring his hand closer to her aching core. His fingers finally found what they were looking for and he plunged them inside her wet heat. She wrenched her mouth from his, gasping against the delicious onslaught.

Her hands found the fasteners of his trousers and nearly ripped the buttons off in her desperation to get rid of the clothing that was in her way. His fingers dipped inside her again, pushing in farther until she succeeded in getting his trousers open. She shoved them down, and he grabbed her hips, pulling her to the edge of the table. She reached between them to help guide him to her entrance and bucked against him as he thrust inside.

She cried out and wrapped her legs around his waist, trying to draw him farther in. The table rattled against the glass wall, and Alex glanced up at the noise. Lavinia choked out a laugh and pressed closer to him, pulling his face back to hers so she could devour his lips again. She didn't care if the table actually went through the wall, as long as he didn't stop.

That delicious, aching pressure was building to a crest so intense she was nearly sobbing against him. He dug his arm under her hips and lifted, deepening his angle, and that's all it took to send her crashing over the edge. He thrust faster, chasing his own release as her shuddering walls gripped him until he came with a shout. She clung to him, her mouth moving over his, their kisses growing less frantic as they held onto each other and tried to catch their breath.

He gazed down at her, seeming almost surprised at the speed with which that came on.

"Are you all right?"

She let out a shaky laugh. She was better than all right. Her body still fluttered lightly around him in tiny aftershocks that had her toes curling.

Should she worry that every time they had an argument, or even the beginnings of one, they seemed to divert their energies to passion of a different sort? One she far preferred. Still. Then again, perhaps it meant their relationship was in a good place. That no matter how annoyed they might be with one another, they could still come together in such a manner.

He leaned down for a kiss, and she cupped his cheek, her heart thumping for reasons that had nothing to do with what they'd just done on that rickety table. She was becoming embarrassingly fond of her husband. Perhaps even more than that. She just wished he put as much effort into their relationship as he did his research. He seemed to care for her. And if she were less of a coward, she would ask him outright exactly what his feelings for her were.

But she was too afraid of the answer.

Instead, she kissed him again. "I think…" She dragged in a tremulous breath. "I think the conservatory is my new favorite place."

Alex laughed and kissed her again. "Mine too. But for all new reasons."

He pulled his shirt off and used it to clean her up before helping her off the table.

She looked at his bare chest and raised her eyebrows. "Won't the servants wonder why you are wandering out of the conservatory half naked?"

He shrugged. "I wouldn't think so. They'll

probably just assume I was showing my new wife the finer aspects of planting."

She laughed and tried to put herself to rights. "You might have to show me a few more times in the very near future."

He raised a brow. "Thank you for the warning. I'll be sure to leave the door unlocked."

She cuddled into him, wishing she could freeze that moment, with them together, their arms about each other. It was the only time she felt he was fully there with her, body, mind, and soul. She knew all too soon, he'd be running off again for his all-important research.

And she hated that she was jealous of his work. But she couldn't help wanting more of him. She could only hope that someday he'd want more of her, too. Perhaps if she continued being the wife he needed, shouldering as much of the social burden for him as she could, as she'd heard him tell Timothy he wanted, then her presence in his life might become not just a necessity, but a desire.

She just needed to stay the course. Be what he needed. And thankfully, she was so far enjoying her wifely duties. From the parties, which were a surprising pleasure, to her private time with her duke…which was both surprising and more of a pleasure than she could have ever imagined.

CHAPTER TWENTY

Lavinia watched as her guests talked and laughed, all appreciating the revelries as far as she could tell. Some were enjoying a musical number in the parlor, card tables were set up in the library, and refreshments were spread out in the dining room.

There were a few glances and titters behind fans at the sight of her in her spectacles. But they were far more comfortable than trying to see through the quizzing glass. And while a woman in spectacles in public was perhaps unfashionable, the fact that that woman's husband of only a few weeks didn't seem it necessary to keep her company seemed a juicier bit of gossip. At least from the whispers she'd managed to overhear.

Far more people had come than Lavinia had expected. She was both gratified that so many would attend her party. And embarrassed that Alex was not there to mingle among the guests along with her. Even Nigel was missing this evening, presumably too busy with his own research. Georgina presided over the festivities with her instead. A welcome substitute. But one that shouldn't have been necessary.

Georgie came to stand beside Lavinia

where she stood near the parlor door, surveying the festivities.

"Everyone seems to be enjoying themselves," Georgie said. "I told you so."

Lavinia gave her sister-in-law a fond look, but before she could answer, Lady Asterly spoke.

"Listen to your sister-in-law, Your Grace," she said. "She knows of what she speaks."

"I'm afraid I haven't had the pleasure," Georgie said, her tone more than implying that there was no pleasure to be had in making her acquaintance.

"Georgie, this is Lady Asterly," Lavinia said. "I'm sure I've mentioned her before."

"I'm honored to make your acquaintance, Lady Georgina," she said with a little bow of her head. "And this is Mrs. Barbara Sewickley." She gestured to a shy-looking woman who stood a little behind her.

"Pleased to meet you," Lavinia said. "I'm sure you know my sister-in-law, Lady Georgina."

Mrs. Sewickley bobbed her head at Georgie and Lavinia and went back to staring at the floor.

Lady Asterly nodded toward Georgie. "I believe we've met at some function or another."

"Have we?" Georgie said with a slight shrug.

Lavinia didn't know what had gotten into her sister-in-law, but it was obvious that Lady Asterly was feeling slighted. And for good reason.

"We were in attendance at your wedding ball, Your Grace," Lady Asterly said.

"You and everyone else in London," Georgie muttered, but Lady Asterly ignored her.

"Such a beautiful event. And an even more beautiful bride."

"Oh," Lavinia said, her cheeks blushing slightly. "Thank you, Lady Asterly. That's very kind."

"I was disappointed you and your mother didn't attend my soiree after we first met, Your Grace. I did so hope we could become friends."

Lavinia sucked in a small breath, her stomach clenching in knots. The reproach was unmistakable in Lady Asterly's voice, and Lavinia couldn't help her gut's reaction to disapproval over her conduct. But to mention it at all seemed impolite, at best. And from Georgina's narrowed eyes and the bright spots of red on her cheeks, Lavinia wasn't the only one to think so.

However, Lady Asterly moved on before anyone could chastise her.

"I do understand, though. You were so busy preparing for your wedding."

Lavinia hadn't thought of it until that moment, but that seemed unforgivably rude to point out.

"Yes, it was a shame to miss it," she said, glancing at Georgie, who was fanning her face hard enough to make her curls dance in the wind.

"Her Grace has had to be very selective with which invitations she accepts," Georgie said, her tone deceptively sweet. "You'll understand, of course."

"Naturally," Lady Asterly said with a smile that threatened to freeze the condensation on Lavinia's glass. "And I'm sure your husband has been monopolizing your company as well. Men are so needy. Though he doesn't seem to be in attendance this evening, is he?" she asked, glancing around with feigned concern. "Then again, mine isn't, either. Men will be men, I suppose. They prefer their own company far more than their wives."

Lavinia's throat closed up, and she swallowed hard. Georgie came to her rescue again.

"My brother is terribly busy with very important research," she explained in that same sickly sweet tone that would have terrified Lavinia had it been aimed at her. "Not everyone is lucky enough to have a husband who has nothing to do all day but indulge in gambling and revelry."

Lady Asterly's smile faded, and she snapped her fan open, glaring at Georgie before turning back to Lavinia.

"In any case, I am so glad we've found each other again, Your Grace. I have been wanting to renew our acquaintance for weeks now, isn't that right, Mrs. Sewickley?"

The other woman nodded, but Lady Asterly turned away from her before she could say anything.

"Anyhow, Your Grace, I do hope you won't think I'm too forward, but I would love to call on you sometime. I am involved in several charity groups, and we are always searching for new patronesses. If you have any time to spare, we would be so grateful."

Lavinia gave her a genuine smile. "Oh! Of course. I would be delighted. I have been looking for some worthwhile projects with which to get involved. I'd be much obliged if you could direct me to some worthy causes."

Lady Asterly practically preened with pride. "It would be my pleasure, Your Grace. I could call on you tomorrow, if that suits?"

She seemed sincerely happy at Lavinia's response. Perhaps she had taken Lady Asterly's other remarks too much to heart. She'd only been making an observation, after all.

Lavinia glanced at Georgie, but she was steadfastly ignoring Lady Asterly, so Lavinia answered. "That would be lovely."

"Well, I won't monopolize any more of your time. Until tomorrow, Your Grace. Lady Georgina," she said, nodding to each of them. "Come along, Mrs. Sewickley."

Georgie watched Lady Asterly leave with a look of sheer exasperation that Lavinia could certainly understand. The woman was a bit like a force of nature, blustering her way through the party and tossing everyone about every which way she wanted before blowing out again. But she seemed nice enough.

And Lavinia truly was interested in getting involved with a few charities. If Lady Asterly could help her navigate some of that, she would be most grateful. Besides, she never really had friends before outside her own family. She would love to meet new people, and if nothing else, Lady Asterly seemed eager to be friends.

"Be careful with that one," Georgie said as they turned back to their guests.

"Lady Asterly? She seems amiable. Mostly."

"What people seem and what they actually are are often two very different things."

Well, that was true enough. "I'll be careful, Georgie, I promise."

Georgie looped her arm through Lavinia's and started pulling her into the crowd. "Come along, Your Grace. We have hours before dawn and a house full of guests to amuse us."

Lavinia laughed, though Lady Asterly's comments about Alex not being there reso-nated rather more than she'd like. She knew that he hated these sorts of things. But they were a necessary evil, for lack of a better word, for people in their position. Every woman in her life had been nothing less than adamant that in order to not only be accepted but become a force in society, they must see and be seen. Host the most impressive parties and balls. Be the ones to impress instead of the ones seeking to impress.

And not just for themselves. They would have children someday. Soon, very likely. And those children would have to navigate these waters as well. Their name and position would get them far. Farther than most, con-sidering who their father would be. But the *ton* could be treacherous. Especially with an eccentric, reclusive father and a mother who had never expected to be in the position she was now in. It wouldn't hurt to ease their way as best they could.

For Lavinia, at least, that was worth a few parties.

For Alex... Lavinia sighed.

For now, she'd try to ignore the whispers and enjoy herself. There was little else she could do.

• • •

"Damn!"

Alex threw down the wilted leaves that had just turned to dust in his fingers. "I was sure that one would have worked."

Timothy scratched at his chin and looked thoughtfully at the failed graft before them.

"Did we use the same wax as the last time to seal the graft?" he asked.

Alex dropped in his seat and grabbed his stack of experiment notes to find the particulars he was looking for. "No. We didn't use wax at all on the last one. The one before that was beeswax."

"Perhaps it's the soil mix."

"No. This is the one we used in the last successful graft."

Timothy sighed and rubbed his temples. "I don't know, then. All I do know is that I could use a spot of tea and a moment or two to rest my eyes."

Alex snorted. "That might be the first time that you wanted to give up before I did."

"I didn't say anything about giving up. But a man's got to eat," Timothy said. "And you know me. The longer I go without food, the more irritable I'll become, and if I get irritable…"

"Yes, yes, I know," Alex said. The man was a terror even when he wasn't irritable.

"All right, then. I suppose there is nothing more we can do for this one now anyway."

He sighed and pushed the plant off to the side for the moment, trying to keep his frustration under control. They were quickly running out of time to find the right combination of plants and soil that would produce the compound they were looking for, and every time they had another failure, it made Alex more desperate to find the right one.

After Timothy left, Alex made his way to his study. Hopefully there wouldn't be anything new or pressing that needed his attention.

There wasn't any paperwork, but there was his wife.

He couldn't stop the smile that spread across his lips as he gazed down at her.

Lavinia had curled up on the chair in front of the fire and fallen asleep. He knelt beside her, not wanting to wake her just yet. She looked so peaceful with her features relaxed. He reached out to brush a hair from her forehead, and she stirred, her eyes opening to blink sleepily at him.

"Hello there," he said. "Long day?"

She groaned. "Your sister came to fetch me before the sun had hardly risen and we were shopping all day. I never knew one could purchase so many hats."

Alex looked at her in alarm, and she smiled and patted his arm. "I reined her in as best I could. But you have no idea how persistent she can be."

That drew a snort from him. "Actually, I do have a good idea. I have accompanied my sister on a shopping trip before."

"You have?"

He nodded. "Once. Exactly once. And it was an experience I never want to repeat again."

She grinned. "I thought I would enjoy it. I've never gone shopping just to buy things. Not like that. If Harriet needed new gloves, we'd perhaps all get a new ribbon or something of the sort while we were there but... store after store."

She gripped his hand. "I did try not to spend too much, but..." Her lips pulled into a frown. "Your sister can be very persuasive."

Alex groaned. "That may just be the understatement of the year. And don't worry about the money." He held up a hand, eyes closing as he belatedly realized he might have just given her carte blanche to spend every dime he had. "That's not to say that I want this to happen every day. But an occasional shopping trip with my sister isn't going to bankrupt us. If there is anything you ever need, you have only to ask."

"That's good to know. And don't worry. I don't think I have the stamina to repeat that experience too often."

"Did you have any fun at all?" he asked.

"Buy anything you are excited about? It would be nice to know that something good came out of all that money."

She sat up, her face instantly alight with an excitement that warmed his heart. "Yes! We went to Hatchard's. Oh, Alex, it was wonderful. Nothing but row upon row of books."

"Ah! Now that is one store that I don't mind spending time in. What did you get?"

"That's what I came in to show you. Well, that's not the only reason I came in, but it's one of them. In any case…" She jumped up and grabbed his hand to pull him back out of the study and to the library.

"I hope it's all right," she said, leading him to a particular shelf. "There are several shelves that were only partially full, so I combined a few to create a shelf just for my volumes." She glanced up at him with worried eyes, and he chuckled and leaned down to kiss her.

"This is your home," he said, smoothing his thumb over her cheek. "I want you to be comfortable and claim spaces as your own. I'd appreciate it if you didn't completely dislodge me in the process," he said with a smile, "but I think I can spare a few bookshelves."

"Wonderful."

She gestured to a newly cleaned shelf that now proudly sported six new books.

"This one discusses the history of the area

in which Wrothlake Park is built. I would like to get to know my new home better, so when I saw that…"

"It's perfect," he said, pleased that she was taking such an interest.

"This one is on painting techniques. I have always loved to paint but never spent much time with it. I would love to try my hand more. Maybe learn a few new techniques."

"A worthy pursuit."

"These three are on botany and horticulture." She frowned, and his eyebrow quirked up.

"Regretting your purchases? I assure you, while not the most diverting of material for the lay person, you should find them interesting enough—"

"No, it's not that. It's just I didn't stop to consider that someone with as great an interest as you might already have copies of these books on your shelves."

"Ah." He nodded. "I'm sure there are quite a few duplicate copies on these shelves. We do have a list somewhere that catalogues all the volumes. But it would be impossible for any person to know each and every title by heart so as to avoid buying more than one copy. Besides, now you have your very own copies to do with as you please."

"Thank you," she said with a smile so sweet it made his heart ache.

"And the sixth book?"

"Hmm? Oh, it's…nothing that would interest you, I'm sure."

His brows lifted again. "You can tell me."

"It's…well…it's a romantic story," she said, her cheeks blushing.

"Romance?"

"Yes. A fictional story about two people who fall in love and the obstacles they must overcome before they can live in happiness."

"Interesting." He picked it up and looked at the title page. "*Sense and Sensibility*, a novel in three volumes, by a lady." He shrugged and handed it back to her. "It sounds very…sensible. I hope you enjoy it."

"I'm sure I will." She bit her lip, her eyes looking everywhere but at him.

"Was there something else?"

She blinked at him and then let out a flood of words that took him a second to decipher.

"I met a new friend who runs a charity, and they are having a charity auction and really needed some items, and I told her we'd be happy to donate a few things, and she was so happy but also somehow assumed that meant I'd help host and you'd be in attendance, and she was so excited about that so I really didn't have the heart to tell her that wasn't what I meant, so now we need to host a charity event and also find a few items to donate." She stopped and pasted on a toothy smile.

Alex just stared at her for a second and then closed his eyes and rubbed his temple. Then he took a deep breath and let it out slowly before going to the door.

"Alex?"

He held up a finger to her and stuck his face into the hallway.

"Bar!—Oh, there you are, Barnes."

"Yes, Your Grace?"

"Apparently, my wife has volunteered to donate several items for a charity auction. Can you find a few appropriate pieces?"

"Certainly, Your Grace."

"Thank you," he said before closing the door and turning back to her.

"Consider my part of this endeavor fulfilled," he said, trying not to sound too short with her.

He wasn't, in truth, incensed. Exasperated, perhaps. This was exactly what he didn't want to happen. Lavinia had seemed like she'd be as happy as he to eschew constant social engagements. Or at the very least involve herself and keep him out of it. Though he supposed as this event was for charity, he could understand her desire to participate.

"Are you cross?" she asked, the anxiety clear in her voice.

He just shook his head, not wanting to start an argument. "No, I'm cursed."

She looked so crestfallen he sighed and

wrapped his arms around her, kissing the top of her head.

"I'm sorry," she mumbled against his chest.

Alex snorted. "You are no longer permitted to shop with my sister. No good comes of it."

She looked up at him with a soft smile and then rose on her tiptoes to kiss his cheek.

He just sighed again and held her tighter. Maybe if he held her tight enough, he could keep her from volunteering for anything else. But somehow, he didn't think he was that lucky.

At least he hadn't had to worry about Nigel lately. The man was apparently too busy with his own work to bother Alex about his. Lavinia hadn't seen him, either, that Alex knew. And there had been no more messengers from the Royal Society with concerns about similar research.

Alex fervently hoped that it was a coincidence that the leaks about his research seemingly stopped just as his wife stopped seeing so much of her dear friend.

If it wasn't…he didn't know what he would do.

CHAPTER TWENTY-ONE

The charity auction was held at the Asterlys' London residence. Which came as a surprise to Lavinia, as she'd been under the impression that as the ball's hostess, it would be held at her home. The event was one of the biggest of the season. Asterly Hall was fashionable, but surely it couldn't hold all the people that Lady Asterly had talked about attending.

However, it worked out well, as Lavinia didn't wish to tax Alex too greatly. He was already balking under the parties she had hosted, and she wanted him in a good mood for his upcoming birthday celebration. That was one soiree he definitely couldn't miss, so she didn't want to exhaust what little goodwill he had for these events. The fact that he'd agreed to attend the charity auction with her had been a small miracle.

They hadn't been there a quarter of an hour when Lavinia realized that when Lady Asterly had said "we" would be putting on a charity event, what she meant was that Mrs. Sewickley, Lavinia, and any other poor person who crossed her path and had the desire to help out would be running things, while Lady Asterly greeted guests and supervised.

Frankly, it wasn't all that dissimilar from

being at home with Harriet and Kitty. But Lavinia had thought this sort of thing would stop once she was a duchess. Then again, she never said no, either. And it was for charity, after all.

Once the guests started arriving, however, Lady Asterly pulled Lavinia from set-up duty and had her stand at the door by her side to welcome everyone.

"This way you'll be able to meet everyone," Lady Asterly pointed out.

It did make sense, although it was a bit irksome that she implied they were much better friends than they actually were.

The auction was what Lady Asterly called a silent auction. Instead of people calling out their bids, the items were displayed on tables and patrons would write their bids on a piece of paper beside the item. At the end, Lady Asterly would read out the winning bidder's name. In the meantime, people would mingle, nibble on refreshments, and hopefully, open their pocketbooks.

Once the auction was underway, Lavinia took a walk around the tables to look at the items and see if there was anything she wanted to bid on. But as she looked, most of the items seemed oddly familiar. And one item in particular was just...odd...

Alex came to stand beside her at the table. "I'm fairly certain that every one of these items came from our house."

Lavinia looked up at him and frowned. "Didn't you approve the items that Barnes sent over?"

"No." Alex shrugged. "I told him to just choose a selection of items from the knick-knacks and things we have on the shelves around the house and to consult with you if he had questions. When you said that you were participating in heading a charity auction, I assumed you meant as part of a committee. I didn't realize we were the entire committee."

"Yes, I didn't realize that myself, either," Lavinia said, glancing around to see where Lady Asterly was. She sighed. "Well, the bright side is that the items seem to be doing well. Every one of them has several bids on it. So, at the very least, we'll have aided in raising a good amount of funds for charity."

And she was performing the duties expected of her as Alex's wife, making those all-important connections and keeping his name mentioned in a good light. She hadn't realized being the perfect duchess would be so exhausting. But she'd do it all and more if it helped Alex and their family. It felt good to be needed, to be making a difference.

Alex grunted. "It would have been easier to just give them the money. At least then we would have gotten to keep our things."

"Oh, hush," she said, playfully slapping him on the arm.

But once again…he wasn't wrong.

"I have been wondering what this thing is, though," Lavinia said. "I don't recall seeing it at the house. But it looks very much like… a… *Oh my*."

She pressed her gloved hand to her mouth and looked around to see if anyone was watching them before she grabbed Alex's arm.

"Is that what I think it is?" she hissed.

Alex stared at it for a minute. "I guess it depends on what you think it is," he said.

She didn't need to answer, though. One look at her face and Alex cracked a grin. "Yes, it is what you think it is."

"Well, what it is doing *here*?" she whispered to him, glancing around to make sure no one was paying attention to them.

But they were the Duke and Duchess of Beaubrooke, newlyweds, and apparently the sole donors of the auction. Of course, everyone was watching them.

Alex shrugged again. "My best guess is either that Barnes just grabbed it along with everything else or that he thought it would be amusing to include it."

Her mouth dropped open. "Amusing?"

"Barnes does have an odd sense of humor."

That was putting it lightly. "This auction is

supposed to be benefitting the widows and orphans fund," she muttered, and Alex's eyebrows hit his hairline.

"Oh dear."

"Indeed," she said. "Putting aside the fact that it ended up here, why did *we* have it to begin with?"

"Ah. Therein lies the bigger problem."

"We have a bigger problem than accidentally donating a stone…object…?"

"The word you are looking for is 'phallus.'"

She pinched her lips together, her cheeks flaming. "I wasn't looking for it. I was avoiding it."

"A bit hard to do that," he said with that wicked little half grin she loved so much. "But no, the problem is that it doesn't really belong to us. I borrowed it from the museum so I could study the art etchings on it."

Lavinia looked at him in horror and leaned in closer so she could whisper. "You mean we are silent auctioning a stolen artifact?"

"Well, it'll only be considered stolen if we can't get it back. I had permission to have it at my home. Just…not to sell it off for charity, no."

"Well, what are we going to do about it? There are bids on it." A distressingly large number of bids as a matter of fact. "We can't just make it disappear. Too many people have seen it."

"We'll have to win the auction, I suppose." He leaned over, took up the quill, and wrote a figure in the spot for the next bid. It was an impressive sum. But not nearly enough.

She picked up the quill next and wrote a bid double what Alex had written.

He gaped at her. "Why did you do that? You just bid against me."

"Yes, and now we have a better chance of winning. And maybe it will teach you to just let your butler go shopping around our house for charity supplies."

They stopped hissing at each other as another couple wandered over. "Lord and Lady Harwood," Alex said, nodding at them. "Fine day for an auction, isn't it?"

"Yes, it is," Lady Harwood said, though her shocked and horrified—or possibly intrigued—gaze was riveted on the phallus.

She bent to write a bid, and Lavinia made a face at Alex, trying to tell him with her eyes to get the couple out of there.

"Lord Harwood, have you seen the set of candlesticks at the end of the next table? I have it under very good authority that they are of the best quality."

Lady Harwood put down the pen and wandered over with her husband, and Lavinia looked down to see that she had raised the bid by a good 25 percent.

"Oh, for the love of God," Lavinia said,

grabbing the pen and doubling the Harwoods' bid.

It was going to cost them a fortune to keep from being art thieves.

For the next hour, Alex ran interference with the guests while Lavinia tried to do what she could to keep those who would not be deterred from bidding. She lost the pen for a good quarter hour until someone found a new one. She spread tales of hauntings and curses and, when that failed, went for straight-up Biblical shaming.

But it was truly inspiring, in a way, what people would do and pay to own a piece of ancient…artistry.

Finally, Lady Asterly called an end to the bids, and Lavinia stood at her post until the sheet was collected and she was assured that Alex's name had been the last on there. She gave him a nod as she came to take her seat beside him in the drawing room where the winning bids would be read out.

"Do I want to know how much I'm paying to buy back my own property?" he asked.

"I shall hazard a guess and say no." She didn't bother pointing out that it wasn't really his property. That point was fairly moot by then.

Lavinia braced herself for abject humiliation when their names were read, but it ended up not being so bad. Most people gave them envious looks, and a few tried to outright buy it from them. Alex determinedly informed them it was not for sale.

Lavinia held it together while they said goodbye to the guests, and Mrs. Sewickley and Lady Asterly. She didn't say another word until she and Alex were safely in their carriage and it was underway.

Then they looked at each other, their gazes locked, and burst out laughing.

When their carriage arrived at home, Alex hopped out to help Lavinia alight but then turned to get back inside.

"Wait," she said, placing a hand on his arm. "Where are you going? We are hosting a dinner for the guests who purchased items at the auction."

Alex frowned down at her. "I was not made aware of these plans. I cannot stay. I'm meeting my contact in town about my plant cuttings. He thinks he's found a solution for a problem we've been having with stems drying... I don't have time to explain it all now. But I can't miss this meeting."

"But..."

"Perhaps if you'd told me about it earlier, I could have made other arrangements."

"I did," Lavinia said, torn between yelling and crying. "Several times, in fact."

"Did I respond?" he asked, his brow creased in confusion.

Lavinia threw her hands up. "I'm sure you did. I'm not in the habit of having conversations with people who do not converse in return."

"Lavinia, I am sorry, but I cannot miss this appointment."

He couldn't really be leaving. Again! She took a deep breath and tried one last time. "What will people think if you are absent?"

He put one foot on the step of the carriage. "I have too many of my own concerns to worry about what others will think. Now I truly must go. We will discuss this when I return."

Lavinia didn't wait for him to say more but turned on her heel and stormed up the steps. Where Harriet was waiting.

Harriet pursed her lips together and reached out to wipe away the tear running down Lavinia's cheek.

"Dry your eyes, Your Grace. Your guests will be arriving shortly, and we must be presentable to greet them." She linked her arm through her sister's and walked her into the house.

Lavinia took a deep breath and blew it out, grateful to have her sister by her side. To have anyone by her side now that Alex was a near ghost in their house. He had been disappearing more and more the closer to the end of the Season they got. Timothy had all but moved into their London home, he was there so often, and he and Alex typically worked late into the night gathering their data, creating graphs, and writing up theories and explanations. Even Nigel was too busy lately to attend her parties.

Lavinia was excited for them. So far, the grafting of their newest plants had been a success. And, by all predictions, looked like the final flowering product would be potent enough to combat all manner of illnesses. A great boon not only for the men who created the plant but for society as a whole. She was incredibly proud.

And more than a little lonely.

Her husband had always been a busy man, but lately, he had no time for anything or anyone but his plants. She understood. And of course, it wouldn't last forever. Once the Royal Society had bestowed its grants, they wouldn't be under such an urgent deadline.

Then again, it wouldn't stop his research. That would never stop.

And she didn't want it to, not really. But she did wish he would spend a little more time with her. She'd enjoyed his company so much today and thought…hoped…that maybe it would warm him up to the idea.

There were many days where she felt like she was back in her parents' house. There, but not really there. And that was a life she had never wanted to return to.

CHAPTER TWENTY-TWO

Lavinia had awoken before dawn on the morning of Alex's birthday. It had been a very long day. But now, most of the preparations were done, and those still in need of doing were handled by teams of servants scurrying about the house with arms laden with flowers and greenery.

Alex had moved his precious grafts out of the conservatory the week before. To where, she didn't know. But thankfully they wouldn't have to worry about those, and she could deck the conservatory out as much as she liked.

She only hoped he liked what she'd done for him. Yes, it was a social event, and she knew that wouldn't be his first choice for a birthday celebration. But she had been very exclusive with the guest list. Family, of course, and all their closest friends.

But she'd also invited several well-respected scholars and lecturers on the subject of botany and plant science. And the entire party was being centered around a garden party theme. The conservatory was overflowing with even more plant life than usual. Minus the flowers that Alex had promised to rescue for her. Those were dead beyond revival.

She pushed the uncharitable thoughts that sprang to her mind when she thought of those plants. In the grand scheme of things, they were a small matter. A broken promise, perhaps. But at the end of the day, not something that was life-altering. Disappointing though it was that he hadn't followed through.

As long as he came to the party. Though of course he would. It was his birthday celebration. And she had a gift she couldn't wait to unveil for him. A massive portrait she'd had commissioned that had only been finished the day before and now stood covered in a place of honor in the conservatory, waiting to be unveiled in front of their guests.

Alex had spent the majority of the day in the library, trying to stay out of the way of all the servants and workers, not to mention both their mothers, her sisters, and Georgie. But he'd need to get dressed for the party soon. The festivities would start earlier than these things usually occurred. The June heat wouldn't be welcome, but Lavinia had wanted to take advantage of the sunset, which was stunning when viewed through the canopies of trees in the conservatory.

She hurried to the library to fetch him but needn't have worried, as he was in the hall, pulling on his gloves and coat.

Her stomach dropped to her feet. "Where are you going?" she asked.

Alex turned to her with a look of contrition. "I'm sorry, Lavinia. I know this is the worst possible moment, but I must go."

She stared at him, horrified. "But you can't leave. Our guests will be arriving any moment."

"I know," he said. "I wouldn't go if I had a choice. I know how important this evening is to you."

"It should be important to you as well," she insisted. "And you *do* have a choice."

"Lavinia, this is a message from the Royal Society," he said, holding up a letter. "I have been summoned to present my research tonight. If I do not go, I am out of the running. I *must* go."

She sucked in a silent, strangled breath, her stomach dropping to her feet, leaving ice in its wake.

"But this entire party is for you, for your birthday. What will I tell everyone?"

His jaw clenched, and he put his hat on his head. "I know you have gone to a lot of trouble, and I appreciate it. I truly do. But this is not something I can ignore."

"I know," she said, swallowing past the lump in her throat. She understood this was his life's work. He couldn't miss his presentation because of a party, no matter how important that party was. She understood. But it still broke her heart to watch him walk away and get in that carriage.

She stood watching the empty doorway until Kitty came up beside her and wrapped an arm about her waist.

"It's no matter," Kitty said. "We will have fun without him. In fact, I doubt anyone will even notice he's not here. There's finally a reason to be grateful he always did what he could to hide from these things in the past."

Lavinia choked out a laugh as Harriet and Georgie approached.

"Don't you worry," Georgie said. "We will make the most of it."

Harriet nodded. "Do not let anyone see you upset. It will only be fuel for the gossip mills. Act as if nothing is wrong and so will everyone else."

"They are right, Livy. Listen to them."

Lavinia turned, relief washing over her when she saw Nigel.

"Nigel! Where have you been?" she said, letting him take her hand.

"I'm sure you already know the answer to that question," he said with a smile. "But I wouldn't miss your big night."

He seemed to realize what he said, because he frowned and opened his mouth to say something else, but Lavinia shook her head.

"It's no matter."

Nigel didn't look pleased about that, nor

did her sisters or Georgie, but they didn't say anything further.

"Come along, Your Grace. It's time to perk you up," Nigel said.

Lavinia straightened her shoulders, took a deep breath, and let Nigel and her sisters lead her to the dining room, where Georgie pressed a glass of champagne into her hand.

"This'll help," she said, taking one herself.

Lavinia made quick work of it, ignoring Nigel's wide eyes as she downed the glass. She took a deep breath as the bubbly liquid warmed her insides and drowned out the worst of her thoughts with a pleasant haze.

"Sit and rest a bit," Harriet said. "We'll fetch you when the festivities get under way."

Lavinia sank gratefully onto a chair in an out-of-the-way corner and nursed a second glass of champagne. And did what she could to keep her mind off her husband.

She didn't know how long it was before Kitty came back to fetch her. But she was feeling marginally better by then, thankfully.

The guests were beginning to mill about the conservatory, and Lavinia tried to take pleasure in how beautifully everything had turned out. The pride in a job well done went some way to easing the ache in her heart, as did the exclamations of the guests who marveled at the beautiful settings.

When it came time to unveil her birthday

gift to her husband, Georgie helped her pull off the sheet covering the painting. It had turned out beautifully. A perfect reminder for Alex of what he held the most dear. And for her, it held hope. Hope for a future she was beginning to fear would never be realized. Everyone gazed dutifully at it and then turned to her. But instead of the heartfelt speech she had planned for Alex, she extolled the virtues of the artist, her new brother-in-law John.

And it seemed like some good would come from the evening after all, as many of the guests wanted to commission paintings from him as well. He and Harriet would be leaving shortly for Prussia. But when he returned, he would have plenty of work waiting. Lavinia could take comfort in that, at least.

For the most part, the evening was a success. Even without the guest of honor.

Lavinia tried to keep up appearances. And for a while it worked. But then the whispers began reaching her.

Whispers about Lavinia and her missing duke. She'd expected it, of course. After all, this wasn't some simple afternoon tea party. This was a special, personal affair. One everyone who attended was aware had been thrown to honor Alex…who hadn't bothered to attend.

Lavinia was walking past one group when

the sound of her name caught her attention, and she stopped near one of the large clumps of trees and plants, looking for all the world like she was surveying the room. She knew she shouldn't listen. People who listened to gossip never heard anything pleasant about themselves. But she couldn't help it.

"Do you think they are having business problems? Something must have happened for the duke to not attend his own party."

"Or perhaps there is something else afoot," someone said with a conspiratorial lilt in their voice.

Lavinia knew that voice. She'd been listening to it almost daily for weeks. Listening to it be often unkind and judgmental. She'd always tried to excuse and dismiss those moments. But she should have known better. After all, if someone was willing to say it to you, they'd likely say it about you as well.

Lady Asterly, Claudette Peregrine. Her supposed friend.

"Perhaps there is something amiss between the duke and his new bride," Lady Asterly said to a chorus of gasps.

"That could be true," someone else said. "After all, they've only been married for three months, and yet, look at her. She seemed so sad and alone today. Constantly looking around the room like she was searching for him. Quite pathetic, really. Surely, she

doesn't expect her husband to dance attendance upon her forever."

"Forever, no," another voice said. "But it
has only been three months. Has she lost his
attention already?"

"Well, there's no accounting for men and
their decisions," someone said to a chorus of
tittering laughs. "Still, a wife should be able to
depend on her husband for important occasions. Especially when so newly married."

"True," yet another voice said. "If there
wasn't something wrong between them, then
why else would her husband so publicly snub
her by not attending a party specifically to
honor him?"

"Well, we all know that their marriage was
arranged," Lady Asterly said.

"No," another voice said. Was that Barbara
Sewickley? "Not really. There was a match
made between the families, but he was free to
choose among the sisters."

"Yes," Lady Asterly said, "but why did he
choose her?"

"Love," Barbara said.

Someone softly snorted.

"Not likely. If he had chosen Lady Kitty,
perhaps. Every man in London is half in love
with her. Or even Lady Harriet. She's formidable, yes, but she commands attention. But
the duchess?" Another scoff.

"Then why?"

"Who could know? The man is hopelessly obsessed with his projects. Perhaps he engaged in some sort of…experiment. Used research and charts and other sorts of strange nonsense to pick his wife."

"No," another said with a laugh. "That's just as bad as going to a fortune teller and letting her pick your spouse."

"It's quite possible. Everyone knows he spends most of his time buried in his work," Lady Asterly said.

"Well to be fair, so does mine," another woman said with a laugh.

"Yes, but your husband isn't a man of science," Lady Asterly pointed out.

"Poor woman. Imagine your husband being so cold and disinterested that he'd let some…experiment pick the woman he had to marry."

"It obviously wasn't a very good experiment. For him to get saddled with her."

Lavinia closed her eyes against the sudden onslaught of pain the women's snickers caused. And the doubt it seeded in her already questioning heart. Nigel had joked that Alex only married her as a way to get back at his rival. But perhaps he'd been in earnest. Now, the women of her inner circle seemingly believed that he only married her because of some failed experiment? If this was what the people closest to her thought, what was the rest of the *ton* saying about her?

"Is it any wonder he keeps his distance?" someone said. "He should have picked someone he actually loved. Or at least liked enough to stomach her company."

"But better for us that he did not. Our dear duchess was so desperate to belong that she'll go along with just about anything I say," Lady Asterly said with a laugh. "Who needs to marry a duke when you can have a duchess at your beck and call?"

Desperate to belong.

That wouldn't hurt so much if it weren't the truth.

Lavinia had heard enough. She'd been such a fool. She turned to walk away but bumped into Nigel. And the look on his face told her he had obviously heard everything.

"Ignore them," he said, moving her farther away from the malicious gossipers. "Their opinions on you and your marriage don't mean anything."

"Don't they?" she said. "She's not wrong. I overlooked many things I probably shouldn't have. I let them manipulate me, while they laughed at me behind my back. They aren't wrong about that, maybe they aren't wrong about my marriage, either. Alex has been so focused on his research…I do not expect to be his only focus, of course. But…"

Nigel shrugged. "Even if that is why he

chose you, that is not a reflection on you. That's just the way that man thinks. If there's not a graph or some pile of research on it somewhere, it doesn't exist. I'd almost be worried if there wasn't some scientific reasoning behind it all. The point is that he chose *you*."

"Only if that's the case, then *he* didn't. His data did. His charts and graphs and research did. They were right. That's not much different than our parents arranging a marriage or a fortune teller giving you a name. It doesn't have anything to do with emotions. With…"

"Love?" Nigel asked. Always so observant.

She took a deep breath and straightened her shoulders, determined to ignore the ache in her heart. "It doesn't matter. I…I should make sure we have enough refreshments."

"Livy…"

"I'll be fine, Nigel, really. Just…keep everyone happy for me. That is what I need the most right now."

He gave her a sad smile and turned back to the guests, leaving her to her thoughts. A dangerous place to be but better than trying to think through everything with everyone watching.

The truth was it didn't really matter why Alex had chosen her. It was said and done. And it wasn't as if anyone else had been lining up for her hand. Of course, she'd prefer if her husband loved her. But they hadn't known each other long. Maybe it would come with time. They had been happy in their private moments, hadn't they? Moments that had been too few of late.

What was worse was the fact that he'd married not just out of duty, but necessity. And for a brief, glorious moment, she'd believed she could be everything he needed. Everything she'd always wanted to be. The shining star. She'd always wondered what it would be like to have people respect her the way they did Harriet. Or love her company the way they did Kitty. Or look to her authority and expertise the way her father did with her mother.

And she'd thought, foolishly perhaps, that she'd achieved that. After all, she was the Duchess of Beaubrooke. She'd not only been accepted but welcomed with alacrity. She was sought after, admired. Flattered. Had the growing love of a husband she was fairly sure she adored. And she had thoughtlessly believed it all. It wasn't her they wanted at all. Just her title and what it could do for them.

As for Alex... She truly didn't know what to think. He'd seemed so happy when she'd said yes to his marriage proposal. It had seemed...personal. Because of *her*. Was it really just because their parents had arranged the match? Regardless of any of that, now that they were wed, shouldn't he show her support, at least while they were in public?

Things had been going so well between them. For the most part. Until lately, that was. She knew Alex hadn't had a choice about leaving this evening. He wouldn't purposely humiliate her. But the whispers still hurt. Especially as she had foolishly started to think perhaps there was something much deeper between them than a few shared interests and physical attraction.

Maybe she shouldn't complain, even inwardly. That was a far sight better than many women had in their marriages. But she had hoped for so much more, and for a moment, it had seemed she'd get it.

But as she was discovering, things weren't always as they seemed.

CHAPTER TWENTY-THREE

Alexander removed his coat and gloves, wanting nothing more than to collapse into bed, pull his wife into his arms, and sleep for a week.

When the message from Timothy had arrived informing him that the Royal Society had moved their review date to that very day, he'd rushed out, unable to do anything else. While the main presentations were only now getting underway, each application had submitted a summary of the research that they would be presenting. And it seemed those questions that had plagued them before had only grown. Now it wasn't just rumors that some of their research might be similar to another's. The board now seemed to fear Alex and Timothy's entire project might be too similar to one that had been presented ahead of theirs...the one belonging to Lord Nigel Bainbridge.

Alex slapped his hat onto the hook in the entry hall, trying to rein in his aggravation that this was still an issue. They had explained everything once before. And the board's continued questions were a stain on his reputation. A reputation he'd worked for years to ensure was beyond reproach.

Damn Bainbridge.

The board wanted more answers.

Hopefully, Alex had been able to mollify their concerns. They were researching the same topic, yes. But both had different emphases, different conclusions. And had different samples, different grafts. Different information entirely.

Or they should, in any case. Alex hadn't seen Nigel's research, certainly, so unless Nigel had seen his, or been told about it…

He rubbed his hand over his face. It was unfathomable. Or at least would have been until recently. Until he'd discovered just how close of friends his wife was with his biggest rival.

He shook his head. That was nothing but stress and paranoia coloring his thoughts.

He needed to look in on Lavinia. She was surely upset about his disappearance, unavoidable though it had been. He'd worried about her the entire time he'd stood in front of that board and presented his research. He had no doubt that her party had been executed magnificently. Lavinia was nothing if not capable and had been growing even more so the more confident she'd become in her new role.

But he did feel guilty that he hadn't been there at her side when she had worked so hard to do something special for him. It had meant so much to her. And having to leave her there with Nigel...

Alex tried to swallow down his jealousy. It was surely misplaced. Nigel was a trusted member of the Wynnburn family, for all intents and purposes. Did it irk him that the man who had always been his deepest rival was closer to his wife in many ways than even Alex himself? Yes. But he trusted Lavinia. With her marriage vows, at least. She had grown up with Nigel, and while Alex hated how close they were, he didn't think it was romantic.

But...they *were* close. And had been since childhood. How much would she do for Nigel? To what lengths would she go to assist the man she loved like a brother? Would she play the spy for him? Share bits of information she may come across now that she shared a home and a bed with Nigel's main competition for the Royal Society grant?

Alex took a bracing breath and dragged his hand through his hair. All this focus on his research was beginning to turn his head. He needed rest. Hopefully, soon he would have it. His presentation had been made. Now, they waited.

He'd assumed he'd feel relief that the project he'd been working so hard toward for so long had finally been delivered. But he wouldn't feel safe until everything was official. Until he'd either won the grant or been passed over so he could publish his findings on his own. Until then, he couldn't let his guard down. His research was too important.

As for Lavinia...he'd make it up to her. They could return to Wrothlake soon, and it could be as it was in the days right after their wedding.

They'd need to talk about cutting back on all the social events she kept planning. Or at least get her to understand that if that was what she truly wanted to spend her time on, she was welcome to it, but he had no desire to join her. He wanted her to be happy, but if he had to spend his life going from one event to another, he'd be miserable.

As miserable as she had looked earlier when he'd left.

He sighed again. He'd rather attend a hundred soirees than hurt his Liv. He'd make it right. Do something to bring a smile back to her lips. In fact, he had an idea brewing that he was sure would do just the thing. As for her upcoming events, now that his project had been presented, he should have a little more time for her. Though they still had to get through their ball at the end of the Season...

He stopped just in front of the staircase, an icy nausea hitting him right in the gut.

Lavinia's flowers. He'd promised to treat them and have them perfect before the party.

He turned down the hall and hurried to the conservatory. The door was slightly ajar when he reached them, and he pushed them open…and stopped dead in his tracks.

The conservatory had been decked out with more plants than he'd ever seen in there. Chairs and benches were scattered throughout the clusters of plants, offering guests semi-private areas in which to talk while other tables and chairs were placed here and there throughout the room. A banquet table had been set up along one side. And toward the front was a large portrait.

He stepped inside and went to stand in front of it, trying to draw in breath, though it felt as if he'd been punched in the lungs.

The painting depicted the interior of his greenhouse at Wrothlake on a beautiful summer day. The artist had captured every bit of the splendid beauty of the place that held his heart. And the person who held it as well.

Lavinia sat inside the greenhouse, her hair unbound and flowing down her back as she stared ahead, a soft smile on her lips. The artist had even painted her wearing her spectacles. And the sight of his beautiful wife in the place he loved most in the world squeezed at his heart until he had to rub at his chest to ease the ache.

"Mr. Riley painted it," Lavinia said quietly, and Alex spun to face her. "When he and

Harriet went to Wrothlake after their wedding. So he was able to get the greenhouse just right. And then he added me in. It's your birthday present."

"It's wonderful," he said, his throat tight as he gazed at his wife. "Thank you."

Lavinia stood wrapped in her robe, staring down at the row of dead flowers that had been hidden among the other plants, her eyes red and puffy. She wasn't crying...but she had been.

Nothing else in his life had ever or probably would ever make him feel as despicable as the defeated look on her face did when she raised her red-rimmed eyes to him. Especially considering his recent thoughts. But she didn't yell. Didn't berate him. Didn't do anything except look back down at the dead flowers.

"Lavinia, I—"

"What happened with the Royal Society?" she asked, her voice steady but quiet. "Did it go well?"

His jaw clenched. "Yes, I think so."

"Good." She nodded. "That's good."

She stared at the flowers a second longer, and then her gaze trained on the ground, and she moved around him to leave.

He stepped in front of her and reached out to lightly grasp her shoulders. When she didn't protest, he pulled her into his arms. She didn't struggle. But she didn't hug him back, either.

"I'm so sorry, Liv. I had to go. I didn't realize it would take so long, but…I couldn't not go…"

"I know," she said. "I'm glad it went well."

She was saying the words he wanted to hear, but her voice sounded so…small. Empty.

"Liv, your flowers, the party…I'm so sorry, I just—"

She pulled away and stepped around him, still not meeting his eyes. "It's all right. It doesn't matter. I'm going to bed now."

"Liv…"

"Good night, Your Grace."

He closed his eyes against the stab of pain her use of his title in that quiet little voice sent searing through him. He had hurt her. Deeply. And he was at a loss at how to make it better.

He spent a few minutes looking over the flowers, but there was little he could do. And frankly, it didn't matter now.

He was more worried about his wife, though he wasn't sure how to remedy the situation. What's done was done, and it couldn't have been helped. He stormed up the stairs after her. Only she wasn't in their room when he opened the door. The bed was still neatly made, his robe laid out and ready on the foot. But his wife was nowhere to be found.

He spun back into the hallway, his eyes

searching until he saw a faint glow from beneath the door on the far end. He marched down the hallway, hesitating briefly at the sudden realization that she may have locked the door against him. And then what would he do? Break the door down?

He warred with himself for several moments, not sure if he should barge in or knock. His first inclination was to shove the door open and retrieve his wife. But the image of how she'd looked downstairs, so unlike herself, so…fragile, made him proceed with caution.

He knocked and waited.

"Enter," she said, her voice barely audible through the heavy door.

He pushed the door open and looked around at the slightly rumpled and empty bed and over to the fireplace where Lavinia was curled up in a chair before the fire. She had her knees tucked under her and a cozy blanket wrapped around her. If it hadn't been for her sad, empty eyes staring into the fire, he might have thought the scene looked relaxing.

"Liv, why aren't you in our room?"

She lifted her shoulders in a slight shrug. "I thought it might be more comfortable if I moved into my own room."

"More comfortable for whom?"

She glanced up at him and said, "For both

of us," before returning her gaze to the fire.

"Lavinia," he said, shoving his hand through his hair. "I know I upset you, but I think you are carrying this too far."

Her forehead furrowed. "I'm not upset with you. I just wanted my own room. My mother has her own room. Most of the couples we know maintain their own spaces. You keep odd hours. This way you could work as late as you wished without disturbing me." She shrugged again. "I just wanted my own room."

His hand drummed against his thigh, his overriding instinct being to smash something or yell at something or—he glanced down at his wife who was staring into the flames again—cuddle something until she stopped looking so miserable.

He dropped to his knees in front of her, putting himself in her line of sight so she had to look at him. Her eyes flinched momentarily, but other than that, she didn't have any reaction.

"Lavinia, you have to talk to me."

Her eyes closed, and she sucked in a deep, shaky breath. "I know. But at this exact moment, I don't have anything to say."

"I am sorry about today…"

She shook her head and stared back at the fire. "I understand. You had to go. I would have liked for you to be there, but I had my family and Nigel."

He bit back a retort at Bainbridge's name. Whatever else Bainbridge was, he was a good friend to Lavinia. Whether or not he was a thief, Alex would deal with later.

"Liv, are you sure—"

"I'm fine, Alex. I'm tired. But I'm not angry, I'm not upset, I'm just…" Her eyes turned back to him, and the pain inside them stole his breath. "I'm just sad," she said, her voice broken. "Things aren't the way I thought they were, with anything, with us. And it makes me sad. And I don't want to talk about it right now. I know we need to, and we will. But for tonight…I just need to be sad."

He sucked in great lungfuls of air, each one burning his throat on the way down, and he shook his head. "I don't want you to be sad."

She gave him a tremulous smile that didn't reach her eyes and reached out to cup his cheek. "Even the great Duke of Beaubrooke doesn't get his way all the time."

He turned his face to kiss her palm and she withdrew it, tucking it back inside her blanket. "Go, Alexander, and leave me in peace."

He stood and backed up until he reached the door. But she didn't look up again.

Fine. He'd give her what she was asking for

then. For tonight. Tomorrow, they were going to talk whether she liked it or not. They couldn't leave things like this. And he knew just what he'd do to get her talking to him again…

• • •

Lavinia didn't watch Alex leave the room. She was tired of watching him walk away from her.

She sighed deeply and rested her head on the chairback. It had all gone so wrong, and she wasn't exactly sure why. She'd done everything everyone had told her was necessary in order to be a good wife and duchess. Everything that Alex needed. And surprisingly, she'd enjoyed it much more than she'd ever thought. The parties and soirees and balls were much more diverting when she participated in them rather than spending the evening hiding in the plants.

But Alex didn't share her sentiments. She hadn't expected him to, necessarily. Just because she'd changed her mind didn't mean he'd follow suit. But she had hoped that on a few rare occasions he'd endeavor to carve a few hours out of his work to spend time together. But it seemed even that was too much to ask.

She stood and paced in front of the dark fireplace. The nights were growing warmer. It would be a relief to escape to the cooler countryside once the weather grew too unbearable in the city. It had been pleasant at Wrothlake. More than pleasant. Her body warmed just remembering the moments she and Alex had spent there.

She stopped pacing. Once they returned to Wrothlake, Alex would be in heaven. His grand greenhouse was there, and new projects and research would be waiting. And while he might have a bit more time without the Royal Society looming over him…what would she spend her time doing?

Oh, there were neighbors not too far away who would visit. And there was always the possibility of a house party with a group of friends who might come to stay for a few days. But, aside from that…

She dropped back into her chair, seeing nothing but empty days stretching out ahead of her.

Truth be told, despite her newfound enjoyment in the social events offered during the Season, the quiet moments in between were often…too quiet.

She rubbed a hand across her forehead, hoping to stave off the ache that was growing behind her eyes. Perhaps she should just retire for the evening and hope the thoughts swirling through her head would calm once she closed her eyes.

Her diary caught her attention on the corner of the small desk in the room. She'd once written in it faithfully every day. Just small notes about what each day had brought. Though she hadn't written in it of late. And she suddenly felt the desire to so do keenly.

She moved to the desk and opened to a fresh page. A few words, perhaps. And then she'd retire for the night.

But as she wrote, the words began to pour from her. Everything she felt. All she'd experienced in the last few weeks. And as she wrote, her own experiences became someone else's entirely. Conversations which had heretofore only taken place within her own thoughts found their way onto the page. Her musings about love and life and duty somehow changed into the tale of another wife in another place but imbued with all the emotions and passions and ruminations that had plagued Lavinia of late.

Before Lavinia realized what she'd done, her candle sputtered, having burned itself nearly out. And she had page upon page of a story that she'd carried around with her for ages.

One of many stories.

Stories that she enjoyed dreaming about from time to time but had never thought to put to paper.

And yet, why not?

Other women wrote their stories. Published them even. Stories that Lavinia loved to read.

Was it so fantastical that she might wish to write her own stories?

The thought filled her with an excitement she hadn't felt in quite some time. She enjoyed her parties. She longed to develop her skill at painting. She even wished to spend more time with Alex in his beloved greenhouse. Though she could not be sure if he shared that wish. And even if he did, the plants were *his* passion. She longed to find her own.

But there would be moments in the long days to come, where she would be alone with her thoughts. And the prospect of writing them down, pouring out the emotions she couldn't quite manage to release in her real life, just yet at least, lightened her spirit. She flipped through the pages she'd written and bit her lip with a hesitant smile. Nothing might come of it. But she had the beginnings of a rather good story.

Lavinia closed the book and laid her quill to the side, already knowing she'd take it up again the next day.

She and Alex still needed to speak. Her heart fractured a little more with every passing hour they were at odds. The cruel words she'd overheard at the party still sat on her soul like a bruise. But their weight wasn't quite as heavy. She had yet to find her place, her purpose.

But for the first time, she had hope she might be on the right path.

CHAPTER TWENTY-FOUR

Alex stood on the steps of the makeshift gallery and watched impatiently as Lavinia's carriage, followed by her family's, pulled to a stop. He'd invited her family along as well, both because he thought it might interest them, Harriet's new husband in particular, and because he thought she might be more willing to come if her sisters did also.

He truly did not care with how many people she arrived. He just wanted her to enjoy the evening. To be happy again. Their lives had been hectic and, especially of late, stressful. He missed the idyllic days of their honeymoon. Hopefully, now that his presentation had been made to the Royal Society, they could spend a bit more time together. Alone. Without all the parties and galas and balls filled with throngs of people. And Nigel. Perhaps they'd return to Wrothlake now that the Season was ending.

And if he found that she had indeed helped Nigel...he'd worry about it then.

For the moment, he'd take one step at a time and hope the evening went well. When he'd chosen their venue, he'd been certain it would delight her. His only goal for the night was to put a smile back on her face. To perhaps make up, at least a little, for the hurt he'd caused the night of the garden party. Though now that she had arrived the doubts came pouring in.

Her parents descended first, followed by her sisters, who all looked around with expressions of polite interest. And in Harriet's case barely masked boredom, though her husband beamed with delight. Georgie and their mother were already inside, hopefully enjoying themselves. Lavinia alighted last. She took one look at the sweeping stone exterior of the Royal Academy and clasped her hands over her bosom with a gasp.

"An art exhibition?" she asked, meeting him on the stairs and peeking around him, trying to see inside.

Alex couldn't help but smile at her excitement. It was good to see after the melancholy of the last few days. "After a fashion?"

She tilted her head, regarding him with impatient curiosity. "It must be an exhibition if it's at the Academy," she insisted.

He gave her a little bow and then turned to greet her parents, who graciously accepted his welcome.

"You arranged this for us?" Lavinia asked, her eyes shining with interest. *Happiness*.

It made him realize how long it had been since he'd seen that look in her eyes. That thought sent an ache through his heart. They still had some things to work out. But she was his wife, for good or ill. That wasn't going to change. And he didn't want either of them to go through the rest of their lives miserable. Hopefully this was the first step in their coming to a new understanding.

"For you," he said. "I called in a favor from a friend."

Seeing the slow smile spread across her lips was like basking in the sun after a rainstorm. When she held out her hand for him to help her up the steps, he brought it to his lips, pressing a lingering kiss to it before tucking it into the crook of his arm. She ducked her head, but the smile stayed, and she gripped his arm tightly.

She made a visible effort to contain herself though her face was still alight with pleasure as they moved through the arched hallways and past rooms overflowing with art. He couldn't help the happy warmth fluttering through him at Lavinia's near-palpable eagerness. Some rooms had been set up to display the best pieces of the different exhibits, though others were used for art instruction. Something he might have enjoyed if he'd been any good at it.

Lavinia's eyes drank everything in as they moved, and more than once he had to gently prod her to keep her moving.

"Aren't we here to see the art?" she asked

as he deftly blocked her from moving into yet another room containing sprawling canvases and several sculptures.

"Yes. But very special art."

Her eyebrow rose. "What kind of special art?"

They finally arrived before a hallway that had been cordoned off with a rope. "The kind that isn't yet available for public viewing," he said, lifting the rope with a flourish.

Lavinia gasped. "A private viewing?"

He leaned in, brushing his lips across her cheek. "Just for you," he said, low enough that only she could hear.

It wasn't strictly true, as her entire family and several other guests were also invited and, in fact, already inside. But the evening had been arranged with her in mind. Lavinia beamed up at him, and his heart stuttered a beat or two.

Within moments of entering the space, Harriet and Kitty had spotted dear friends among the dozen or so other attendees and were already making their way toward the chattering groups, John in tow. Lord and Lady Abberforth looked indulgently on at their offspring before heading over to mingle themselves. Leaving Lavinia standing with Alex.

"These are lovely," she said, leaning closer to look at a trio of miniatures that were propped on black velvet.

"Thank you," a feminine voice said from behind them.

Alex turned with a smile to greet the newcomer, and Lavinia glanced up with an embarrassed smile.

"It is always a treat to have one's work admired," the woman said.

Lavinia's eyes widened. "Are you the artist? These are wonderful," she gushed, not giving the woman a chance to answer.

Alex smiled and drew his friend forward. "I'd like to introduce you to an old friend of mine, Mrs. Clara Pope."

"I protest the old part, but the rest is true enough," she said, giving him a fond smile before bowing her head to Lavinia. "It's my great pleasure, Your Grace."

Lavinia flashed Alex a startled look before turning to Clara with a gleaming smile. "Oh, Mrs. Pope, it is wonderful to meet you. Your work is truly beautiful. In truth, I've admired you for years. It's an honor to make your acquaintance."

"Thank you, Your Grace," Mrs. Pope said with a gracious bow of her head. "That is most kind of you."

"We haven't shown you all of them yet," Alex said, his heart near to bursting at the sheer joy shining from Lavinia's eyes.

"Oh, please do," she said, all but bouncing

before them.

Alex smiled indulgently at his wife and led both ladies around the room, stopping to admire more of Clara's work. Her miniature portraits were exquisite, but Alex had a particular affinity for her botanical works and paused when they'd reached a wall that showcased several of them.

"Oh, how lovely," Lavinia breathed, stepping closer to admire Clara's technique.

"I quite agree," Alex said quietly, though he was looking not at the paintings, but at Lavinia. She was by far the loveliest thing in the room.

He tore his gaze from her with an effort and turned back to the paintings. "Is this a new piece?" he said, leaning in closer to a painting of daisies.

"Yes," Clara said. "Just finished last week as a matter of fact."

Lavinia moved closer to admire it along with him, pulling out her quizzing glass. It pained Alex to see she had returned to using the glass in public instead of her spectacles. Her confidence seemed shaken since the night of the garden party. But that moment was not the one to address it.

He also peered closer, muttering and mumbling under his breath as he absorbed the picture before him. Painted for the most part on neutral backgrounds, most of the paintings depicted nothing but the flowers themselves. They had a clinical air to them, as though they were meant more for education than beauty, though they were beautifully rendered. The minimalist approach to featuring each plant showcased the beauty of the flowers themselves without anything in the background to detract from them. Quite exquisite. And it spoke to his scientific heart.

From the corner of his eye, he caught a slight movement and glanced over just in time to catch a smile shared between Lavinia and Clara.

He straightened and cleared his throat. He hadn't meant to get caught up in the artwork himself. "Yes, well…an admirable job, as usual, Mrs. Pope," he said, clasping his hands behind his ramrod-straight back.

"Thank you for those rousing words of admiration, Your Grace. I shan't recover from the honor for weeks," Clara said, her lips twitching.

He frowned down at her, and she turned to Lavinia with a smile. "It was lovely to meet you, Your Grace. Please feel free to stop by my studio any time. Perhaps we can paint a flower or two while we share the latest gossip."

Alex looked in surprise between the two women, but Lavinia beamed. "It would be my true pleasure, thank you, Mrs. Pope."

Clara nodded. "Now I must go see to my other guests. Have fun, dearies."

Alex watched Clara walk off, a slight frown furrowing his brow. He didn't notice Lavinia had moved closer until she spoke mere inches from him.

"Have I committed another social faux pas?" she asked.

He frowned. "What do you mean?"

She nodded toward Clara's retreating back. "Accepting her invitation to paint together? I suppose a duchess does not typically befriend an artist, let alone arrange to spend time painting with them. I wouldn't want to do anything that would shame you."

His frown deepened, and he drew her closer. "What do you mean? You could never shame me."

He wasn't sure where this was coming from, and he didn't like that it immediately sparked the suspicion that she'd already, perhaps, done something about which she felt guilty. He shoved the thought aside.

She took a deep breath and let it out slowly. "I have…been informed recently that my behavior isn't always…as befitting a duchess. I should like to remedy my errors when possible."

"Who dared say such a thing?" he asked, a burning ball of rage building in his gut.

She waved her hand to dismiss it. "It's no

matter. Just gossip I know I shouldn't listen to. I just…I wouldn't want to ever embarrass you."

He took her chin in his fingers and lifted her face so she met his eyes. "You could never embarrass me. Even if you spent the entire evening carrying on a conversation with a potted palm in full view of the entire assembly."

She choked out a laugh, and though her eyes were still suspiciously bright, she smiled up at him. "That is good to know, Your Grace, as I'm afraid I can't promise I won't do just that at some point in the future."

He brushed his thumb across her cheek. "You are my wife, Lavinia. Your place is at my side. If you make a misstep, it matters not to me. We can be social pariahs together."

The hesitant but hopeful smile she gave him simultaneously warmed and broke his heart. "I am most grateful, Your Grace." She took another deep breath and then looped her hand back through his arm.

"Well, then. Show me the rest of these gorgeous paintings and then point me in the direction of the nearest potted palm," she said. "I'm sure there's room for two."

She grinned up at him, and he steeled himself against the little flip his heart did at the sight.

"Are we discussing potted palms again?"

Bainbridge said, coming to join them before the painting of dianthus flowers.

"Oh, who let you in?" Alex said before he could stop himself.

Bainbridge barely registered he'd spoken—it was hardly the harshest thing he'd said to him over the years. But Alex had startled a laugh out of Lavinia that she quickly covered with her gloved hand.

"I was invited by the indomitable Mrs. Pope, Your Grace. Who you are well aware is just as much of a particular friend of mine as she is of yours. Really, why do you insist on pretending we have not run in the same circles since we were children? Honestly," he said, turning to Lavinia. "This one acting as though it were a strange happenstance for two botanists to befriend the same botanical artist." He huffed out an exasperated breath before turning back to Alex. "Do not worry, I have no intention of impeding anyone's plans."

Alex muttered, "Since when?"

Bainbridge's eyes widened. "Are you suggesting I've purposely impeded before?"

"No, I'm suggesting you deliberately stole research and passed it off as your own."

Bainbridge gasped, though Alex was nearly certain he wasn't actually offended. The man took nothing seriously. Lavinia, however, looked back and forth between them with growing concern.

"I've never done any such thing," Bainbridge protested.

Alex's eyes narrowed, but now was not the place to accuse Bainbridge of theft. Especially as he had no proof. He hadn't meant to say anything at all, but now that he had, he couldn't leave it at that.

"The summer we were twelve," he said. "We were supposed to write an essay on the pollination process of the apple tree. I did my assignment. You frolicked in the orchard with the groom's daughter the whole time. Yet somehow you ended up with a fully completed paper. Despite doing no research."

Bainbridge pressed an offended hand to his chest. "I have never frolicked in my life."

"*That* is the part of my accusation with which you take umbrage?" Alex asked, his eyebrow quirking up.

Bainbridge shrugged. "The rest is utter nonsense."

"It is not."

"You truly think I stole your research?" Bainbridge folded his arms across his chest in righteous indignation. Very convincing.

Alex glared at him. "I know you did." Then and possibly now, though he wouldn't add that…just yet.

"I did no such thing," Bainbridge said, his eyes narrowed, though they still twinkled with an amused light that drove Alex to drink.

He threw up his hands. "Then how did you get the information on the orchard?"

"It was *my* orchard!"

Lavinia opened her mouth to say something, but Clara stopped her, apparently drawn back to their corner by the men's absurdity.

"Better let them have it out, Your Grace. It's always something with the two of them. Sometimes you can get lucky and they'll wear themselves out before the fighting gets too terribly bad."

Alex and Bainbridge looked at each other and then back at the women. "We're not fighting," they said simultaneously.

Lavinia bit her lip, though she apparently couldn't hide the smile that threatened to break free. Clara rolled her eyes. "They'll be at this all night if they aren't stopped."

Alex straightened up and cleared his throat. Clara was right. Bainbridge did enjoy goading him. And he could admit that he somewhat enjoyed letting him. Sometimes.

But not when he was supposed to be entertaining his wife—who may or may not be working in tandem with the bane of his existence in order to steal his research. And not a schoolboy's project, but his life's work. A thought that seemed more ludicrous every time it occurred to him. Yet…she was much closer to Bainbridge than she was to Alex. And anyone who was connected that closely to Bainbridge was suspect.

Or had been.

He sighed, his head beginning to ache.

He didn't know how well this evening had gone toward redeeming him in Lavinia's eyes. Or how much it had erased, or stoked, the suspicion in his own mind about the possible alliance between his wife and his greatest rival. But he had certainly enjoyed himself far more this evening than he had since…well, since the last time he'd spent time in her company. Unhurried, relaxed time, that is. Time where he wasn't looking at his pocket watch with the Royal Society's deadline pulling him away.

They spent another couple hours perusing the art, having rousing discussions with Clara and John. The way Lavinia lit up during the discussions made Alex think that her interest in painting was more than just a passing whim. There was a room at home that would make an excellent art studio. He must arrange to have it set up as a studio for her.

When the night drew to a close, he escorted her to her carriage, and she lingered after Harriet and John had climbed inside.

"Thank you for this evening, Alex," she said. "I truly enjoyed it."

He took her hand and brought it to his lips. "It was my pleasure, Your Grace."

"We have much we need to discuss," she said, her brow furrowed slightly.

"Yes…"

"Tomorrow, perhaps. We can sit down and…talk."

He gave her hand a squeeze. "I look forward to it."

She smiled shyly and half turned to go but hesitated. "Will you be home soon?"

"I'll be but a moment behind you, as soon as I collect a few things."

She nodded. "I'll wait for you, then. In our room."

He sucked in a breath, though it took everything in him not to betray any other sign of the emotional wave crashing through him. He knew that this one night hadn't fixed everything that was wrong. But he was glad it had given them an opening. It was a start.

He pulled her to him for a gentle kiss and then helped her into the carriage. It pulled out into the night, and he jogged up the few steps, stopping to watch as the carriage drove out of sight.

He'd almost turned to go back inside when someone ran up to it and the carriage pulled to a halt. Lavinia popped her head out the window as Bainbridge approached, standing close as they exchanged a few words. Lavinia passed a folded piece of paper out the window to him, and he took it, then caught her hand to press a kiss to it before stepping back and waving as the carriage pulled away again.

Bainbridge glanced down at the paper in his hand and then tucked it into his pocket with a smile before turning to walk off into the night.

And Alex was left standing on the stairs, wondering if he'd just seen an innocent exchange between friends. Or if he'd just witnessed the death of his career...and his marriage.

CHAPTER TWENTY-FIVE

Lavinia woke in the middle of the night, alone. Still. She'd waited up as long as she could, but she'd finally fallen asleep.

What had happened? She'd thought these nights of Alex disappearing would be over now that his project had been presented. And while she was still upset about the events of the last several weeks, they'd taken an important step tonight at the art gallery. Found some common ground with each other again. He'd seemed to care about repairing their relationship. Seemed eager to come home to her.

So where was he?

She threw the blankets off and got out of bed. She'd never be able to sleep until she knew if he'd bothered to return home or not.

She wrapped her heavy velvet robe around her and tied it tight against the cool night air, tucked her feet into her slippers, and padded downstairs. He wasn't in his study, though she hadn't really expected him to be. In an effort to keep his ducal duties separate from his scientific life, he'd set up his research in the library while keeping everything pertaining to his estates in his study. Before their marriage, he'd simply kept everything at his

Oxford office. But he had made an effort to be more present.

It hadn't felt like it at times. Most times. But he had tried.

The library was in shadows, many of the candles sputtering out in their own wax. The fire still roared away in the fireplace, likely built up by Barnes before he retired for the evening. The table was covered in paperwork, as usual. But Alex…

She looked around the room and then followed the sound of faint snoring to the chaise near the fireplace. He lay sprawled across the surface, and the papers that had been in the hand that was now dangling were strewn about the floor. She covered her mouth and smiled down at him. He was always so adorable when asleep. Even when she was angry at him.

Why was he going through all these papers now that the presentation had already been given?

She bent and carefully picked up the papers and piled them on his desk and then took a blanket from a nearby chair and covered him with it. He'd likely be more comfortable if he were up in his bed, but she had no doubt that if she woke him, he'd just go right back to work. At least this way, he'd get some rest.

Once she'd tucked the blanket around him,

she lightly kissed his head and then went to the desk to see if she could tidy it up a bit. How they found anything with the papers just tossed about willy-nilly, she had no idea. But maybe if she organized things a little, it would help.

As she gathered papers, trying to keep them in the areas she found them while leaving them a little tidier, she saw what someone had been working on. It looked as though Timothy perhaps (as the handwriting was not Alex's) had been transcribing passages from a manuscript. She sat down and pulled it to her with interest.

While she knew next to nothing about plant grafting and merging plants and whatever else it was that Alex did (and the little she did know came from him), she did find the topic interesting. Not devote-her-life-to-it-so-nothing-else-exists interesting like Alex. But interesting.

She read for a minute and then glanced at the transcriptions they'd been working on. It looked as though they were making note of the passages that discussed the origins of the plant they had grafted to the indigenous variety. And they hadn't gotten very far before giving up for the evening.

She bit her lip and looked back at her exhausted husband. If she outright asked if she could help, he'd most likely say no. Probably not because he didn't think she was capable. But the man was almost rabidly territorial when it came to his work. She wasn't even sure the passages still needed to be transcribed now that the presentation was done. But she assumed they'd still need the information for the future, else it wouldn't be on the desk.

They really needed to hire an assistant. Poor Timothy could only do so much. Despite working all his spare hours on the project, he did, in fact, have another occupation with which he had to concern himself. So, like it or not, Alex might just have to accept her help.

Or she could go ahead and provide it while he was asleep and couldn't argue with her.

Yes, that was a much better plan. As Nigel said, it's always better to beg forgiveness after the fact than ask permission before. A phrase she detested under normal circumstances but that served her very well at the moment.

She took the manuscript and notes and gathered a few candles to set up on a small desk in the corner. She was close enough to the fireplace to still feel its warmth but wouldn't be in Alex's direct line of sight if he were to wake before she left.

And then she got to work.

• • •

"Your Grace," Barnes said, probably not for the first time.

Alex blinked sleepily and then jolted back, instantly wide awake as he realized he'd fallen asleep.

"Barnes! What time is it?"

"Half past seven, Your Grace. I knew you wished to be up early this morning in order to get to your solicitor's early."

"Yes, yes, thank you, Barnes."

The butler bowed his head and turned to go wherever it was he went when Alex wasn't pestering him. Alex glanced down, drawing the blanket that covered him closer for a moment. Then he frowned.

"Barnes?" he called.

The butler stopped near the door. "Yes, Your Grace?"

"Did you cover me with the blanket last night?"

"No, Your Grace. You were still toiling over your paperwork, I believe, when I retired for the evening."

"Thank you, Barnes."

The butler made his escape, and Alex fingered the blanket again. Lavinia must have come looking for him last night and tucked him in when she found him.

A shard of guilt speared through his chest. The only reason she'd had to come looking for him was because he'd left her waiting for him in their room. After the wonderful evening they'd had.

Which had ended with catching her giving something to Bainbridge under cover of night.

He hadn't meant to leave her alone all night. Despite the misgivings he couldn't shake, especially after what he'd seen at the gallery, he'd meant to go to her. Have their long-overdue talk no matter how late it was.

But he'd had to know what she might have given Bainbridge. If it was indeed from his research as he suspected. Though hours of going through his paperwork hadn't turned up anything missing. He must have fallen asleep reading through one of the stacks.

In fact…

He glanced down at his hands. Hadn't he been reading something when he'd fallen asleep? Lavinia must have seen the papers when she covered him. Perhaps she had moved them…

He looked over at his desk and his stomach dropped at the sight of the neat piles. Oh no. She'd cleaned.

Not a typical reaction under normal circumstances, but these were not normal circumstances. As messy as the piles had looked, they had been organized in a sort of chaotic fashion. Strewn about in piles, perhaps, but they were very specific piles, and he knew what each and every one of them had contained. And now…

Now, it would make it that much more difficult to discover if anything was missing. Especially since she could have just copied something over and left the original.

He raked a hand through his hair, staring at the manuscript in the center of his desk that he'd been working on. And the page of neat transcriptions that sat beside it.

It wasn't his handwriting, and it definitely wasn't Timothy's. Lavinia must have sat up last night after finding him and transcribed…

He flipped through the transcriptions and silently marveled. She'd transcribed not just the passage he'd been working on, but every passage within the chapter that discussed the plant they needed. She had saved him *hours* of work.

Or saved Bainbridge from having to do the work at all.

He marched to the library door and wrenched it open. "Barnes!" he bellowed.

"Yes, Your Grace," the butler said, appearing from the hallway just a few feet away.

"Oh," Alex said, jerking back a little at the man's sudden appearance. "Where is the duchess?"

"I believe she's in the study, Your Grace."

"My study?"

"Yes. Going over her plans for the grand ball. She didn't wish to disturb you."

He jerked his head in a nod and said,

"Thank you," before turning to march down the hall to his study.

The door to the study was mostly closed, but not latched, so he didn't bother to knock. Not that he would have, anyway. It was his study, after all. But when he pushed the door open and moved far enough into the room to see the table set up on the far end of the room…the table where he currently had his research notes…

His heart dropped into his gut with a wave of shock and anger so intense he shook from it.

They still hadn't seen him. His wife and his greatest rival, his enemy since childhood, bent over the table while they shuffled through papers, pausing every few seconds so Lavinia could show something to Bainbridge.

His research. It must be his research they were studying.

"Get out," he all but growled as he stalked into the room.

They both glanced up at him, startled, dropping the papers they held in their hands.

"Alex?" Lavinia asked. "Whatever is wrong? We were just—"

"I know what you were doing," he said, though he directed his words to Bainbridge. "The same thing you've been trying to do our whole lives. You already have the Royal Society questioning my integrity and the authenticity of my research—"

"What are you talking about? I've never said a word to the Royal Society about any—"

"You've never had to. All you had to do was present research that was eerily similar to my own. And I wondered…how could our research be so similar that they might suspect something untoward?"

Bainbridge stared at him, and the genuine shock on his face made Alex pause for the first time.

"You think I stole your research, truly?" Bainbridge said, obviously shaken.

His eyes flicked to his wife. "Or were given it," he said, the words he'd kept pent up for so long slipping out before he could stop them.

Both Bainbridge and Lavinia went completely still, stunned into silence.

"Alex," Lavinia said, the tremor in her voice driving another stake in his heart.

Bainbridge slowly shook his head. "You're mad. We've always jested in the past, but I never believed you truly thought me capable of something so despicable. And even worse, that you could think so of your own wife."

Their obvious calm in the face of his fury gave Alex pause. Either they were incredible actors or he might be mistaken.

But there was too much evidence…circumstantial, possibly. But it was still there.

"You can say that, when the two of you

were in my study, going through my notes while I slept across the hall?"

Lavinia picked up one of the papers from the top of the pile and handed it to him with a stony face.

He glanced down and his heart sank. "These…"

"Are the plans for the ball, yes," Lavinia said. "That particular sheet you are holding is a sketch from Mrs. Pope for the chalk design on the floors."

Alex glanced over at the other papers on the table, and while he couldn't see exactly what they all were, he could make out several lists, diagrams, cost sheets. Nothing that resembled his research.

He sucked in a breath through his nose. "The transcriptions I found…"

A choked sound that might have been a sob came from Lavinia, and Alex nearly flinched. "I simply wanted to help. To be of use to you. To do something nice after the wonderful gift you gave me last night."

Alex's head dropped. "The paper that you gave him last night, when he stopped your carriage?"

Lavinia's eyes widened, but there was no guilt there, no fear. Anger. Shock, perhaps. Sorrow, certainly. But no guilt.

Bainbridge pulled the folded paper from his vest pocket, unfolded it, and dropped it to the table.

"A letter of introduction," he said, biting out the words. "For a young lady I briefly made the acquaintance of the night of your garden party who I found pretty and wished to get to know better. Lavinia was gracious enough to offer to champion me to the lady."

The pit of dread in his gut opened wide, spreading its cold tendrils throughout his body.

"The Royal Society…"

Bainbridge finally lost his temper and threw his hands up. "We are researching the same plant, Beaubrooke! Trying for the same graft, using much of the same information. Is it really so surprising that our presentations might contain similar information? Once they look more closely, they will see we do have some differing information and have reached different conclusions. You just happen to be further along than I."

Alex's head jerked up in surprise that Bainbridge would admit to that.

And just like that, the fight went out of him. Bainbridge had been right. He *was* foolish. Irrational. He'd allowed his ambitions to color his perceptions and jumped to conclusions that he should have known better than to entertain.

He let out a deep breath. "Bainbridge, I'd like a moment alone with my wife," he said, curbing his desire to demand Bainbridge leave. He owed the man an apology; being polite was the least he could do.

Bainbridge glanced at Lavinia, waiting for her nod before he headed for the door. "Send for me if you need me," he said before he left, and Alex had to bite his tongue to keep from saying anything. He had no right to say anything just then. Not until he'd apologized for what he'd accused them of. And even then, he wasn't sure they, *she*, would forgive him.

He wasn't sure he would if he were in her place.

. . .

Lavinia couldn't do more than stare at her husband and try to figure out where she'd gone wrong. What misstep had she made that would not only suggest to Alex that she couldn't be trusted, but that she was so untrustworthy that she would stoop to stealing her own husband's life work? She truly couldn't fathom what he'd been thinking.

As soon as Nigel had left, Alex turned to her.

"Liv, I—"

But she held out a hand to cut him off and then closed her eyes and took a deep breath. "How?" Her voice cracked, and she cleared her throat and tried again. "How could you think I would steal something so precious from you? That I would hurt you in that way?"

Alex shook his head and dropped into a chair. "I don't know." He looked back up at her. "I know that answer isn't satisfactory, but it's the only one I have. I suppose I added two and two together and got thirteen. And then when I saw you in here with him, it all just came to the surface."

She shook her head. "The analogy would be better if you were to add an apple and orange and get the letter T. You saw a few completely unrelated, harmless activities and twisted them to fit the story you'd already made up in your head."

He frowned. "The activities weren't exactly harmless. Whispering in corners with your husband's business rival, for all intents and purposes. Passing that same man notes on dark London streets. Staying up until the wee hours of the morning transcribing information that is vital to your husband's research?"

Lavinia's careful facade finally cracked. She had been trying to keep herself together and not lose her temper from the moment Alex had stomped into his study with his wild accusations. "I did that to try and help you," she said, her voice raised, though she wasn't exactly yelling at him...yet.

"It was a help, one I would have greatly appreciated, if you'd actually told me you were doing it," he lobbied back. "It would have been a great deal more helpful than all the dreadful gatherings you've been dragging me to over the last several months."

"I thought I was doing what you wanted me to do!"

He blinked at her in total confusion. "Why would you think that?"

"I heard you. That day we came to meet you at your office in Oxford. I heard you and Timothy talking about how you needed a social secretary. You needed someone to navigate the society functions, someone who could take care of all that for you. I knew you didn't particularly enjoy them, but you are also still expected to make appearances, so I was doing what I could to make it easier for you. I was doing exactly what you said you wanted."

"That's not what I wanted. If it was, we likely wouldn't have married. I thought—"

She froze again, her body going numb. "What do you mean?" she asked, her voice strained.

He sighed again. "Lavinia, I think we both need to—"

"No," she said, with as much force as she could muster without shouting. "What do you mean we wouldn't have married?"

"I didn't mean anything by it, Liv."

She shook her head. "You aren't the person I thought you were."

"Neither are you," he shot back.

"I am exactly who I have always been."

"No, you aren't. The reason I married you was because we were alike. Or so I thought. You craved quiet and solitude. You hated social events. You'd rather hide in corners and read, remember? Yet the moment we married, you changed into someone I didn't recognize. The only thing on your mind was the next ball or soiree. You were obsessed with hosting your own, and worse, you kept dragging me into all of it with you. Forcing me to live a life I never wanted."

The pain that tore through her heart ripped a gasp from her throat, and she pressed a hand to her mouth.

Alex blanched. "Liv, that's not—"

She coughed out a mirthless laugh. "I've been a fool. I thought you were like some sort of knight in a fairy story, come to rescue me from a life of loneliness." She looked up at him finally and shook her head. "But you didn't want to rescue me. You merely wanted to change the location of my prison. You wanted me to stay just as I was. Quiet. Overlooked. Amiable. Someone who wouldn't disturb your precious, peaceful life."

Alex recoiled, denial etched on his face. "No. Liv, that's not what I meant." He tried to reach for her, but she stepped out of his grasp.

She nodded her head slowly, her hands clenched into fists in her skirts. She wouldn't let him see how much he'd just hurt her. How much those words had torn through every shred of confidence and happiness she'd managed to scrape together over the last few months.

She took another step back. "Do not worry, Your Grace. I shan't disturb you again."

"Liv…"

But she didn't listen to him. She couldn't listen to any more or she'd break down. And she refused to let him see that.

She'd never wanted anything but to give him what he wanted. Maybe she'd gotten it wrong. She could concede that. But her heart had been in the right place.

Regardless, she wouldn't make that mistake again. He wanted peace and solitude?

He'd have it.

CHAPTER TWENTY-SIX

Lavinia and Georgina paused before the door to yet another shop, and Georgie pointed at the hat in the window, waggling her eyebrows at her. Her sister-in-law had decided that what she needed was to get out of the house and into the fresh air and had kidnapped her for a day of shopping.

They had amassed a truly embarrassing number of parcels in the back of the carriage. And Georgie showed no signs of slowing down.

"But I don't need another hat, Georgie," Lavinia insisted.

"No one needs another hat, silly. But we are here, the hats are here…seems a shame to let them sit and go to waste."

Lavinia sighed. "I appreciate you trying to cheer me up, Georgie. Truly. But I…I think I'm just tired. Perhaps we should return home."

Georgie regarded her for a moment. "One more stop."

Lavinia opened her mouth to protest, but Georgie held up a hand. "Only one more. If you still wish to return home after that, I promise I will grant your wish."

"Very well," Lavinia said, forcing a smile.

Georgie meant well. Ever since the night of her fight with Alex, she hadn't been the same. When she'd woken the next morning to find him gone, she'd known it was over. For a brief moment, she'd thought they'd have a marriage like her parents. One where they truly enjoyed one another. Perhaps even loved each other.

But after that dreadful night...it didn't seem as if that was to be.

The pain that knowledge caused was staggering in its intensity. She hadn't realized just how much she'd come to hope that they would find a way to make their marriage work. Instead, it seemed as though they'd be one of those couples who were married in name only.

It wasn't what she'd wanted. But...she would survive. Despite the pain ripping through her heart every time she thought of him.

When their carriage pulled to a stop again, Lavinia glanced out the window. Georgie was watching her, her face bright with a hopeful smile. Hatchard's sat just outside, books gleaming in the windows. A few weeks ago, the sight would have filled her with glee. In fact, she hadn't realized just how miserable she truly was until that moment. Because the only thing she felt was an overwhelming, soul-crushing fatigue.

Georgie sucked in a deep breath through her nose and then hung her head out the window and told the driver to take them home.

"I'm sorry, Georgie," she said, her voice cracking.

Georgie reached over and patted her hand. "You don't have anything to be sorry for," she said. "I just want you to feel better."

Lavinia sighed. The only thing that would truly make her feel better would be if she could go back and change things. Though she wasn't sure what she wanted to change. Would she wish that she'd never married Alex?

The thought of that sent a pain through her so deep she nearly gasped. No. She'd never wish that. But she wanted to go back to when they'd been happy. At Wrothlake, perhaps. Before all the pressures of their marriage had overwhelmed them. Before he'd gotten so engrossed in his research that nothing else existed. Before she'd tried so hard to gain his attention and approval, and that of everyone else, that she'd pushed him even farther away.

If she could do things differently, she would. She'd thought she was being a good wife, a good duchess. And frankly, she'd enjoyed a lot of the more social aspects of her new life. Far more than she'd anticipated. But Alex, obviously, did not feel the same. And perhaps she shouldn't have pushed it on him, no matter what anyone had told her. Perhaps she'd listened to too many people and hadn't listened enough to *him*.

"What would make you feel better?" Georgie asked as the carriage stopped in front of Beaubrooke Hall.

Nothing.

But poor Georgie wanted so desperately to help.

"If I could rest maybe…"

Georgie nodded and ushered her inside and straight up to her room. Within half an hour, Georgie had her ensconced in a comforting nest of pillows and blankets, blinds drawn tight across the windows.

Lavinia sighed and burrowed deep. She wanted nothing more than to stay curled up and sleep for a week.

And with Alex gone, there was no reason why she couldn't.

She closed her eyes, willing herself to drift off and wishing she could close off her broken heart as easily.

• • •

Alex sat in front of the cold fireplace at Wrothlake, a whisky tumbler in one hand and the nearly empty decanter in the other. He'd brought the portrait of Lavinia at the greenhouse back with him and had had it installed over the mantle in the library. And he'd been staring at it ever since.

He'd lost track of how long he'd sat there, staring at the portrait of the perfect life that he'd had and lost. Lost through his own doing. Through his neglect and suspicion. For one brief moment, he'd had everything he had ever wished for, and he'd pushed it away.

He wished he could go back and change things. His research was still important to him, of course, and it always would be. And regarding the past three months, at least, it was still something that he couldn't have given up. But he should have tried harder to find a balance. He should have tried harder to make sure that Lavinia knew that even with his project deadline looming, she was still important to him. Instead of neglecting and ignoring her just as badly as her family had ever done.

It didn't matter that it had not been his intention to do so. He doubted her family had ever meant to hurt her, either. They loved her. And…so did he. And now, he may have just lost the most precious gift he'd ever been given. But there was little he could do about it now…except maybe drink more.

He turned slightly when the door opened and a footman announced, "Lady Georgina Reddington."

Alex groaned and laid his head back on

the chair. Georgie came to stand in front of him, blocking his view of the portrait.

"Well, this is a nice sight," she said, her hands on her hips.

"Go away, Georgie," he said, taking another drink.

His sister huffed and dropped into a nearby chair.

"I came to talk to you about your wife. But apparently, you're in even worse shape than she is."

Alex cocked an eyebrow at her. "I am?"

Georgie snorted. "She is plenty miserable," she assured him. "But so far she hasn't resorted to drinking herself into a stupor."

Alex grunted. "She should try it."

"It doesn't seem to be helping you much," she said, lifting a brow.

Alex took another swig directly from the decanter and pointed a finger at his sister, squinting one eye. "Not yet. But I'm hopeful."

Georgie shook her head. "You two are infuriating. Lavinia is London, burying herself in her bed, refusing to even buy new books…"

Alex raised his brows at that. That sounded serious indeed.

"And you are out here drowning in whisky and self-pity."

He frowned. "I am not. This is brandy."

Georgie glanced at the bottle in his hand

and then at the empty decanter on the table.

"Look again, brother dear."

He squinted again, trying to focus his eyes enough to see the bottle clearly. Was this how the world looked to Lavinia without her glasses? Poor Liv.

He squinted again at the bottle in his hand. "Oh, look at that. You are correct. In that case, then yes. I *am* trying to drown myself in whisky."

Georgie shook her head with well-placed disgust. "You need to sober up and figure out what you're going to do to get your wife back," she said.

Alex sighed deeply. "I already tried to figure that out. There's nothing I can do."

Georgie frowned, her disappointment in him palpable. He knew how she felt. "Well, this plan of yours certainly isn't going to work," she said. "I can barely stand to be within six feet of you and I *want* to be here. You're definitely not going to convince a woman who is still angry with you to suffer your presence."

Alex shrugged. "She has every right to be angry with me. *I'm* angry with me."

"So am I," Georgie said. "That doesn't mean I don't still love you."

That gave him pause. "You think she loves me?"

"Of course she does, you dolt!" She threw

her hands up. "Why is it that the people involved are always the last ones to know
what's going on?"

"Well, she has a funny way of showing it,"
Alex said.

"Do you blame her?" Georgie asked. "You
spent three months doing everything in your
power to push her away. And I understand
that not everything she did was your particular cup of tea, but she thought she was doing
what *you* wanted and needed her to do. You
didn't ever say otherwise that I'm aware of.

"Oh, you complained about having to go
to these occasions. But you never bothered to
explain to her that your position in society
meant nothing to you or that throwing a party would do nothing to help you in the ways
that you needed it. She might have gotten
some bad advice, but she thought she was
helping. Her intentions were good. And she
knew that you didn't like these occasions, so
she did try to tailor the ones that she hosted
to evenings that would best suit you so that
you wouldn't be as miserable as you might
have otherwise been."

Alex frowned, though her words rang true.
"I will never be able to make amends for everything."

"Well, you certainly can't try if you're sitting in here wallowing in whisky."

He snorted at that. Another good point.

"Do you want to get your wife back?" she asked him.

"Of course I do!"

"Then put the bottle down and try and figure out what you can do to make that happen."

Alex put the bottle on the table with a thump along with his glass and rubbed his hands over his face, raking them through his hair. "I just don't know," he said. "That is…I think I know how I can prove my sincerity to her. But how do I get her to listen to me? And what if I make matters even worse?"

Georgie sat back. "Well, I can't help you there, brother. I have only known her as long as you, and you've certainly spent more time with her than I. What you need to do is talk to somebody who knows her better."

"Her sisters, perhaps?"

Georgie snorted. "I doubt Kitty would even let you in the door, and Harriet might well shoot you where you stand."

Alex grunted. "And I would deserve it."

There was someone else he could talk to. But no, he wasn't that desperate.

He groaned and rubbed his hands over his face again.

Yes, actually he was.

But he couldn't imagine actually getting help from that quarter, not after the accusations he'd made. Unless he made some sort of conciliatory gesture that proved he was sincere in his desire to make Lavinia happy. And there was one thing that he could think of that would prove his intentions.

His gaze strayed to the overflowing stack of papers on the desk. Was he really willing to do that?

He looked again at the portrait over his fireplace. At the picture that held his heart in its brushstrokes. Yes. He'd give up anything to have her back. Nothing less than everything.

CHAPTER TWENTY-SEVEN

Alex lasted three more days before he cracked and returned to London to do the unthinkable.

He packed up all his research and then threw his coat, gloves, and hat on and marched out into the balmy summer night. Thankfully, the place he sought wasn't too far away. Just a few houses down from his own, though with the size of the houses involved it was still a good brisk walk to get him to his destination within a quarter hour.

He raised a fist and banged on the door until it flew open.

"Wha—! Oh, it's you," Bainbridge said, leaning against the doorframe with his shirt half undone and untucked from his trousers and a glass half full of whisky in his hand. "What are you doing here?"

Alex frowned. "What are you doing answering your own door?"

"It's the middle of the night. My servants are all asleep."

"I'm sorry, my lord," a voice came from down the hall. "I'll be right there."

"Don't bother, Johnson. I've got it."

"Very good," Johnson said, his voice already retreating. "Good night, my lord."

Bainbridge looked Alex up and down and shook his head. "Well, come in then before the neighbors catch sight of me consorting with the likes of you. I might die of embarrassment"

Alex walked in and removed his coat and hat, handing them to Bainbridge.

"Although that would be handy, wouldn't it? One of us popping off. It would save the other quite a bit of trouble with this Royal Society debacle."

He took Alex's coat and hat and tossed them in the general direction of the coat hooks near the door. They fell in a heap on the floor.

Alex raised a brow, but Bainbridge merely turned on his heel and lifted his glass. "This way."

He led the way down the hall to his study, where he dropped back into the seat he must have been in when Alex interrupted him.

"Sit," he said, gesturing to the other chair.

Alex slumped down into it.

"What are you doing here, then?"

Alex shook his head where it rested on the back of the chair. "I think I may have made a mistake."

Bainbridge snorted. "I'd wager you've made several. Starting with your accusations against me. But let's see to what you're referring, and I'll tell you if I agree or not."

Alex cracked an eye open at him but then

went back to staring at the ceiling.

"Right. Well then," Bainbridge said, taking another healthy swallow of his drink. "Since I am vastly more knowledgeable than you, let me help you narrow it down. You are either here over the Royal Society grant, or Livy."

Alex's body jolted at the sound of her name, and Bainbridge chuckled.

"Ah. Yes. Our lovely Lavinia. I should have known you'd come to me for help one of these days."

Alex sat up at that. "She is not *our* anything, and I'm not asking for help."

Bainbridge snorted. "First of all, yes, you are. And second, you may be her husband and you certainly love her in a different way than I do, but I have loved her longer, and like it or not you can't do anything about that. I know that darling woman better than I know myself, and I suspect that is why you are here."

Alex blinked at him, stunned. "I didn't say…"

"That you loved her?" Bainbridge nodded, draining the rest of his glass. "I know. That's part of the problem."

He sat forward to put the glass down and then swept his hair out of his face. "Let me ask you something. Why did you marry her?"

Alex grimaced at him. "That's none of your business."

Bainbridge rolled his eyes. "You really must stop your denials, or we shall be here all night. Why did you marry her?"

Alex took in a deep breath. "Because…she makes me laugh. I like the way she thinks. I can almost see the thought processes in her mind, and it's fascinating to watch. She's kind and intelligent and likes to read. She talks to plants and pretends to be interested in what I do. And she's so beautiful that she makes me ache."

Bainbridge blinked at him. "That's a very specific list."

Alex shrugged.

"Have you told her any of that?"

He opened his mouth, ready to say of course he had, but then snapped it shut with a frown.

Bainbridge nodded. "I thought so."

Alex frowned harder. "But she should know all that."

"How?" Bainbridge laughed. "How would she know all that?"

"Because she's more intelligent than either you or I, and I have no talent for hiding my emotions. The woman can tell when I'm angry or hungry or tired just by the way I breathe, and you're telling me she can't figure out on her own that I love her?"

Bainbridge just stared at him. Waiting.

Waiting for what, Alex didn't know. He

was probably waiting for…oh…

"Took you long enough," Bainbridge said, then shook his head. "And you're the one they want to give the grant to."

Alex sat in stunned silence, the words he'd just said reverberating in his head. He loved her. *Loved* her. And how would she know that when he'd only just realized it himself?

He let out a bone-weary sigh and rubbed his hand over his face. "I really am an insufferable fool."

"Don't expect me to argue with you," Bainbridge said. "By the by, did you imply at some point that she was little more than an inept social secretary?"

Alex didn't answer, but apparently the look on his face was enough, because Bainbridge's eyes grew wide, and he shook his head again.

"Well, that didn't help matters."

"I'm aware."

"Are you sure? Also, if you'd like to have a relationship, you have to *be* there occasionally."

"I tried—"

"Well, try harder. She's a woman, Beaubrooke. Not a hydrangea."

Alex groaned. "Again, I'm aware."

"Glad to hear it. Because she's been neglected enough in her life, and I'm not sure *she's* aware that you think of her as anything but another inanimate object you've acquired. Another plant to water occasionally and then forget about."

Which was exactly how he'd been treating her. Even if it wasn't his intention or had seemed unavoidable at the time. And then he'd gotten angry and complained when she tried to do what she thought he wanted and spend time with him in the process. No wonder she didn't want to be near him. *He* didn't want to be near him.

"I have to go," he said, half standing.

But Bainbridge waved him back down. "There's something else you should know."

He filled Alex in on what he'd overheard Lady Asterly and her parcel of harpies saying at the garden party, and by the time he was done, Alex was ready to march over to each of those women's houses and give them an earful they'd never forget.

"Breathe through it, Beaubrooke," Bainbridge said. "If I can refrain from scratching their eyes out after actually hearing it, you can hold it together as well."

Alex glared at him but sat back down. And then groaned and dropped his head in his hands. "How do I fix this?"

Bainbridge sighed again. "I need more whisky."

When he sat back down, he handed Alex a glass as well. Alex grunted his thanks and took a bracing shot of the amber liquid, savoring the woodsy burn as it trickled down his throat.

"You already know what to do. You just need to stop feeling sorry for yourself and start using the brain in that oversize head of yours. What does Livy want more than anything in the world?"

Alex sighed and rolled the cool whisky glass along his forehead for a moment. Liv. Her excitement at the art gallery. Her surprise and joy whenever someone acknowledged her or her contributions. The way she'd blossomed and gained confidence once she'd gotten away from her family.

Oh, his poor, sweet Lavinia. The neglected middle daughter her whole life. Watching her sisters get all the attention. Being chosen over her.

"She wants to be wanted. Seen. Loved." He flinched, thinking of everything she'd learned over the last couple days, everything he'd said. "Chosen. For who she is."

Bainbridge nodded. "Correct."

"And I chose my research over her need of me. Repeatedly. And she overheard her supposed friends confirming she was nothing more than a social ladder they didn't like or respect. Good God."

He downed the rest of the whisky.

"I doubt she resents you over the project,

if it eases your mind at all. She knows how important it is," Bainbridge said.

"I know. And that somehow makes it better and worse."

"Well…now you know what's wrong. What are you going to do to remedy the situation?"

Alex pinned Bainbridge with a steely stare. "I'm going to make sure she knows how I feel about her."

"Right…" Bainbridge lifted his brows. Waiting. "And…how will you accomplish this magnificent feat?"

Alex frowned. "That is a very good question. The answer to which I do not yet possess."

"And what is in your little satchel there?" he asked, pointing at the case Alex had brought.

The sigh Alex loosed came from the very depths of his soul. "That's your payment for helping me win back my wife."

Bainbridge just stared at him, unblinking, for so long Alex's eyes began to water. Then he finally closed his eyes and shook his head before pushing out of his chair.

"We're going to need more whisky."

CHAPTER TWENTY-EIGHT

Lavinia knocked on Harriet's door, poking her head in when her sister answered.

"Just wanted to see if you needed any help with packing."

Harriet smiled. "I think we have it well in hand," she said, nodding toward the two maids that were carefully stowing all her belongings in several trunks that were strewn about her old bedroom in her parents' home.

Lavinia sat on the edge of the bed and watched them bustle about for a moment. Harriet and John would be leaving for the Continent immediately after the ball. She and Harriet had never been particularly close, but she had always been there. The thought of her being gone, even if not permanently, was a strange and unsettling adjustment.

"Can you leave us a moment?" Harriet said to the maids.

Lavinia looked up in surprise but didn't say anything as they went out and Harriet sat beside her on the bed.

"So, what is this face about?" Harriet said, waving her finger at Lavinia.

She put her hands to her cheeks. "There's something wrong with my face?"

"Yes. It's looked dreadful for days. And

you've been avoiding your husband. I don't think I've seen the two of you in the same room since he returned. Are you still upset with him over the garden party? Or has something else occurred?"

Lavinia scowled. "Perhaps I've just realized I shall miss you."

Harriet's stern expression softened, but before she could say anything, Kitty came flying from out of the dressing room, a beribboned hat trailing its ribbons behind her.

"I shall miss you, too, Harriet," Kitty said, launching herself at Harriet so she could wrap her up in a hug. "Why must you go so far away?"

Harriet chuckled. "Oh, come now. It's not like we've all been particularly close. Though…I'll admit…I will miss you both as well."

"I knew she loved us," Kitty said, winking at Lavinia.

"Of course I love you, you foolish girls. And as for why I must leave, you know why. My husband must work for a living, and so I must go where his work takes him. Work that we are most grateful for," she added, giving Lavinia's hand a squeeze. "Besides, do you think it will be a hardship living in the most beautiful palaces in Europe and mingling with all those interesting people? I shall miss you, but…I do confess I'm looking forward to it."

"I envy you," Lavinia said. "Traveling to such beautiful places with the man you love. It's so romantic."

"You could come visit me, you know," Harriet pointed out. "Your husband has both the means and now the time to show you the world. If he can tear himself from his plants long enough to do so."

Kitty laughed, but Lavinia could only muster a bare smile.

"That. That expression right there. I insist you tell me what's going on immediately."

Lavinia threw up her hands. "I haven't said anything because there's really nothing to say. I've just been feeling a bit sorry for myself lately, and I'm having a difficult time pulling myself out of it."

"Oh, I do understand that," Kitty said. "Why don't you visit some of your friends? I'm sure they would cheer you."

Harriet snorted. "Those women aren't her friends."

Lavinia's gaze shot to her sister's, and Harriet lifted her brows. "My dear Lavinia, it was obvious to anyone who was looking that Lady Asterly, whoever she is, and her collection of social-climbing harridans care only for those who can improve their status in life."

Lavinia swallowed hard against the nausea

rising in her gut. She really had been the only one who hadn't seen it. Harriet would have made a much better duchess. She wouldn't have been taken in by them.

Though, looking at how happy Harriet was with her painter, Lavinia didn't think she regretted losing the duke.

"Is that what all this moping has been about?" Harriet asked. "Because a gaggle of wicked women finally showed their true colors?"

Lavinia sighed. "Partly. I know it is silly."

Harriet looked like she wanted to agree, but Kitty shook her head. "No, it's not. You thought they were your friends. You thought they cared for you, and you found out they only cared for what you could do for them."

"Yes," Lavinia said, that lump rising in her throat again. "Yes, that's it."

Kitty nodded. "I could see how things were once you married. You used to be so quiet. Sometimes we'd even forget you were in the room," she said with a smile, though it faded quickly. "That was actually rather thoughtless of us now that I hear it out loud. You were always an important part of our family. But I have a feeling you didn't feel that way very often."

Lavinia sucked in a tremulous breath. "No, I didn't."

"And then here comes along a handsome

duke who sweeps you off your feet and makes you his duchess. And suddenly everyone wants your attention. When a few weeks before they couldn't be bothered to recognize you if they walked by."

"Yes." Lavinia's voice was a mere whisper now. "It felt nice to be wanted at last. To be everyone's first choice instead of the last. Or the never. Or chosen only because someone doesn't think you'll make enough of a difference in his life that it will affect him in any way."

Harriet's eyebrows rose at that. "The duke said something monumentally asinine, didn't he?"

Lavinia threw her hands up. "Yes. But that was who he saw when we married. To be fair, I didn't expect to change."

"You haven't really changed," Kitty said. "You just aren't being kept in the corner any longer."

Lavinia reached for her sister's hand and gave it a squeeze. "If that's true, then Alex would have known I wasn't what he wanted before he married me."

Harriet scoffed. "He knew exactly what he was getting."

Lavinia frowned. "How? I didn't even know."

"Because he was in the corner with you," Kitty said. "The rest of us passed you by, didn't pay attention as we should have. But he was there with you. He always saw the real you."

Lavinia blinked, opened her mouth to refute what her sister said, then frowned. "But...he said..."

Harriet waved that off. "He said he didn't like going to all the parties you were dragging him to. He just neglected to ask if *you* liked going to them yourself and equated the attendance as interest. A miscalculation on both your parts."

Lavinia sighed. "And why didn't I see any of this until now?"

Kitty chuckled. "Because no one else cares as much as you. It's easy to see solutions when you aren't the one seeking them."

Lavinia stared at her. "When did you get so wise?

Kitty shrugged. "It comes and goes. Don't get used to it."

That had them all giggling for a few moments. When they sobered down, Harriet took Livy's hands. "Let me tell you something I've learned. It's not the big choices that matter. Big choices are easy, even the hard ones. They only come along a few times in your life. They are easy to spot and easy to focus on because they are so rare. It's the little ones that people make every day; those are the choices that matter. Those are the choices that show you how a person really feels. Anyone can pretend for a day. It's much harder to do so forever.

"Perhaps the duke didn't choose you for the reasons you thought. Any more than you may have chosen him for the reasons he thought. Neither of you knew the other well and, in the end, the why doesn't matter. Think about every day since then. Think of all the hundreds of choices we make every day, for ourselves and for others. How many times in those moments has he chosen you?"

Oh God. She was right.

Lavinia thought back over the last three months. Thought of all the times he had made sure there were fresh flowers in her rooms or let her help him even though she was pretty sure he was cringing the whole time. Or how he put up with Nigel's presence even though they were mortal enemies (who really loved each other like brothers, Lavinia just didn't have the heart to tell them that yet) just because it made her happy. Or how many social events he attended, and let her host in their home, though he despised them more than anything.

In all the little ways, he had chosen her over and over and over again. And she'd thrown a tantrum the one time he'd had to make a big choice and he'd chosen his life's passion project instead of a party he never wanted, and then made it worse by being offended when he'd gotten overzealous protecting that work. If she was honest, it *had* looked like something nefarious was afoot from his perspective. He'd still said hurtful things. Done hurtful things. Wanted or not, she'd put so much effort into that party, and to have him shun it completely still stung.

But she had made mistakes as well. And instead of staying to try and fix it like he'd wanted, she'd run.

She sighed deeply. "I'm a right bloody ass, aren't I?"

Kitty gasped, her face flaming bright red. "Lavinia Elizabeth Carlotta Beaubrooke! Our mother will be rolling in her grave."

Harriet broke out laughing, and Lavinia followed. "Our mother isn't dead yet," Harriet reminded her younger sister.

"Yes, well, she'll be rolling as soon as she is."

"But I'm not wrong," Lavinia said.

Harriet patted her sister's cheek. "No, dear, you aren't wrong."

Lavinia groaned, and Harriet just smiled. "So, what are you going to do about it?"

"Make the right choice for once in my life, I hope."

"After the ball."

"Oh my goodness. I have to go get ready," Lavinia said, jumping to her feet.

Her sisters laughed. "Yes, you do," Harriet said. "We will see you in a few hours."

She gave both of them a kiss on their cheeks and hurried out. She had so looked forward to this damn ball, for months. Now she just wanted it over with so she could sit down with her husband and start making a few new choices.

She hurried downstairs so she could quickly check on the preparations just as Nigel came through the front door.

"Nigel! You're early. The ball doesn't start for a couple hours yet."

He laughed but caught her hand before she could pull away. "I need to tell you something."

CHAPTER TWENTY-NINE

Lavinia sat at the mirror while Marta put the finishing touches on her ensemble. She'd dressed with care this evening, for all that she was rushed. Tonight was special. It was a new beginning for them. She hoped. Wearing her wedding gown seemed fitting, though she hadn't planned it for that reason originally. It was their first grand ball, their first of what would hopefully be an annual end-of-Season ball. And her wedding dress was both her best and most poetic as the gown to wear for the beginning of a tradition. Now, it seemed to have even more significance.

She'd had the dress modified a bit. A good portion of the lace had gone to trim Harriet's wedding gown. Now, her pale blue bridal gown was much less elaborate and more subtly elegant, in her mind. Her jewelry, she'd kept simple. A pearl necklace, pearl and diamond drop earrings, and on her head, a thin silver headband fashioned to look like palm leaves.

"You look very beautiful, Your Grace," Marta said with a tentative smile.

"Thank you, Marta. I hope the duke likes it."

Marta gave her a knowing smile. "Every

man in there will like it, Your Grace. His Grace most of all."

Lavinia's heart skipped a few beats at the thought of seeing Alex and what he might think. She hoped he'd like what he saw. She beamed at her maid and then took a deep breath, slowly blowing it out. She didn't know why she was having a sudden attack of the nerves. But her belly was flipping like she'd eaten live eels and her hands had begun to tremble.

A knock at her door shook her out of her reverie, and she nodded at Marta to open it. Harriet and Kitty bustled in, each looking stunning in their white gowns.

"Oh, Livy, you look perfect," Kitty said.

Harriet gave her a cool kiss on her cheek. "Every woman in there will want to scratch your eyes out."

Lavinia laughed and quickly pulled on her long kidskin gloves. "Shall we?"

"After you, Your Grace," Harriet said with a twinkle in her eye.

Lavinia led them out into the hallway and down the stairs, and when they reached the bottom, Alex stood waiting, his bright eyes fixed on her.

She stopped just before reaching the bottom step. She'd hoped he'd be at the ball, of course. But given his history with social events and the current status of their relationship, she hadn't been positive he'd be there. Let alone waiting for her.

He held out his hand, hope evident on his face. "Will you permit me to escort you in?" he asked.

She hesitated only a second before taking it, biting her lip as he placed her hand in the crook of his arm. "Thank you, Your Grace." She wanted to say so much more but didn't want to rush whatever tenuous peace they were forging.

They greeted their guests for several minutes before Alex put an arm around her waist and leaned down to murmur in her ear.

"Lady Asterly has arrived. Shall I deal with her?"

Lavinia glanced at him in surprise but shook her head. "Thank you for the offer, but I can handle her."

He nodded and stepped back to let her deal with the woman she'd thought was her friend.

There was only one way to deal with that type of woman, Lavinia had decided. And that was in the only way she'd understand.

Lady Asterly stepped forward to greet Lavinia, smiling at her like she hadn't been spreading malicious gossip about her behind her back for weeks.

"Ah, Lady Asterly," Lavinia said, pretending not to notice her rival's widening eyes at the icy tone she infused into her words. "You were able to come, after all. I'd heard that you were indisposed. Some stomach trouble or other."

Lady Asterly looked a bit taken aback but kept her smile on her face, though it didn't come near to reaching her eyes.

"No, no, Your Grace. I am quite well, thank you."

Lavinia nodded sharply. "Glad to hear it."

Then she turned her attention to the woman standing behind her. "Oh, Mrs. Sewickley, what a pleasure to see you. You must come meet the duke."

She looped her arm through Mrs. Sewickley's and all but dragged her to where Alex stood, close enough should she need him but far enough away that he wasn't hovering.

He turned to her with a warm smile when she approached. "Ah, my love, I see you've brought me a new friend. And who is this lovely lady?" he asked, giving Mrs. Sewickley a gallant bow.

He might just be playing along with the game Lavinia was playing, and splendidly too, she might add, but her heart still thrilled at hearing that four-letter word on his lips.

"Your Grace, allow me to present my dear friend, Mrs. Sewickley. I'm afraid her husband has been feeling poorly of late and doesn't attend many events. But my darling Barbara was telling me all about a new venture of his that just sounded fascinating. Perhaps we could call on them sometime soon and he could tell you more."

Alex lifted a brow subtly enough to show he was surprised, but he continued to play gamely along.

"If my wife says it's fascinating, then I would be happy to come hear more. I trust her judgment implicitly."

"Oh, Your Graces, that would be…well, just wonderful," Barbara stammered.

"Excellent!" Lavinia declared. "And do call me Lavinia, please. I also wished to discuss with you a new venture of my own. I have decided to organize a series of charity events built around the arts—"

"Charity events are a noble cause, indeed," Lady Asterly interrupted. Sneaky little thing. Lavinia hadn't even seen her approach. "But centered around the arts is something that has been done before. I'm not sure you'll get much interest. I should be happy to help—"

"No, thank you, Lady Asterly. My mind is set." She turned back to Barbara. "I was just discussing a few ideas with the Duchesses of Devonshire, Norfolk, and Hampton, who are all eager to begin. As is my husband's cousin, Lady Elizabeth, the new Princess Leopold. We do not want the committee to grow too large, of course, but we could accommodate one more patron if you would be interested."

Barbara looked as if she were about ready to faint. But she admirably managed to hold herself together. "Your Grace, I would be honored. Thank you."

"Excellent. Well, then—"

"I think I would actually have a few ideas that might serve you well, Your Grace," Lady Asterly again broke in. "I'm sure your friends wouldn't mind another patron joining, as it is for charity, after all—"

"That is very kind of you, but I know how dreadfully busy you are, Lady Asterly. We couldn't possibly impose."

And then she turned her back on her. Right there in front of the entire assemblage.

Lavinia looped her arm through Barbara's and led her farther into the ballroom.

"Your Grace…"

"Call me Lavinia, please."

"Lavin…" Barbara stuttered, not quite able to get it all out. "I am terribly grateful…"

Lavinia patted her hand. "Believe me, it was absolutely my pleasure." She turned to the woman with a warm smile. "You were one of the few who has been genuinely kind and stood up for me when no one else would. It's a rare thing to find a true friend in this world. I'd be happy to count you among them."

Barbara nodded, her eyes growing a little

moist in the corners.

"Wonderful."

The orchestra began to strike a few chords, signaling the beginning of the dancing, so Lavinia squeezed Barbara's arm and went to ensure everything went smoothly. She didn't expect Alex to be waiting for her near the dance floor.

He took her hand and gave her fingers a little squeeze. She looked up at him.

"Is something the matter?"

"Not at all. At least I hope not. I have a surprise for you, if you'll allow me."

He began to pull her onto the dance floor, and she hesitated. "You cannot mean to dance with your own wife, Your Grace."

He gave her that half grin that she so dearly loved. "Grant me but a moment, my dear wife."

Bewildered, Lavinia followed him to the dais where the band sat and stepped up.

"Ladies and gentlemen!" he called, waving with his hands to gather people as best he could.

"I pray you'll indulge me for a moment tonight."

He waited for the crowd to gather and the talking to die down as much as possible while Lavinia stared, a mix of apprehension and excitement churning in her belly. Alex was not one for public speeches. He wasn't one for the public, period. What on earth was he doing?

"Ladies and gentlemen," he said again. "Someone once told me that there existed people in the world who enjoyed creating a fuss. Who would insist on throwing a grand ball every time a Tuesday rolled around."

There was a tittering of laughter, and Lavinia, recognizing her own words, wondered anew what was happening.

"Well, as you know, it *is* a Tuesday, so it seems a perfect day for a ball. Even more so because there stands before me an incredible woman who is the most deserving of having a fuss created for her than anyone I know. My beautiful wife, the Duchess of Beaubrooke."

He gestured to her, and the room broke out in applause.

Lavinia's cheeks burned hot, and she could have sworn she could feel each individual set of eyes on her.

"Your Grace," she murmured, reaching up to take the hand he offered.

"Our wedding was beautiful," he said, "and I loved it because it made this wonderful woman mine," he continued. "But it was also a bit impersonal. Planned by others and intended for others."

She nodded, understanding his meaning. She had loved their wedding, as well. It was exciting and sensational. But it was also more spectacle than wedding. And he was right that there had been very little in it that had anything to do with them.

"I wished for something more special and meaningful. I haven't always appreciated the gift I received that day. But I have seen you. I may not have always told you. But I've *seen* you. I've seen how kind you are. How you try to include those who may not be included. Accept those who might be difficult to accept…namely myself," he said with a wry smile.

Lavinia laughed, though her throat was tight with unshed tears.

"I love to watch your sharp mind work through a problem and find a solution. Whether it's in organizing a grand ball such as this extraordinary gathering, or in helping your anxious husband find a few moments of rest. You've offered me comfort, even when I had nothing to offer in return.

"I've seen your love of the beauty around you, beauty that you find even in places where others might overlook it. I've seen your interest in my work and my projects. You've been patient and tolerant and more understanding than I ever deserved. I think I took that for granted far too often. But now, I vow that I will never take you for granted again. And I will endeavor to listen to you at least as much as I speak…"

There was another chorus of laughter, along with some sniffling. But Lavinia only had eyes for the wonderful man who was standing in front of the entire *ton* and telling the world how he felt about her. She wasn't sure her heart could take it. But she would remember every word for the rest of her days.

"I am a scientific man. Which means I tend to focus on research and information. Tangible evidence that I can prove. Unfortunately, it also means I do not always do well expressing my emotions."

Nigel snorted, and Alex glowered at him before continuing. "However," he said, looking back at Lavinia, "after observing you all these months, gathering my data, if you will…"

Lavinia laughed, her heart pounding so hard it took her breath away.

"There is only one conclusion I can reach," Alex said. "I know I do not deserve you, and I will most assuredly make more mistakes in the future. But I also know that I am hopelessly and unequivocally in love with you."

Lavinia sucked in a breath, releasing it with an exhalation that was half laugh and half sob. Her tear-filled eyes locked with Alex's. "You love me?" she whispered, pressing a hand to her lips.

He stepped closer to her and leaned his forehead against hers. "More and more every day. And if you will still have me, I would like to pledge myself to you again, in front of all our guests, to show you just how much."

"People will be telling their grandchildren about this, mark my words," Nigel muttered to Kitty, who nodded with wide, shining eyes.

"Oh, Alex," she said, standing on her tiptoes so she could kiss him, ignoring the smattering of outraged gasps. What was the point of being a duchess if you couldn't be a little eccentric and inappropriate at times?

"I love you, too," she said. A sound escaped her lips that was somehow both a sob and a laugh, full of too much happiness for one sound to contain. "And all this…this is simply wonderful, Alex. It's perfect. And beautiful. And I love it so much. Thank you." She reached up to kiss him again.

"I believe that part is supposed to come after the ceremony," Nigel said, and Lavinia dropped back to her feet, joining the others in a laugh.

"Ceremony?" she asked.

He nodded and lifted a hand. The band began to play as their family members lined up to form a short aisle at the head of which stood a vicar who had appeared from somewhere.

"You brought a vicar?" she asked with a laugh as Harriet came over and handed her a small bouquet of camellias before joining the others in their makeshift aisle.

Alex winked at her and went to take his place by the vicar while her father, Lord Abberforth, stood beside her and offered her his arm. The crowd around them was abuzz. Never had anything like this been seen before.

"Seems a bit odd to be doing this all again, but if the Duke of Beaubrooke says he wants to marry your daughter again, one doesn't say no."

Lavinia laughed and squeezed her father's arm as he walked her up the short aisle to where Alex now stood waiting.

They recited their vows to each other again, and though they were surrounded by half of London it seemed, everyone else faded away, and it was only her, and only him, as they pledged to love and cherish each other to their dying day.

Alex placed another gold band on her finger, this one fashioned to resemble a twisted vine, sprinkled with tiny diamond dew drops. And when the vicar presented them to their guests, Alex turned and kissed his bride, again ignoring the uproar. There were few who would chastise the Duke of Beaubrooke. And while kissing one's wife in public wasn't often done, it was hardly something to be too offended about.

As Alex pressed one more sweet kiss to

her lips, something clicked into place in Lavinia's soul, and for the first time, she felt truly and wholly wanted. Complete.

Their guests clapped and cheered for them as Alex gestured for the band to begin playing again and couples filtered onto the dance floor.

"Shall we dance, my wife?"

Her jaw dropped. "You cannot dance with your own wife, Your Grace."

He gave her a decidedly wicked grin. "I have decided that from now on, I shall do exactly what I please. And what would please me is a dance with my darling wife."

Lavinia swallowed past yet another lump in her throat. At some point, she was going to have to excuse herself and have a good cry. But that could wait until later. "In that case, I would be honored, my husband."

Nigel appeared at her elbow and looked between them. "Are you two going to keep that up all night? Because I'm not sure how much more I can stand."

Alex glowered at him, but Harriet snorted. "I concur."

John came to stand beside his wife and shrugged. "I don't know. I find it romantic."

Harriet just rolled her eyes and muttered something about hopeless romantic artists. But her happiness was unmistakable when she gazed at her husband.

Lavinia stepped into her own husband's arms and followed his lead around the floor for a truly scandalous two songs, before he led her off the dance floor.

"I have one more surprise for you," he said, taking her hand and escorting her into the hall.

She couldn't imagine what else he could have in store for her.

Alex stopped in front of the open conservatory doors, and Lavinia gasped at the sight that met her.

The plants had been rearranged, moved to the outer edges of the room so that a small dance floor was formed in the middle. Candles were placed throughout the room, bathing the room in golden light, while above, snow could be seen falling on the glass. The effect was simply magnificent.

"Oh, Alex," she breathed. "This is incredible."

"So are you," he said, drawing her into his arms. "I am so sorry that I missed my birthday celebration."

"It's all right—"

"No," he said. "It's not. There wasn't much else I could do at the moment, but that doesn't mean that it was all right. I know it hurt you. And I never want that to happen again."

Lavinia cupped his cheek and looked into

his eyes. "It will probably happen again," she said, smiling at the instant denial that rose to his lips. "We are only human, Alex. It is inevitable that we will both hurt the other again at some point over the course of our lives. But perhaps we can endeavor to communicate with each other better before things get to the breaking point."

He pulled her to him for a kiss so sweet her toes curled in her slippers.

"Dance with me," he murmured against her lips.

"Gladly," she whispered, wrapping her arms about his neck so they could sway to the music together in their own private ballroom.

The music filtered in to them from the ballroom, and Lavinia settled against Alex, laying her head on his chest. Alex tightened his arms about her. Nothing had ever felt so wonderful.

They danced for a moment, and then Lavinia took a deep breath. "Nigel told me what you did," she said. "The deal you made with him."

CHAPTER THIRTY

Alex stopped dancing and looked down at her with a frown. "He promised to never speak of it."

She gave him the look that comment deserved, and he huffed. "Yes, I should have known better, I suppose."

"Even if he hadn't said a word, did you truly think I wouldn't have noticed? I can't let you give up all your research, Alex. It's too much."

He gazed down at her and tucked a strand of hair behind her ear, letting his fingers linger on her cheek. "It's not enough. There is nothing in this world I wouldn't give up to make you happy."

She turned into the touch, eyes fluttering closed, and giddy hope speared him through the chest so strong he nearly gasped with it.

"I want you to be happy, too," she said.

"I *am* happy," he insisted. "You are all I need. And my work isn't gone. Bainbridge is a…competent researcher." He swallowed. That was tough to get out.

Lavinia laughed quietly. "Did that hurt as much as it sounded like it did?"

Alex chuckled. "More."

"Well, as I said, I want you to be happy as

well, and I know — Alex, are you listening?" she asked with a giggle when he nibbled at her earlobe.

"I'm listening." His lips brushed against the column of her neck, and she shivered, her breath catching in her throat.

"No, you're not," she said, pushing him away with a laugh.

He sighed. "All right, then. Say what you must."

She blew out a breath and started again. "I spoke with Nigel and — "

This time his finger stopped her lips. "No more talk of Bainbridge."

She laughed and snuggled against him. "Agreed. For now." She leaned in farther and brushed the tip of her nose up along his jawline.

"I've missed you," he said, his mouth hovering over hers until she opened for him, leaning in to meet his lips only for him to move away.

"You knew where to find me."

"Hmm. I know. I was an idiot. Forgive me."

"Only if you kiss me again."

He chuckled, low and deep, and this time when she pressed against him, he didn't tease her. He licked at her lips, his hand cupping her jaw, his thumb pressing on her chin to open her mouth wider for him. She whimpered in the back of her throat, and he groaned, lips and tongue meeting hers with a ferocity made of all the nights of frustration and longing.

She broke away for a second to catch her breath. "I think we talk too much."

"Agreed," he said, kissing her again. "We need to work on listening."

She met him, her passion matching his. "Agreed."

He wrapped his arms about her and walked them backward until the backs of his legs bumped against a bench that was nestled among the plants. He sat, and she immediately climbed on his lap, straddling him so she could wrap her arms around his neck and keep him captive while her lips devoured him.

"Ah, Liv," he groaned, his hands taking advantage of her low-cut bodice. "We don't have time for this right now, love."

His palm closed over a breast, and she arched into him with a gasp. "I know. We need to stop right now." She sucked his earlobe into her mouth, her teeth lightly nipping.

"God, woman," he said, licking at the tight bud of her nipple. "If we don't return, we're going to miss our own ball."

"All right." She reached down and yanked her dress up to her thighs. "Let's be late."

Before she could grab anything else, someone pounded on the door, and they both sucked in ragged breaths, pressing farther back into the potted palms that shielded them.

"You two have exactly five minutes to get back out here before you become the scandal of the season!" Harriet called from the hallway.

"Coming!" Alex shouted.

He dragged her against him for a quick but very thorough kiss that had him wanting to forget about their guests and everything else but showing his wife just how much he'd missed her until the sun came up. But he couldn't do that.

"We will finish this later," he said, giving her bottom a soft slap before moving her off his lap.

She yelped and then pulled her dress back into place with a pout. And she looked so adorable he couldn't help but lean down for another kiss.

"I promise you once this ball is over, a ball that you insisted on hosting and have been planning for months, I'll remind you, I will personally hide all your clothes and we can stay naked in bed for a week."

Her face lit up at that. "I accept."

• • •

They made it back to the dance floor without anyone catching them in an...awkward position. Though there were plenty of knowing smiles. Lavinia slipped her hand into Alex's, and he led her out. Their guests applauded, but they had eyes only for each other. And when he pulled her into his arms and began to sway, she closed her eyes to savor the sheer happiness that flowed through her.

"So," Alex said, gazing down at her with a heat in his eyes that made her knees weak. "You have hosted your first ball. Is it everything you dreamed?"

She chuckled a little. "And quite a bit more."

"Good," he said. "Just don't expect a wedding every time we host a ball."

"Ah, that means you'll agree to hosting more?" Before he could answer, she hurried on. "To be fair, it's more work than it's probably worth. And you needn't worry about our home being filled to the brim with guests every night as I do wish to spend more time on my paintings, and my book, as well."

Alex blinked at her, stunned. "Book?"

"But I confess, I do enjoy these social occasions vastly more than I expected," she said, ignoring his question for the moment. She'd tell him all about her newfound passion later. It would do him some good to wonder for a bit. "Will you hate it too terribly much if I continue to entertain?"

"Yes," he said, but he was laughing. "But that is one of the reasons I needed a wife in the first place. I need someone to drag me out of my greenhouse occasionally."

"Hmm, perhaps," she said. Then she leaned in closer. "But only if I can drag you back in sometimes as well."

His laughter rang out through the ballroom, drawing everyone's eyes as they twirled around the room.

"Everyone is staring, Your Grace."

"Good," he said, holding her a little closer. "Let them stare. Far too few of them know what a man in love with his wife actually looks like. I am more than happy to educate them."

"As am I."

"Wonderful! It would do them good to see what real happiness looks like."

She beamed up at him. "And are you truly happy, husband?"

He leaned in and kissed the tip of her nose. "Only when you are by my side, my love."

"Then I shall never leave you."

"Excellent." He paused for a second, a slight frown on his brow. "I would be obliged if you'd bring a potted palm or two with you, though."

She gasped and then laughed along with him, letting the sound of their happiness fill the room.

EPILOGUE

Six months later

The scene was far too familiar for Alex's comfort. Bainbridge, at his desk, riffling around yet again. That was it. He'd tried to get along with the man for Lavinia's sake, but enough was enough!

Alex had asked him repeatedly to keep his hands off his desk. He had a system, damn it all, and every time Bainbridge went riffling through the paperwork, it took Alex days to repair the chaos.

He needed...a weapon of some kind. He slapped his hands to his thighs. Patted his chest. As if he usually strolled about London with daggers at his hips or a broadsword strapped to his back.

Bainbridge picked up another sheet of paper, his face alight with interest, and Alex rushed fully into the room, grabbing the first thing he could lay his hands on. He marched right up to the desk and pointed the...palm frond?—he stared at his hand and sighed—the palm frond at Bainbridge.

"Drop that paper right now!" he shouted.

Lavinia, who Alex hadn't seen near the fireplace, and Bainbridge both froze, their eyes as wide as a barn owl's. And then

Lavinia's forehead crinkled in confusion.

"Alex, what are you—"

"Don't move!" he shouted at Bainbridge, who had folded one sheet of paper and put it into his vest pocket. "Drop it, I say!"

"Drop what? You've gone mad, Beau-brooke."

"I just finished cataloging that pile last night. Now, unhand my research, you...you... knave! Before you destroy my entire system!"

He shook the frond at him again, and Bainbridge raised his hands and backed up. Right into the matching vase that held the other oversize palm fronds.

He seized one himself and brandished it. "Stay back, Beaubrooke! I'm warning you. I know how to defend myself. I was the fencing champion of our class in fourth year."

Alex swung his frond at Bainbridge, whacking at him the way he would with a fencing sabre. "*I* was the champion fourth year. You were the champion third year. And only because I didn't fence that year."

Bainbridge parried and thrusted back. "Your memory is getting a bit spotty there, old sport. Perhaps you need a little refresher."

He lunged with his frond, narrowly missing Alex who sucked in his gut and jumped backward just in time. "A coward's move! Just admit it, you're already beaten."

"Coward? You're the one dodging my blows. Stand still and take it, you scoundrel!"

They both swung, their fronds connecting with a crash of leaves and a cloud of dust.

"What are you two doing?" Lavinia shouted. "Will you sto—"

She paused mid-yell, which made Alex and Bainbridge pause to see what was wrong. She stood frozen for a second, her eyes blinking rapidly, before her face scrunched up in an impressive feat of contortionism and she released a sneeze that reverberated through the room.

· · ·

All three stood stock still for a moment, and then Alex and Nigel started wrestling again, trying to disentangle their fronds so they could have another go at it.

Lavinia pulled her handkerchief from her pocket and blew her nose. They had lost their minds. That was the only explanation. What in the name of all the holy saints were they *doing*?

Marta had come in with a fresh vase full of garden flowers for Alex's desk but had frozen at the sight of two grown men dueling with dusty shrubbery. Though somewhere between her sneeze and her nose blow they had abandoned the fronds and were now just rolling around on the floor, trying to pin the other.

Lavinia went over to Marta, removed the flowers from the vase, and took the vase from her. And then handed back the flowers.

"Thank you, Marta."

Marta nodded at her, bemused, though her eyes went right back to the men on the floor.

Lavinia marched over to them and stood above them for a moment. When neither acknowledged her presence, she nodded. "Right then."

And dumped the vase full of water right in their faces.

They stopped wrestling and started swiping at their faces. Unfortunately, it only stopped them for a second and they looked like they were about to have another go at each other.

"Freeze!" Lavinia shouted.

Finally, they listened.

She glared down at them. "Either one of you moves again and I'll use the actual vase."

They blinked up at her, faces dripping, and she gave them a sharp nod before handing the vase back to Marta.

"Thank you, Marta. That will be all."

The maid bobbed a curtsy, said, "Yes, Your Grace," and scuttled out of the room as fast as she could. No doubt to spread the fantastical story to everyone downstairs. As well she should. Lavinia couldn't wait to tell a few people herself.

She stood over them with her fists on her hips. "Are you two quite finished?"

They both started talking over each other, and all she could hear was, "All I was doing was minding my own business and he comes storming in attacking me with a palm frond—"

"He was ruining my categorizing; we'll never be able to find anything if he keeps destroying—"

"I wasn't destroying anything, you tw—"

"I saw you clear as day, bending right over my desk, elbows deep in the paperwor—"

"How can I destroy piles of paperwork, you ninny?"

"There is a system to those piles, *as I said*. You just never listen. And since you don't know that system, every time you touch anythi—"

"I only moved one paper. One! And it was from the non-filed pile. See? I pay attention! Livy made sure of it."

"No, you don't... Wait...you did?" Alex asked, turning to her.

"Oh, are you ready to actually listen now?"

He had the grace to look sheepish, at least. Bainbridge seemed to be having a more difficult time with that.

"You, sit there," she said, gesturing Bainbridge over to an armchair on one side of the fireplace. "And you sit there." She pointed Alex to the other one.

She sat on the chaise that was between them and looked between the two most important men in her life.

"Now. I'm going to speak, and I don't want to hear one wor—"

"But—" Alex started, but she held up a finger.

"Not one word from either of you until I'm finished. Is that clear?"

They both muttered yes, and Lavinia took a deep breath, letting it out slowly.

"Alex. Nigel is your partner now. You must stop being so territorial with every scrap of paper that crosses your desk."

Alex nodded and scrubbed a hand over his face. He made to stand up but froze just as he leaned forward.

"May I approach?" he asked, the question sounding sincere though there was a definite sparkle in his eyes that wasn't there a moment ago.

"Not just yet," she said. Then she turned to Nigel. "You."

"What did I do? I was the victim here!"

"You continuously rile him. You knew what he'd think if he saw you riffling through those papers. Because you've given him good reason to think it."

Nigel sat back and folded his arms with a grumble. "I'm just trying to have a little fun."

"You call this fun?" She gestured at the

mess all around them, and Nigel shrugged and glanced at Alex with a naughty half grin.

"Well, yes, a bit."

Alex snorted, but his lips twitched just as much. Lavinia threw her hands up in the air and looked skyward. "Men," she muttered.

"Now, can I safely approach?" Alex asked again.

"No. Sit," she ordered, pointing to the chairs in front of her.

He and Nigel both sat, though they didn't go quietly.

"You two are incorrigible. Everyone's lives would be so much easier and you two would probably get further ahead with your research if you would just accept that you are now working together."

They looked at her with twin expressions of…not horror exactly. But something close.

"Really, the two of you are worse than children. You heard what the Royal Society said. Alex's experimentation and plant grafts are invaluable and could change a great deal of what we know of medicinal plants, but Nigel's research on the origins of the best plants and methods is also necessary to continue with the research needed. Like it or not, the two of you go hand in hand. So you *will* learn to work together, or the Society will give the project to Lord Threwsbury, and I know neither of you wants that."

She crossed her arms, accentuating the small bump of her belly as she glared down at the two men seated before her. "Well. I'm waiting."

"Lavinia, you can't truly mean," Alex started, and she held a hand up to silence him.

"I can and I do. The two of you have been at this for close to two decades now. I think it is time to stop looking for any minute reason to argue and call a truce."

"I don't know. I think we could get another decade out of it easily enough," Nigel said, glancing at Alex with a shrug.

Lavinia glared daggers at him, and he huffed like a petulant child, but he stopped talking.

Nigel and Alex both grumbled, nodding their heads.

"Good."

She took a cautious step backward. Which seemed to act like a trigger of some sort, because the moment she did, they both erupted with more complaints.

"Now listen up, both of you! I have enough to deal with between the charity ball next month, Harriet and John coming for a visit, the paintings I must do to accompany your manuscript, and the final revisions of my book. Not to mention the fact that I am quite busy carrying your child and will soon be caring for him outside of my womb as well. I simply do not have time to supervise the two of you. Nor will I pass along some ridiculous vendetta to our children," she said, resting her hand on her belly. "So, if either of you ever cared for me at all, you will just have to let bygones be bygones and get to work. Is that understood?"

Nigel and Alex both grumbled an agreement and sighed heavily. "All right, then," Alex said. "Truce."

Nigel rolled his eyes but muttered, "Truce."

"For you," Alex added with that half smile she loved so much.

"Agreed. For you," Nigel said.

Lavinia released a sigh of relief. "Good. Thank you."

Alex waited all of two seconds before he leaned toward her and said, "You know, we could solve this whole problem if we just kept the door locked."

That startled a laugh out of her. "Alex!"

He raised his brows, looking for all the world like a naughty child who'd been caught and didn't want to admit he'd done anything wrong. She just stared back at him until he sighed and looked back at Nigel.

"Welcome to my home, Bainbridge. I am happy to accept your help with my research." He spoke in a straight monotone, face expressionless, and from the vacant look in his eyes, Lavinia was fairly sure he wasn't even looking at Nigel.

Nigel cocked an eyebrow. "My thanks, Your Grace. I am most honored to accept *your* help with *my* research."

Then they both glanced at her for approval.

Lavinia looked heavenward. Lord help her with these two. "Just…try not to kill each other. And stay away from the family heirlooms. Now I must go. Clara… Oh, there she is."

Lavinia looked up with a smile as Clara entered the room.

"Lavinia, dear, you look wonderful. How are you fee— Oh no, not again," she said with a sigh, having just caught sight of Nigel and Alex and the mess of the library.

"Yes," Lavinia said, gathering up her notebook. "They have exhausted all my patience."

"Hmm, I don't doubt it. I guess it's a good thing we are going to be gone for a few hours."

"Yes, it is." Lavinia looked at the men again. "Clara and I are going to be working on the artwork for the manuscript until teatime. Do you think you can be civil until then?"

They both nodded grumpily, but Lavinia would take it. She hurried out of the room before either of them changed their minds and called her back. She hadn't yet reached the front door when she heard Nigel exclaim, "Put that palm frond down, Beaubrooke!"

Lavinia rolled her eyes, took a deep breath, and left them to it.

"It's a good thing I love them," she said with a laugh.

"As much as they love each other," Clara added. "No two brothers could be closer, blood related or not. Think we should tell them?"

"No," Lavinia said with a laugh. "Let them continue to think they hate each other. They are happiest that way."

. . .

Alex had fully intended to obey Lavinia's wishes and work nicely with Bainbridge, but the man was insufferable!

And they had managed to behave for a good hour or so. A record for them.

But by the time Lavinia returned, their truce had devolved again. When she walked into the library, it was to find them facing off, Nigel armed with a large sofa pillow in each hand while Alex squared off against him holding the bouquet of long-stemmed flowers he'd brought her from his greenhouse that morning, their naked heads drooping on broken stems.

Nigel straightened and tried to hide the pillows behind his back. Alex snorted, then realized he still held the flowers and quickly dropped them on the table behind him.

Lavinia stared open-mouthed for a moment before her eyes narrowed into dangerous slits and she folded her arms, staring them both down.

Alex didn't wait for permission this time, though he did approach cautiously enough that she had to bite her lips to keep from smiling. When he got close, he reached out and slowly drew her into his arms.

"I'm sorry," he said, pressing a kiss to her temple. "Forgive me?" He pressed another kiss to her forehead.

"Not just yet," she muttered.

"What about now?" He kissed her cheek.

"I'll think about it."

"Hmm." He kissed her jaw. "Now?"

"Perhaps a little."

The slow, sensual grin she gave him sent a bolt of heat down through his core, and he nipped at her earlobe to elicit that quiet gasp that he loved so much before he brushed a feather-soft kiss across her lips.

"Now?" he said, his voice a gruff whisper.

"I'm still in the room," Nigel said, his voice half amused and half exasperated. Or disgusted. It was hard to tell. Either way, she didn't care.

"Nigel," Lavinia said, speaking between the kisses Alex was pressing to her lips, her throat, her collarbone.

"Yes, Livy?"

"Go home."

He stood with a chuckle and saw his way to the door. Where he paused. Leaned back in. And said, "Remember the apple orchard? It's possible I saw at least one of your note sheets."

And then he fled into the hallway.

Alex, startled, nearly jerked away from Lavinia, but she just laughed and pulled him back.

"Oh no, you don't," she said. "You have some forgiveness to beg, remember?"

"Ah, yes," he said, bending her over the desk and knocking everything off it in the process. "Where was I?"

She smiled up at him, her heart overflowing with happiness. "Right where you belong."

ACKNOWLEDGMENTS

So you know that moment during the Oscars, when the winner is at the podium taking way too long so they start playing the music to get them off the stage? Yeah, this moment is the equivalent of that. The music is playing, my editors are frantically waving at me, and the crumpled paper in my hand is too sweaty and tear-stained to read. I want to thank everyone, but deadlines are looming, and we ran out of time days ago. Therefore, we are going to do this fast and sweet LOL.

My undying thanks to Liz Pelletier, Lydia Sharp, the amazing team at Entangled, Stacy, Jessica, Riki, Debbie, Curtis, Meredith, Heather, Katie, and all the incredible people behind the scenes, Elizabeth, Bree, and my oldest and dearest friend (and formatter) Toni, my wonderful agent, Janna Bonikowski, my historical gals—Lexi Post, Eva Devon, and the woman who keeps me sane, Lisa Rayne. I truly could not do this without you! And of course to my partner in crime, Tom, and my amazing kids, Connor and Ryanna, I love you more than you will ever know. To my parents, siblings, and family who have loved and supported me from day one—you'll never know how much it means. Thank you all!

And most of all, to my dear readers—you guys are why I get to do what I do. Thank you for all the love and support!

*Two unlikely allies make for one
scandalous courtship...*

HOW
NOT TO
Marry A
DUKE

TINA GABRIELLE

From the moment her pet pig attacks him, Adeline
Foster knows she does not care at all for the Duke
of Warwick. Certainly the man is handsome, but
such an arrogant arse. But when her scoundrel half
brother demands she marry a stranger over a failed
investment, the duke does something shocking...he
announces *he's* courting her.

One moment, Daniel Millstone is enjoying tinker-
ing with his inventions in his quiet country home
with relative anonymity. The next, he's courting the
willful Miss Adeline. It might have begun as a way to
vex her half brother—his childhood nemesis—but
her striking beauty and kissable lips prove an irresistible temptation.

Now Adeline and her faux beau must convince the
ton and their families that they're an item. It doesn't
matter if they can barely tolerate each other. It
doesn't matter that scandal is only a touch away.
Because if this charade doesn't work, Adeline will
find herself in dangerous hands...

A bright, lively tale about daring to be more than just a lady...

THE DUKE'S SECRET CINDERELLA

USA TODAY BESTSELLING AUTHOR
EVA DEVON

Charlotte Browne could just kick herself. What on earth possessed her to tell the Duke of Rockford that she is a lady? But something about the duke's handsomeness and kind intelligence makes Charlotte blurt out the teeniest, tiniest falsehood. Now it's too late to admit she's just plain Charlotte of no particular importance—with cinder-stained hands, a wretched stepfather, and no prospects for marriage.

Rafe Dorchester, Duke of Rockford, has done what every self-respecting duke must do—avoid marriage at all costs. But the only thing stronger than the duke is his mother, and she lays down the highest ultimatum, he'll need to find a duchess. Immediately. Only, when he calls on a potential bride, he instead finds the pert, fresh-faced Lady Charlotte. Rafe was warned to never mix the business of marriage with pleasure, but when it comes to Lady Charlotte...oh, business would be a splendid pleasure.

Except Charlotte knows that true life is nothing like the penny romances she reads. The duke can't actually end up with a maid. When her vile stepbrother catches her coming from the gardens with the duke close on her heels, Charlotte knows just what he'll do. And there's only one way to save them all from scandal...

*London's most successful matchmaker is
about to break the biggest rule of all...*

THE
DUKE'S
RULES OF
ENGAGEMENT

USA TODAY BESTSELLING AUTHOR
JENNIFER HAYMORE

Joanna Porter is in love with love. As one of
London's most promising matchmakers, it's her job
to ensure her clients are blissfully happy. Now Jo's
about to make the match of the season—*if* she se-
cures the "perfect duchess" for the handsome and
irritatingly stubborn Duke of Crestmont. Surely it
can't be *that* difficult...

If the Duke of Crestmont doesn't produce an heir
soon, his dukedom will fall to his loathsome uncle.
Step one? Acquire the perfect duchess. Which is
where his new matchmaker comes in. If he wasn't so
distracted by the opinionated, infuriating, and utterly kissable Jo—who is more carriage saleswoman
than duchess—he might be able to focus on the perfectly eligible young ladies Jo parades before him...

Jo is not immune. She needs to match the duke—
not fall in love with him. And yet, here she is. But a
romance between them would ruin her reputation,
her business, and the support she provides her family...not to mention exposing the secret that would
push her past ruin straight into pure devastation.

*A chance encounter leads to a game of
desire in this irresistible romance...*

A Matter of Temptation

USA TODAY BESTSELLING AUTHOR
STACY REID

Miss Wilhelmina "Mina" Crawford is desperate.
Having been ruined in the eyes of society years ago
for one foolish, starry-eyed mistake, she spends her
days secreted away at her family's crumbling estate,
helping her brother manage the land but not able to
truly live life the way she's always dreamed. When
her brother admits to just how dire their finances
have gotten, she takes it upon herself to procure employment...but the only one who will even consider
the scandalous idea of a female secretary is the brilliant, ruthless, and infuriating Earl of Creswick.

Simon Loughton, the Earl of Creswick, needs help
if he wants to finally pass the reform bill he's been
championing for years and secure the vote for
England's most vulnerable constituents. Too bad help
comes in the form of a woman with breathtaking
nerve, fiery red hair, and a sense of humor to match.

Now temptation—disguised as a lovely, clever-
mouthed devil—lives and works under Simon's very
roof. And Mina finally feels as though she's truly living life to her wildest dreams. But even the most
incendiary of kisses can't incinerate Mina's past...or
the shocking secret that could ruin them both.

AMARA
an imprint of Entangled Publishing LLC